Mack said, "Tomorrow night then?"

He gritted his teeth in agony.

"Okay," she said, looking as if she'd just been given ten to fifteen years in federal prison. "Tomorrow night."

She wasn't exactly brimming with enthusiasm.

Maybe this wasn't going to be as easy as he'd thought. After all, she was choosing to abstain from sex. There had to be a reason. A reason he had to get around. Even if it took all night.

Speaking of which, that needed to be stated clearly. "You have to guarantee me at least twelve hours to make my case, Kindra."

Kindra blinked. Twelve hours? She would have been happy with ten minutes and a wave on his way out.

"Isn't that a little long?"

He was leaning casually against her desk, and when he shifted, his leg brushed against hers. Kindra shivered and recrossed her legs in the opposite direction to move them away from him.

A slow knowing smile moved across his face. "To get it right, sometimes you need to take it slow. And sometimes it's so good you want time to do it again."

<u>BOOK YOUR PLACE ON OUR WEBSITE</u>
<u>AND MAKE THE</u>
<u>READING CONNECTION!</u>

We've created a customized website just for our very special readers, where you can get the inside scoop on everything that's going on with Zebra, Pinnacle and Kensington books.

When you come online, you'll have the exciting opportunity to:

- View covers of upcoming books
- Read sample chapters
- Learn about our future publishing schedule (listed by publication month *and author*)
- Find out when your favorite authors will be visiting a city near you
- Search for and order backlist books from our online catalog
- Check out author bios and background information
- Send e-mail to your favorite authors
- Meet the Kensington staff online
- Join us in weekly chats with authors, readers and other guests
- Get writing guidelines
- AND MUCH MORE!

Visit our website at
http://www.kensingtonbooks.com

Bad Boys Online

Erin
McCarthy

BRAVA

KENSINGTON PUBLISHING CORP.
http://www.kensingtonbooks.com

Contents

HARD DRIVE

7

PRESS ANY KEY

95

USER FRIENDLY

191

HARD DRIVE

Chapter One

"I want to lick your nipples until you . . ."

Kindra jumped in her swivel seat as a low voice spoke over her shoulder.

Please don't let that be who she thought it was.

She turned. It was. "Ohmigod. Mack!"

Whipping the mouse around on her desktop, she tried frantically to close the e-mail that was up on her computer screen. The dirty e-mail from her cyber partner, Russ. The dirty e-mail that was being read by her real live crush and coworker, Mack Stone.

God, where was the minimize button?

"Come like a rocket, hot and wet . . ." Mack's amused voice trailed off. "What is this?"

"Spam," she managed to say, a sweat breaking out under her white blouse and black jacket. "I get all kinds of junk e-mail."

Kindra clicked the CLOSE button as Mack's finger touched the screen.

"Then why does it have your name on it?"

"I don't think it did," she lied without compunction. There was no way she was admitting to Mack "different girlfriend every week" Stone, that she had been engaging in a cyberaffair.

"Yes, it did," he insisted.

Annoyed, she looked over her shoulder at him and gritted her teeth at his total and utter perfection. Why? Why did she have to spend every day for eight hours looking at this paragon of masculinity? From his short black hair, past the strong jaw, down to the broad chest and gorgeous pecs covered in *GQ*-inspired clothing, and continuing on down . . . lower, he was perfect.

And very out of her league.

She glared at him, willing him to back away from her chair and take his arousing aftershave scent with him.

A grin spread out across his face, showing off perfect white teeth. He probably never even got cavities. "Kindra Hill, are you having cybersex? I never would have guessed."

Her impulse was to just push him out of the way and run down the hall and hide in the ladies' room until he left the building. But that hadn't worked in ninth grade when Tommy Slade had pantsed her in front of her geometry class, and she didn't think it would work now.

Two choices here. Deny. Or brazen it out.

Being a proverbial wallflower, she had never brazened anything out in her life. It was time to try.

Taking a deep breath to gather some courage, she said, "So what if I am?"

Okay, what was meant to sound seductive came out defensive. She sounded like a bitter divorcée who goes through a vibrator battery a week.

His ice blue eyes went wide. "Then I'd say there's more to you than meets the eye."

Then he shook his head, clearly curious. "But I figure, why talk about it online, when you can be doing it live and in person?"

Yeah, if she had him to do it with. But Kindra's choices had never been so appealing. After a few mishaps that had ranged from yawn inspiring to borderline gruesome, she had decided she was better off snuggling up with the blue light on her computer screen every night.

"It's easier this way . . . safer, cleaner," she mumbled. Then she straightened up and turned back to her computer, on the verge of collapsing from mortification. Had she said that out loud?

She had. Mack leaned over her, his hot breath tickling across her ear. His tie fell forward and brushed against the back of her hair, sending a shiver through her.

"But it's so much more fun the old-fashioned way."

"Sometimes. And sometimes it's messy and complicated and just plain lousy." She gave a shrug that was meant to be worldly and nonchalant, as if she'd sampled men aplenty and found them all lacking. Instead she managed to clip him in the chin.

He grunted. "I think you're wrong."

"I don't care." She scooted forward, away from him. *Hint, hint, take it please. Go away and take your hot bod with you.*

"I can prove it to you."

She froze. He couldn't possibly mean . . . no. Mack Stone had never given her the time of day before.

But if he did mean *that*, did she want to take him up on it? Her head said of course not, you naïve and greedy slut. Her inner thighs had an altogether different answer, one that had her pantyhose turning into a mini-oven.

He wasn't serious though.

"I'm serious," he said.

Help.

Kindra opened her mouth, knowing full well her brain had ceased to exist and her crotch was in complete control.

"What kind of proof are you talking about?"

She fought the urge to clap a hand over her mouth. Now she'd done it.

He'd think she was actually interested.

Which, of course, she was.

But she shouldn't let *him* know that.

Mack was still leaning over her. He said in a low voice laced with amusement, "I think you know what kind of proof I'm talking about."

Well, she thought he was talking about having sex with her. But if she said it out loud, and she was wrong, she would have to quit her job and move to Europe.

Kindra cleared her throat. "Maybe, if you explain it to me?"

Mack's hands gripped the back of her chair and she found herself slowly being turned around. Since grabbing the desk and clinging for dear life would be rude, she settled for crossing her legs and folding her hands in her lap.

Perfect position for a woman claiming to be disinterested in live-action sex.

Except that somehow Mack had managed to place a leg on either side of her chair and his . . . pants were eye level. Fascinated, she took a long look. Kindra licked her lips. Mack's pants jumped.

Oh, my.

She forced her eyes upward. He no longer looked amused. His legs and other body parts took a large step backward, removing the masculine scent of him from her personal space.

"If I'm going to prove to you that one-on-one sex is better than cybersex, I can only think of one way to do that."

Here it was. It was coming. "Oh?" she squeaked.

Mack nodded, his hands sliding into his pockets. "Yes, that's right, Kindra. It looks like I'm going to have to have sex with you."

Wow. If this was a dream, may she never wake up.

Mack watched shock cross Kindra's face and he fought the urge to smile. Because behind the shock, right there in those fascinating green eyes of hers was . . . interest.

He had her interested.

Strolling into Kindra's office to borrow some software CDs he wanted to install on his computer had been a much better idea than he could have ever anticipated. It was a pure stroke of luck to find her staring intently at her screen, biting her lip as she read a dirty e-mail. An unoriginal dirty e-mail, in his opinion.

He had read about half of it before he had announced his presence by speaking out loud. He would have expected Kindra to blush, but she hadn't, even though she had clearly been flustered.

Kindra Hill was a mystery. One he had been studying for a year, since he had accepted the position at Ohio MicroDesign, a graphic design company in Cleveland. Kindra gave every appearance of being shy and quiet, but when she thought no one was looking, he had been watching her.

Instead of being demure, Kindra rolled her eyes a lot and snorted to herself. She crossed her arms and slouched in her chair when she was alone. If he was quick enough, he could catch her green eyes spitting fire sometimes.

But she always banked it.

And he wanted to know why.

Kindra closed her mouth, then reopened it. Her eyes narrowed. "Why would you want to do that?"

"Are you kidding?" Now he was the one in shock.

Hadn't she looked in a mirror lately? "What guy wouldn't want to?"

She appeared to mull this over and nodded. "That's probably true. Guys are like that."

Her feet pushed on the floor, inching her chair back farther away from him. "But so you know, to prove what you want to prove, well . . . you're really going to have your work cut out for you."

Damn. His groin tightened painfully. Somehow he didn't think he'd mind the extra effort. Besides, he had twelve months' worth of spontaneous hard-ons caused by Kindra to ease. He stuck his foot behind the wheel of her chair so it stopped moving.

Gripping each arm of the chair, he bent over and murmured alongside her cheek, "I think I'm up for the challenge."

She shivered and leaned back in her chair as if she needed distance. Her eyes were half closed and Mack reminded himself to ease up. Take it slow.

Kindra wanted this. But he wanted to make sure nothing changed her mind.

Just because he had a year's worth of frustration wasn't a good excuse to throw charm and finesse out the window and just attack her in a fit of adolescent lust.

If he wasn't careful, he would screw up this perfect opportunity. And he didn't want that. What he wanted was to see what Kindra kept hidden under those boxy suits she always wore. He wanted to pull down that hair she kept tightly bound in a clip and see if it really had auburn highlights like he suspected.

He wanted her.

With deliberate steps, he moved a few feet over to her desk and leaned against it. "So, what do you think? Can I prove you wrong? Or are you perfectly satisfied with what you're getting right now?"

He held his breath.

"Well . . ." She fiddled with the clip on her head, forcing her jacket to rise up a little and give him a hint of her curves.

"So, what did you have in mind?"

Yes. Mack mentally spiked a football in the end zone. "Tonight. Dinner. Then your place."

She would feel safer in her own apartment, he rationalized. More comfortable. And he didn't care where he was as long as he was naked with Kindra.

But her head was shaking no. "I have plans tonight. It's Friday. I bowl on a league on Fridays."

Kindra bowling? That struck him as odd. Maybe because he'd never seen her wearing anything but black or navy suits and high heels.

Bowling was hard for him to understand. You stood there and threw a ball at plastic pins. Now golf was a different story. That was a game.

"Can't you skip tonight?" Damn, he sounded eager. Maybe he should rein that in a little.

"No. My team will lose my score if I don't show. I can't do that."

Fine. It's not like he was in a huge hurry or anything. He wasn't desperate. He'd had plenty lately. Sort of. Well, not really.

And not with Kindra.

He said, "Tomorrow night then?"

She licked her lips again.

Soft, plump lips that were made for kissing and sucking and biting. Lips that would feel fantastic sliding across his cock.

He gritted his teeth in agony.

"Okay," she said, looking as if she'd just been given ten to fifteen years in federal prison. "Tomorrow night."

She wasn't exactly brimming with enthusiasm.

Maybe this wasn't going to be as easy as he'd thought. After all, she was choosing to abstain from sex. There had to be a reason. A reason he had to get around. Even if it took all night.

Speaking of which, that needed to be stated clearly. "You have to guarantee me at least twelve hours to make my case, Kindra."

Kindra blinked. Twelve hours? He was planning on proving it to her for twelve hours? She would have been happy with ten minutes and a wave on his way out.

"Isn't that a little long?"

He was leaning casually against her desk, and when he shifted, his leg brushed against hers. Kindra shivered and recrossed her legs in the opposite direction to move them away from him.

A slow knowing smile moved across his face. "To get it right, sometimes you need to take it slow. And sometimes it's so good, you want time to do it again."

That hadn't happened yet to Kindra. In her experience, the first time had never been worthy of an encore performance.

A sudden vision of Mack coming at her over and over again for twelve hours, determined to squeak an orgasm out of her, flashed through her head. Maybe this was a really bad idea.

If she slept with Mack and it was just awful, well, then what fantasies would she have left? She didn't even want to count how many times it had been Mack's face she'd pictured when chatting intimately with Russ online.

Plus, if this was a disaster, she would have to see Mack every day in awkward hallway encounters where he would avert his eyes and she would blush. They were designing on the coffeehouse website project together, which put them in each other's company constantly.

It would be horrid, awful, migraine inspiring . . .

"Kindra."

"Yes?" She shot Mack a panicked look.

"Don't panic. It doesn't have to be twelve hours. It can be as little or as much as you want." He leaned forward and took her hand.

But it wasn't a gentle caress. Or an understanding squeeze. It was a forceful pull. With little effort, he tugged her to her feet. Kindra swallowed hard as he slid his arms around her waist and pulled her up against him.

This couldn't be happening.

She was in her office in the middle of the day wrapped in Mack Stone's arms from neck to calf. His body was as hard as it looked, and she put her hands on his chest to create a barrier between them.

Instead of pushing him away, her traitorous little fingers gripped his crisp dress shirt and rubbed against the solid muscle underneath. His thigh moved across hers restlessly.

"I have this feeling," he whispered, his lips brushing against the lobe of her ear, "that we're not going to need anywhere near twelve hours to prove my point."

His tongue dipped into her ear and Kindra gasped.

"But I think we're going to want twelve hours."

Kindra suddenly wanted a lot of things, most of all Mack to throw her down on her office floor and put his theory to the test right now.

With a whimper, she pushed her waist forward, bumping his erection.

Mack groaned.

Heat surged through her body. She had made Mack Stone groan out loud. Could there be a bigger turn-on?

"Shit," he said fiercely, his hands gripping her shoulders. "I'm going too fast."

Said who?

If she were gutsy, she would grab him and force him

to go fast again, but Kindra had never claimed to be gutsy. Not in her career, or her social life, and certainly not when it came to sex.

"I want this to be right," he said, setting her away from him. "After all, I've just promised you the best sex of your life."

Kindra struggled not to collapse on the floor in an anticipatory seizure at Mack's words. She couldn't speak. She gulped.

Mack rammed his hands in his pocket. Then pulled them back out. "Ah, hell. Are you sure you're busy tonight?"

He looked desperate. He sounded desperate. Mack Stone. Desperate. For her.

The words were on her lips. She was about to say, *Screw the bowling and take me,* when Kindra's office door flung open. She watched in horror as her friend Ashley walked in.

Ashley took three perky steps before she realized Kindra wasn't alone.

"Oh! Sorry. I didn't know you were in here with Kindra, Mack."

Kindra stood there, inches from Mack, sure her face was a picture of guilt. She might as well have a sign on her forehead saying DESPERATELY SEEKING SEX.

Mack gave Ashley a light charming smile. "No problem. Can you just give us a minute alone? Then I'll be out of your way."

Kindra crossed her arms and took a step back. Did Mack have to be so obvious? Long after he had his twelve hours, she had to work with these people. She didn't relish the idea of being office gossip, even if Ashley was a good friend. If he was this obvious in front of Ashley, who else would he embarrass her in front of?

She said tightly, "What did you need, Ashley?"

Ashley looked startled, and smoothed down her wild blond curls. She looked back and forth between the two of them, her eyes wide. "I wanted to see if you were ready to go to lunch."

"I'm ready." Maybe a cool soft drink could douse this fire Mack had started in her stomach.

Her feet were already carrying her toward the door when Mack's hand stopped her. "We haven't finished our business."

His voice was like fingers down her spine, tickling and teasing. Kindra froze. "What else is there to discuss?"

His thumb stroked her hand. "What time I'm picking you up tomorrow."

She shouldn't have asked. Now Ashley was doing an imitation of a hooked trout.

"We can discuss that later," she said in a high, strangled voice.

He moved around her, letting go of her hand. His eyes followed hers as he headed to the door. There was a wicked grin on his face. She didn't trust that grin.

"Okay," he said with a nod.

Then he strolled out the door in a powerful masculine strut, tossing back, "Bye, Ashley. Later, Kindra."

Kindra was so over her head with him.

"What was that all about?" Ashley demanded, whispering fiercely.

"Mack asked me out." Sort of. As a precursor to twelve hours of horizontal research.

"No kidding?" Ashley fanned herself. "Whoa. You go, girl! Now you've got to tell me every single thing he said, you know."

Not a chance. "Hey, listen, Ash, can I meet you in

your office in five minutes? I've got some stuff to finish up real quick."

Like deleting the e-mail from Russ so she wouldn't get caught again.

Ashley gave her a curious look, but shrugged. "Okay."

"Thanks."

The second Ashley left, Kindra sat back down in her chair and reopened her e-mail. For the last two months she had been exchanging sexy e-mails with Russ, and on Friday and Saturday nights they went into a private chat room and talked "live."

It had been harmless. Until now.

She quickly deleted the e-mail, intending to dash off a quick note back to Russ saying she was busy at work, but would meet him at their usual time and place after bowling tonight. Her finger was on the mouse, ready to create an e-mail, when she noticed a new message in her in-box.

From Mack Stone.

Her body ignited like a blowtorch in response to just seeing his name.

Shoot, she was really in trouble.

Glancing back over her shoulder to make sure no one had crept up on her, she clicked on the message with trepidation.

I'll pick you up at seven. Dinner at Mojo's. What's your address?
—M
Kindra, I ache from wanting you.

No greeting, no preamble, no electronic smiley faces. Just . . . wham. Right between the thighs.

Kindra inserted an address in the send field. Subject: *Date.*

Then she typed:

Russ, I'm so sorry, but I'm going to have to cancel our date tonight. I have a headache.

Mack hadn't even touched her yet and he had already ruined her for other men.

Chapter Two

"I cannot believe you decided to come bowling when you could be on a date right now with Mack Stone." Ashley shook her head at Kindra as she pulled her hot pink bowling ball out of the ball return.

Kindra rubbed her eyes. Her friends had been grilling her for the last forty minutes about her date with Mack. And that was after a similar interrogation from Ashley earlier at lunch.

Trish, who was wearing jeans and a deep red shirt that matched her bowling shoes, set down her beer with a snort. "Seriously, Kindra, why play with bowling balls when you can be playing with Mack Stone's balls?"

"Trish!" Kindra felt herself flushing.

Ashley and Trish laughed. Even Violet, who was even quieter than Kindra, looked shocked, but amused.

If they only knew how much she wanted to play with Mack Stone and all his body parts, they would be beyond shocked. They would stop breathing.

"I didn't want to let the team down. I'm going out with Mack tomorrow night."

"We wouldn't have minded," Violet said, patting Kindra's leg as she sat down on the bench next to her.

Kindra knew her friends wouldn't have minded. And she was actually the worst bowler of the four of them, so they would hardly miss her. But she'd been glad for the excuse. She needed twenty-four hours before she could face Mack.

If she faced Mack. Part of her was still wondering if she should cancel the whole thing and go back to Russ.

She knew what she was getting with Russ. Safe, clean, uncomplicated. He didn't even know her last name or where she lived. For all she knew, Russ lived in Alaska. She would never have to encounter Russ over the water cooler or be cornered by him in her office.

Ashley stomped back from her turn, hands on her hips. "Spare. That's the third one in a row."

"I think I'm going to cancel," Kindra blurted out.

Trish dropped her bowling ball on the floor. It crashed, spun, and landed in the gutter. "Crap, Kindra! You made me throw a gutter ball!"

While Trish's ball rolled slowly down the lane, her friends rounded on her.

"You're nuts," Ashley said.

"Certifiable," Trish said.

Kindra turned to Violet. "What do you think?" Violet would probably be on her side.

Violet brushed her long dark hair out of her face. "I don't blame you, Kindra. He sounds like the kind of guy I wouldn't want to go out with. I like the gentle type."

"You like the dorky type," Trish said disparagingly.

Though Trish and her bad boy types weren't exactly Kindra's style, she had to agree that Violet went for quiet and uninteresting. Sort of like mild salsa. Why even bother? You'd be better off just biting a tomato.

"That's not true." Violet pulled on her turtleneck decorated with miniature pumpkins and shook her head.

Violet was even better at camouflage clothing than

she was. Granted, it was October, and slightly cool, so perhaps a turtleneck might be warranted. But the pumpkins? Kindra couldn't figure that out. She was not into revealing clothes personally, tending to favor conservative suits at work and track pants on the weekends, but never once had she felt the urge to wear tiny pumpkins on her breasts.

"Well." Trish waved her hand. "From what Ashley says about this guy, he's hotter than hot, so if you cancel you're just plain crazy." She grinned. "Or chicken shit."

It was true. She was chicken shit. And she had sworn to herself on her twenty-sixth birthday in July that she was going to stop doing that. She was going to take charge.

That had been the reason for going out and finding Russ, since real men hadn't been working out for the last decade or so. Of course, Russ was real, he just wasn't actually physically there with her. But at any rate, the point was, she had put her foot down on being chicken shit.

And here she was doing it again.

She squeezed her eyes closed. The feel of Mack pressed against her came rushing back.

"Fine, I won't cancel."

"Alright!" Ashley gave her a high five and said, "Now what are you going to wear? Because if you wear those track pants, I will beat you."

Eliminating work clothes and the wind suits didn't leave her many options. "Jeans?" she asked, biting her lip.

Trish said, "It depends on the jeans." She tossed her thumb toward the lane. "Violet, you're up."

Ashley eyed her long and hard and said, "Don't worry. We'll fix you up. By the time we're done with you, Mack Stone will be eating out of your hand."

Her hand was not what she wanted Mack to be eating out.

Kindra mentally groaned. Help her, she was turning into a total pervert. And liking it.

When seven o'clock rolled around on Saturday, Mack was nervous and horny. Not necessarily in that order.

Nervous, because he wanted to do this right.

Horny, because, well, because he was going to have sex with Kindra.

As Mack drove through the West Park neighborhood of neat and tidy houses, he wondered again why a woman like Kindra had sworn off sex. He didn't doubt for a minute that she had. The look on her face had been too serious.

It could be as simple as a sour relationship or just that no man had ever taken the time to give her pleasure. It made him angry that there were men who would just take and never give a thought to a woman's pleasure. He wasn't satisfied until the woman he was with was satisfied.

If Kindra had suffered through a string of lousy lovers, it was no wonder she was disinterested. He could fix that. He could satisfy her. He'd given himself twelve hours after all.

Mack pulled into the driveway of a white Cape Cod with gray shutters. It was tiny but well kept, and there were a couple of pumpkins sitting on the front steps. He'd never pictured Kindra as the homeowner type.

They had worked together a lot over the past year, and about the only thing he could say about her for sure was that she was intelligent. She did her job well. Quickly and with little fuss.

Other than that, he couldn't claim to know Kindra at all.

He wanted to know her. And not just in the physical sense. He was drawn to her, attracted to that flash in her eyes that popped up from time to time.

Parking his black SUV in the driveway, he got out and rang the doorbell. He waited. And waited. He rang the bell again.

Rocking on the balls of his feet, he peeked in the window. He couldn't tell if she was home or not. Had he been stood up? That hadn't happened to him since . . . ever.

The door flew open. Kindra hovered there, her face pale and her eyes huge. Her hair was still tightly bound in a clip, and she wore no makeup that he could tell, but she had on a denim skirt.

It hugged her hips and ended with a naughty little slit in the middle an inch or two above her knees. Mack swallowed hard. He'd seen Kindra's legs plenty of times at work. But covered in nylons and sticking out from under a shapeless black skirt.

Now her smooth, creamy legs were bare, making his hand ache to run along her calf. She wore sandals with straps and her toenails were painted a chestnut color, giving rise to images of her feet sliding across a white sheet.

Above the skirt rested a navy blue tank top. Which was not revealing in any way. But given that Mack was used to having all of Kindra covered in layers of business boring, this was enticing.

The cotton top was straining against her lush chest. He stared in appreciation. Kindra had been hiding some great tits.

"Hi," she said breathlessly.

"Hi," he said with a glance up, then couldn't stop himself from zeroing back in on her chest. Why had she been covering those up? It defied logic.

Her arms covered her chest and a pink hue tinted her cheeks. Her embarrassment was evident. It was also arousing.

With a smile, he reached out and pulled her arms away with a light tug. "No, don't cover up. I'm enjoying the view. You have a beautiful body, Kindra."

She tugged her arms back. "You're making me uncomfortable."

"I'm going to see it all anyway, sooner or later."

"Later," she whispered.

"So, you haven't changed your mind?" He needed to hear her say it, having had twenty-four hours to think about it, that this was what she wanted to do.

Her chest rose and fell. Her hand crept up to fiddle with the clip on her head. Finally, she took a deep breath and said, "No. I haven't changed my mind."

Thank God. Mack tried not to fall on the ground and kiss her feet in gratitude. But hell, for a second there, he had feared for his sexual safety. If she had said no, he might have actually suffered some real damage from lack of release.

He smiled at her. "I'm glad. Now are you ready for dinner?"

They didn't talk on the ten-minute drive to the restaurant in a trendy rejuvenated old neighborhood. Kindra seemed to be concentrating on breathing, and keeping her legs crossed and far away from him. Mack was concentrating on driving and accidentally-on-purpose bumping her with various parts of his body as often as he could.

A thigh brush here, an arm rub there. At one point he stretched all the way across the front of her, brushing everything, to retrieve his sunglasses from the glove compartment. Kindra sucked in her breath and froze.

Whether or not it was arousing Kindra, he couldn't tell, but it sure had him hot and bothered.

Mack had called Mojo's ahead of time and had requested the smallest table in the darkest corner. As he guided Kindra to the table, his hand on the small of her back, he was happy to see they had followed his instructions.

Once seated, they were sitting almost next to each other, plants and shadows separating them from the nearby tables. Their knees were touching.

Mack slipped his hand under the table and stroked Kindra's bare knee. Smooth and soft.

She jerked it away.

Now he intended to find out exactly why Kindra had chosen cybersex over the real thing. And what would be his best strategy to please her. To make her moan. To have her begging for more.

He shifted as his black pants swelled beneath the table. Damn. If he kept this up, he was going to knock the whole table over with his dick.

"So how does a nice girl like you wind up having online sex?" he said, going with the element of surprise.

Kindra nearly swallowed the lemon wedge in her iced tea. Eyes watering, she coughed and sputtered. She should have known Mack would be curious and questioning. He certainly was at work, and it made him a good designer. But they weren't talking about download times here, they were talking about *sex*.

But this was not like a normal date.

Mack Stone was a cut-to-the-chase kind of guy. Working with him had shown her that. The encounter in her office the day before had confirmed that.

He was also a flirt and something of an expert on

women. Everywhere he went, there was bound to be one or two dangling after him, giggling and smiling and offering to fetch and carry for him.

To Mack, this was probably just mild, everyday kind of stuff. Eat dinner, talk about sex, then do it. But for her, little Kindra Hill, this wasn't exactly the kind of conversation she had on a regular basis. She didn't talk about sex.

Well, if you didn't count Russ, that is. But that was different. That was like an outlet, a hobby. Some women scuba dived, some women knitted. Kindra talked dirty to Russ.

Which somehow made her seem frighteningly sad and twisted. Maybe it wasn't too late to take up chess or spelunking. Tennis could be fun.

In answer to his question, she said carefully, "I'm not sure that's any of your business."

His ice blue eyes never left hers. "You're my business. For tonight anyway. I want to know you."

Kindra shivered and wished she hadn't let Ashley talk her into wearing this tank top. It was clingy and totally ridiculous for October, even if the temperature had peaked at seventy degrees that afternoon. She had worn a denim jacket with the tank top at home, but the cut was so narrow, it had made her feel as if she were stuffed in a straitjacket, so she had taken it off.

Now she wished she were covered in head-to-toe denim. Loose denim. A denim sack. Then maybe she wouldn't feel like Mack was looking at her, picturing her naked.

Of course, the whole point was that she wanted him to see her naked. No—correction—she wanted to see *him* naked.

But getting from here to there was the hard part. She almost wished he had just jumped her bones the minute she had opened her front door and had forgotten all about this wine-and-dine part.

But that would make her a really cheap date. She was being cheap enough already; she supposed she should at least spend the guy's money first. A flush started hiking up her face. She wasn't so good at this in-person business.

"Well," Mack said. "If you're going to talk dirty, you should at least find someone who knows how."

While this sounded interesting, Kindra was aware that though they were in a dark corner, they were still in a public place. With other people around. Mack's voice sounded really, really loud to her.

She opened her mouth to shush him.

"I mean, that guy is completely unoriginal. Come on." His voice rose another notch. "I want to lick your nipples until you come like a rocket, hot and wet . . ."

Yikes. Did he want a microphone in case the chef didn't hear? Or maybe he could take out a billboard ad or start an *Embarrass the Shit out of Kindra* website. She darted a glance around and nearly hid under the table-cloth when she saw that two different tables of people were gawking at them.

Mack was oblivious to her horror. Or the shocked looks of their fellow diners.

"That sounds like he just typed a passage right from a porno."

Kindra fisted her hands and whispered, "Mack!" Couldn't he see she was mortified?

"Now if I was going to say something to you, it would be something like, 'I can't sleep without seeing you in my dreams.'"

Wait a minute. Hold the phone. She looked at him in surprise. Was he trying to get poetic on her? That wasn't part of their bargain. She couldn't handle him saying loverlike things as if he actually cared about her. It would be too much like what she really wanted.

Kindra sat up straight, startled at her thoughts. What did she really want? Sex with Mack, right? Nothing else.

Right?

Mack brushed against her knee with his leg, and she felt it reverberate through every inch of her body.

"No? Not your style? How about, 'You're a beautiful woman and I want you so bad I ache to taste you.' "

Kindra had known she was no match for him. This confirmed it. He seemed to be teasing her, a little smile playing around the corner of his mouth. She sat stock still, afraid to move, afraid to say something needy and grasping, which was how she suddenly felt.

Vulnerable.

"Not doing it for you?" Mack smiled patiently. "Do you like it dirty? I can talk dirty to you, Kindra. How about . . . 'You've got a sweet little ass and I can't wait to fuck it.' "

Her mouth dropped. She felt it clunk down onto her chest. She found her voice. "I don't think, uh, dirty, is my style."

Not that she had a style. But Mack using words like *that* when talking about her was too much. Way too much. So Russ used them with her all the time. But Russ wasn't real. Russ was like her computer screen had just gotten really smart and was talking with her. Real, but not real at all.

Russ wasn't looking her in the face. With gorgeous blue eyes and muscles rippling in his short-sleeve rayon shirt. Russ didn't have a low, powerful voice that made women want to stand up and howl at the moon.

Russ wasn't Mack. Oh, so real, and oh, so close.

Mack grinned. "Dirty's not your style? Not yet, anyway."

If she were inclined to be honest, which she wasn't, she kind of liked it when he talked like that. But nothing was going to make her admit that. Not in public. If he tried really hard in private, using all his powers of naked persuasion, she might concede the point.

The waiter stopped next to them, brandishing plates of food. "Oh, look, our dinner is here!" she beamed at the waiter, then took a nice long swallow of her iced tea.

Maybe she should have accepted the wine Mack had suggested instead. She was a little tense.

When the waiter moved away, leaving the steaming fajitas in front of her, Kindra busied herself with filling and rolling up a tortilla.

As Mack did the same, he suddenly asked, "How old are you?"

Pausing with a pepper on her fork, Kindra looked at him. He wasn't looking at her, but was cutting his chicken. It was a harmless question.

She answered, "I'm twenty-six."

"How long have you worked for MicroDesign?"

"Four years." Kindra took a bite of her fajita and savored the spicy flavor.

"So do you own your house or do you rent?"

Was this a loan application?

She swallowed her food and said suspiciously, "Why do you ask?"

He shrugged and leaned back against his chair. "I'm just trying to get to know you, that's all."

Well, stop it. That was the last thing she wanted.

This was supposed to be like the live version of Russ. Anonymous. Sex for the sake of sex. Mack would try and prove his point, she would get to fulfill a year-long fantasy, and everything would be hunky dory. On Monday they would pretend this had never happened, and life would go on.

Instead of telling him that, Kindra found herself saying, "I just bought the house six months ago. I was tired of living in an apartment."

"I know what you mean. I have these neighbors who are always yelling at each other. And I'd like to get a dog, but my building has this ten-pound rule. What kind of a dog is under ten pounds?" He shook his head. "Not any kind of dog I'd want."

The image of Mack with a poodle popped into her head. She giggled before she could stop it.

"What?" He paused with his fork halfway to his mouth.

"Nothing." Kindra put her napkin in front of her so he wouldn't see her smiling.

"Tell me."

"Okay." She dropped the napkin. "I was just picturing you walking a poodle. With bows in its fur and a little hot pink sweater."

Mack's lips twitched. "Hey! I don't think so."

Kindra laughed. "You could call her Bitsy. She could ride in your backpack with your laptop."

Mack looked amused. He grinned and said, "You'd like to see that, wouldn't you?"

"I'd love to," she said with relish, not stopping to temper her words. For a minute, she'd forgotten that he was Mack Stone, and she shouldn't be herself with him. She had forgotten that over the years she'd learned it was better to fade into a corner than draw attention to herself.

Her philosophy at MicroDesign had been put up and shut up. Do her job and leave the office politics to those who were capable of handling it.

Hide the bod and the brain.

It had worked.

But it also left her feeling unfulfilled and restless. Daring. Reckless.

Capable of throwing herself into a one-night stand with Mack Stone.

"I like you, Kindra," Mack said, his tone changing from amused to aroused.

Her laugh cut off. His hand was on her knee. My God, he was stroking up her leg, past her thigh, to her . . .

A gurgling sound left her mouth.

"Mack."

Did that ridiculous breathy voice belong to her? She'd never heard that kitten purr emerge from her mouth in her life.

Flustered and hot, Kindra tried to back her chair out. She hit the wall.

Mack's hand settled onto her inner thigh above the knee, stroking lightly back and forth. Her skirt was bunching a little. He was barely even leaning to reach her and she felt a little like how a fish on a hook must feel. She could thrash about, but that would only make it worse.

Besides, it felt . . . good. Naughty. If anyone was glancing their way, it would look like he was resting his hand on her knee under the table. No big deal, people did that all the time.

Gripping the table, she strove to act normal. Mack was eating more chicken with his free hand, his face a delicious combination of feigned innocence and wicked intent.

She wanted him. His fingers were a vicious little tease, so close yet so far, and she was having trouble breathing. Her nipples were beading painfully against her tank top, and she ached and throbbed.

With a deep breath, she reached for her fajita.

Mack pinched her inner thigh lightly, sending a jolt of heat surging between her legs. Her hand jerked and the fajita fell on the table, beef tumbling out.

Mack, his blue eyes clouded with desire, said, "I think we're skipping dessert, aren't we?"

Yeah, yes, uh-huh, that would be correct.

Would it look pathetic if she called for the check now?

Mack said, "I'm not really hungry. Let's get this to go."

She was liking him more and more each minute.

Chapter Three

Mack was having a little trouble keeping his eyes on the road. They kept wanting to drift over to Kindra, who had her legs crossed again in the passenger seat, but whose skirt had hiked up way past the point of indifference.

Just one hand in and under the denim, and he would be touching her panties. He should have bought an automatic transmission instead of stick. Then his hand would be free to roam about the cabin, right under Kindra's skirt.

They weren't talking, but the air was filled with Mexican spices from their boxed dinners, and a healthy dose of sexual tension.

Every inch of him was aware of her. Her soft breasts rising and falling, her small hands clasping and unclasping, and her sweet floral smell.

He was hard and heading out of control.

Kindra peeked at him from underneath long lashes.

His SUV flew into her driveway at forty miles an hour and he slammed on the brakes.

Kindra grabbed the dashboard and gasped. "That was fast."

"Can you get something out of the glove compartment for me?" If he had to lean across her tits, he was not going to be able to resist a kiss. Or a suck. Right here in her driveway.

"Sure." She popped it open. "Oh!"

She had spotted the big box of condoms he had thrown in there. Magnum size. Not that he was bragging or anything, but the regular kind just weren't comfortable.

"Yeah, just grab those, Kindra, and we'll go on in."

"Okay," she squeaked.

She gingerly pulled them out and held them away from her as if they were moldy cheese.

They got out of the car, and he followed her up the walk to the front door. Kindra, in her eagerness to keep the condoms away from her, had forgotten to push her skirt back down.

It was sliding and curving and moving, hugging her tight little ass and showing off a lot of thigh. It was made more alluring by the fact that Kindra was completely unaware that she looked hotter than hell.

On the front step, she took her key and bent her head to unlock the door.

The skirt cupped her ass. He could see her panty line. The last remaining threads of his control snapped.

When the door opened, he put his hands on her waist and pushed her in. She barely had time for a startled cry before he had spun her around and placed his mouth on hers.

Damn, she tasted good. Like sweet and hot and spicy, her plump lips falling open with a sigh of capitulation. He pushed his tongue in and plundered deep into her mouth.

His hands gripped her waist, pulling her against him, and he moved his legs around hers to cage her in with his body. He caressed her ass, grinding her against him as his fingers slid over the denim of her skirt. Too many clothes. They needed to come off.

Her breath came hot and fast in his ear as he pulled back and she whimpered.

That needy sound made him reach out and pull her bottom lip into his mouth and suck gently. He eased her against the nearest wall.

Her head fell back. She groaned. He pulsed with need. He wanted her more than he had ever wanted any woman, ever.

He was going to have her.

His hand shot out, ready to grip her tank top and rip it off, when she whispered, "Mack."

Kindra's shy, trembling voice stopped him cold. He was supposed to be doing this right, taking his time and showing her that making love could be a wonderful thing, better than anything you could ever talk about in a chat room.

Don't blow this for her, he told himself harshly. His dick could wait five minutes.

Taking a deep breath, he stepped back. He shoved his hands in his pockets and cleared his throat. He counted to five.

Then he said in what was almost a normal voice, "Where's your computer, Kindra?"

Kindra blinked. What the heck was he talking about? She clung to the wall, her knee jutting out from where his leg had shoved her thighs apart.

He was moving into her living room, looking around, as if nothing had just happened between them. He said, "Are you connected all the time, or do you need to dial up?"

Why? Did he want to order a CD? Check his e-mail? Torture her?

She peeled herself off the wall and wiped her wet lips. "What?"

Though his stance was casual, Kindra could clearly see his huge erection pressing against his black casual pants. Good to see he wasn't totally unaffected.

"Cybersex, remember? If I'm going to prove to you that the real thing is better, I have to know what that guy is saying to you." He rubbed his jaw slowly. "I'll read what he says . . . then do whatever it is to you."

Hello. Kindra felt her knees go weak. She flopped against the wall again. Mack was four feet away from her and he was still causing her body to tingle.

His eyes ran up and down the length of her. His voice was hard. "Then you can decide which way is better."

"It's in the spare bedroom." She pointed down her hall. "My bedroom is upstairs, in one big room, because this is a Cape Cod, the other two bedrooms are down here, I use one for an office."

Clapping her mouth shut on her verbal diarrhea, Kindra let Mack take her hand and pull her toward the office. Her computer was on. She left it running all the time, and she had a twenty-four-hour connection, so it was just sitting there, humming happily, waiting for her.

Mack said, "Open one of his e-mails."

Kindra hesitated, hovering in the middle of the room. There was some graphic stuff in those. "I delete them all."

Mack smiled, his eyebrow raising. "Just retrieve them from the trash, Kindra. Come on, there's got to be some in there."

The room was small, and cluttered with the desk, a file cabinet, and a swivel chair. It had thick brown carpet that she had been meaning to replace, and she stumbled, her heel caught in a loose loop of the carpet. Mack caught her and held her for a heartbeat, then released her.

With trembling fingers, still standing, she went into her mailbox and fished around in her trash can.

"Here's one." Mack pointed to her screen.

There was more than one. There were a dozen at least. Russ's e-mail address stared back at her in black print, mocking her. Could she do this? Shy Kindra?

Could she indulge herself, enjoy this without guilt, and relegate Kindra the wallflower to the closet for one night?

"Open this one."

His voice was commanding, but soft. Titillating, but not frightening. She knew he wouldn't do anything she didn't want to.

Her finger clicked on the mouse.

The mail popped up.

" 'Kindra, what are you wearing?' " Mack read. He chuckled. "I told you, not very original."

He turned to look her over. "But let's see. What are you wearing?"

Kindra stood still in front of the desk while Mack moved around her, his finger trailing across her back.

"Sexy tank top in blue." He went around the front, his fingertip dragging over her arm and falling onto her breast. "A bra. Definitely wearing a bra."

He brushed her nipple. She gasped, then bit her lip nervously. The finger dipped down between her breasts, causing her to shiver, and headed down to her skirt, where Mack tugged at the waistband.

"Denim skirt."

Down, down he went while she narrowed her eyes and clenched her fists. Oh, help, he was on his knees now in front of her. She knew what he was going to do, and yet she didn't. Whatever it was, it would be a tease.

She wanted his hands on her, both of them, touching, stroking, not this furtive brush with one finger.

She guessed that was the point. To make her ache. His finger wiggled into the slit of her skirt and rose vertically again, dragging the skirt up with him.

She felt cool air on her thighs, and then the pad of his finger reached out and pressed against her sweet spot through her panties. Moisture flooded her.

"Panties." He studied her. "Very hot, very see-through panties."

It had been a dare to herself. They were brand-new, never-been-worn-before, sheer black panties. She'd seen what they looked like on her in the mirror. She knew exactly what Mack was staring at right now. His face was only inches away from her curls. All he would have to do was pull the panties aside, then touch her . . .

He dropped the skirt back into place. Kindra could have sobbed with disappointment.

His hand caressed against her foot. "Sandals."

Then he rose up in front of her, brushing but never fully touching as he rose to his full height. Taller and taller until he hovered over her powerfully, despite the heels of her shoes.

Bending down over her, lips parted. Kindra closed her eyes, waiting for his mouth to take hers again. He moved past her mouth and she opened her eyes in confusion. Her head yanked back.

With a startled cry, she realized he was undoing her hair from its twist.

"One hair clip, no longer in place." Mack tossed it over his shoulder and drove his fingers into her hair.

It hurt a little. He wasn't gentle and the hair tugged and pulled, but Kindra barely noticed, so arousing was the look on his face.

Mack was murmuring, "I love your hair. I've been dying to see it down. I just knew it would have red streaks in it."

Her hair could be purple and green for all she cared. Kindra boldly reached for him, wrapping her arms around his neck, urging him toward her mouth.

Mack brushed her lips, his tongue flicking across her quickly before he pulled back. She stumbled again as he let her go.

"Let's see what else your friend has to say."

Kindra stood in fascination, watching Mack scroll down through her e-mails. He was serious about this. He was going to act out Russ's e-mails.

Mack was going to touch and tease and stroke her until she either died from pleasure or begged for mercy, whichever came first.

Either of those worked for her.

"Here we go." Mack stood up straight again and read, " 'I bet you have great tits, Kindra.' "

Mack glanced at her tank top. "I can attest to that."

Kindra rubbed her hands on her skirt and tried not to cross her arms over her chest. She didn't remember those exact words from Russ, so she didn't know what was coming next. That was both frightening and arousing.

Mack went on. " 'They're probably round and full, with hard, taut nipples that want to be sucked. I'll suck them hard and fast, my tongue tasting you everywhere.' "

His mouth quirked up at the corner. "Hard and taut are redundant, and I don't think your nipples have a mind of their own, but we get the point."

He closed the distance between them, and before Kindra could even think, his mouth was on her. He was sucking and pulling through her shirt, without warning or preparation.

"Oh my God!" she said, then closed her mouth in mortification at her words.

Mortification quickly gave way to pleasure.

His hands were on her waist and he pushed the tank top up, the arm on his hair tickling her skin. Another second and he had tugged her bra down, and her breasts were spilling out.

His firm, wet tongue flickered across her. Kindra gripped his shoulders and whimpered. He wasn't being gentle, but was raking across her with his tongue, before pulling her breast back into his mouth.

Oh, yes.

Teeth nipped her and she felt an odd mix of pleasure and pain that was new and downright interesting. When he stood up, she rocked back toward him. She didn't want him to stop, not now when she was hot and aching and desperate for completion.

Mack's eyes were dark, the normally ice blue a lustful royal shade. He wiped the moisture from his mouth and said, "He said to suck hard."

Likely excuse. Kindra was starting to suspect Mack was getting off on this just as much as she was.

Which was a lot.

"Hard and fast," she repeated, tossing her hair back out of her eyes.

Mack was damn near to exploding. He wanted Kindra and he wanted her yesterday, but he was having a fucking good time turning her on like this, nice and slow.

It was obvious no man had ever bothered to take the time to get Kindra good and ready, and Mack was enjoying watching her. She looked shocked, but damn if she didn't look like she was basking in it.

Those green eyes were round and stunned, glazed with passion. She kept making little sounds of encouragement and pleasure, then looked embarrassed to realize she had. And she was completely letting him take the lead.

He was doing, and she was taking.

Until today, Mack had thought he'd had a lot of great sex in his life, even if his reputation had been exaggerated. He did date a lot, but there hadn't been that many women he had actually slept with. But he had considered those times to be damn great sex.

He had been wrong. That had been good sex. But nothing had made him this edgy, this eager, this nervous to please, this out of control.

Sex in the past had ultimately always been about him. Sure, he'd prided himself on pleasing his partner, but he had been in it for him.

This was a new thing, this pleasure from pleasuring someone else. He wanted to get Kindra off all night and just watch.

He turned back to the computer screen. Kindra seemed to like this method of acting out her online fantasies.

" 'Take your bra off for me.' " He smiled at Kindra. "Oh, I like this one."

She stood still in front of him, her rich auburn hair sliding across her shoulders. Her hands rubbed across her skirt again.

"It doesn't say anything about taking your top off, so leave that on."

Hands on the bottom of her tank top, she said, "You can't watch."

Laughing, he closed his eyes. "Fine." He was going to see it all anyway. He'd already had his mouth on her nipple, but hey, if she wanted to be shy, he didn't mind.

Eyes shut, he leaned back against the computer desk and crossed his feet.

"Have you ever had great sex, Kindra?"

Kindra, busy wrestling with her bra straps, said without thinking, "No."

She mentally groaned. She hadn't meant to say that out loud. She didn't want Mack to think there was something wrong with her, or that she was difficult to please.

He said, "That's not your fault, you know. That's his fault, whoever he was."

Tugging her bra down her arm and freeing it from the tank top, Kindra watched Mack leaning there, eyes still closed. Could he see somehow? He looked like he was smirking.

"Maybe it was my fault. Maybe I'm hard to please." She didn't know why she said that, her private fear, but once out there, she couldn't take it back.

Mack's mouth curved up. "I don't think so. You seem to be enjoying yourself so far. Are you? Enjoying yourself?"

"Yes." It was so much easier to be honest when he wasn't staring at her. And she was enjoying herself. More than she had thought possible.

"Good."

His eyes popped open. "Have you ever had an orgasm?"

With a man in the room? She froze, her bra dangling in her hands, the urge to laugh overcoming her. Let's see, she could count the times on one hand . . . no, make that one finger.

Once. And she was convinced it was a pure accident, since it had yet to be repeated.

"What do you mean?" she hedged, twisting her bra between her hands.

He laughed. He straightened up. Shoot. He was coming toward her. She took a step back.

"It's a simple question. Have you ever had an orgasm?"

"Yes."

"During sex? Were you on top, the bottom, from behind maybe?"

Her face started to burn. From behind? He could not be serious. "None of the above."

He stopped right in front of her, and his fingers wrapped around the bra and yanked it away from her. He dropped it on the floor.

"With his finger then? His tongue?"

There was no way she could answer that. Not with him standing so close her breasts were rubbing across the softness of his shirt. Not when his erection pressed lightly against her mound, then pulled back.

Forward, back, forward, a soft light rhythm that echoed the primal urges she felt.

She couldn't admit out loud that she seemed incapable of an orgasm. He might give up and go home. So she whispered, "I don't think that's in the e-mails, is it?"

His eyes darkened. "Oh, good point. So let's see what's next, shall we?"

When he turned, she breathed a sigh of relief. She couldn't think when he was that close to her. Her body was heavy and feverish and she was starting to feel the pangs of desperation.

Mack looked like he could play like this all night. For twelve hours.

Kindra didn't think she could take much more. Mack was going so damn slow, and he was teasing her with more foreplay than she'd had in a year-long relationship with her ex-boyfriend.

It was now a fact in her mind that she had been robbed. To have made it to the age of twenty-six and never felt this kind of pleasure before was a crying shame. She had a mind to call up the three different men she had slept with and tell them they'd been doing it wrong.

Very wrong.

Maybe Mack could give them some tips. He certainly knew what he was doing.

And if the number of smiling women he had dated in the past were any indication, she wasn't the only one who thought so.

Jealousy surged up in Kindra, catching her off guard. She didn't like the thought of Mack looking at another woman the way he did her. But he wasn't hers.

He was hers for only twelve hours. She had to remember that.

So she should do her best to enjoy him for the time she had, then worry about the after later.

Mack's profile was toward her, and she watched his lips move as he read silently. Admiring his strong jaw and straight nose, she was distracted by the urge to bury her hands in that short black hair and tug.

"You know what?" he said, glancing over at her. "We've been doing this wrong, I think."

It was working for her. "Why?"

"Because this isn't how you would be doing this normally, is it? I mean, when you're here by yourself, reading these e-mails."

She stared at him, not sure what he meant. "I don't know . . ."

A finger came out and landed on her mouth. "Shh. I'll show you what I mean."

The scent of his skin, a salty sweet smell with remnants of spices, rose to her nostrils.

Guided by instinct, she slipped her tongue out between her lips and licked his finger.

It was a tossup who was more surprised.

"*Shit,*" he exclaimed, his eyes half closed.

Her sentiments exactly.

He slid his finger in between her lips.

Kindra wrapped herself around it and sucked, gently. Mack hovered over her. She could feel his control wavering as he struggled to hold himself still.

She sucked harder, pulling his finger down deep, gliding her tongue up and down. It occurred to her exactly what she was mimicking and the thought had her aching for him inside her.

When he yanked his finger back, she cried out in disappointment.

"Naughty, naughty," he taunted. "I can see I'm going to have to keep a closer eye on you."

Kindra wished he would. An eye, and a hand, and a tongue . . .

Her aggressive move had startled her. She wasn't used to taking the lead with men.

But she also knew it wasn't in her nature to be so obedient. It was something she had trained herself to do, until she had lost sight of herself in her shy persona.

Mack made her feel bold.

"Sorry," she lied with a grin.

"No, you're not."

Shaking her head, she admitted, "No."

He brushed her mouth with a hot kiss. "Good. You're free to do whatever you want here, Kindra. Sex with me is never having to say you're sorry."

It sounded funny and she let out a soft laugh.

With a grin, he said, "Are you laughing at me?"

"Not *at* you. With you," she corrected, remembering the reprimands she used to receive from her mother.

He snorted. "I wasn't laughing." He squeezed her hand. "But don't worry, you won't be laughing in a minute. Not when you're having the greatest sex you've ever had."

She was ready. Bring it on. "I promise not to laugh." She let her eyes drop down to his erection.

He got the implied joke. "Hey!"

She found herself pressed up hard against him, his mouth on her neck, his impressive male parts bumping her in the perfect spot.

He was chuckling. "You're going to regret that, Kindra Hill. No more Mr. Nice Guy."

She didn't want nice. She wanted hard. She wanted down and dirty.

"Sorry." Then she said in a soft meek voice that was anything but, "I'll be good."

Mack made a strangled sound as he moved back a step, shaking his head. "I can't wait to see how good you're going to be."

Neither could she.

Chapter Four

Damn, damn, damn. Did she know what she had just done to him? He had almost lost it right then and there without her even laying a finger on him.

Hell, he knew there was more to Kindra than the up-tight woman she was at work. Hadn't he seen that flash in her eyes? It was there now, as her eyes defied her words.

Kindra was dynamite, just waiting to explode.

Her mouth said she would be good, but her eyes said she wanted to be bad, very bad.

Perfect.

He pulled her forward. "I was talking about the e-mails, remember? I want you to show me how you read them."

Confusion crossed her face.

"Do you sit in the chair? Do you stand up?" It had given him a sleepless night last night imagining her reading those e-mails, getting all hot and bothered, with no one to satisfy her.

Fuck. Now *he* was hot and bothered. Again. Maybe he had never stopped being turned on since the minute he'd walked into her office the day before.

"I sit in the chair."

"Have a seat then." He gestured to the chair, pulled out in front of the computer.

"What do you wear? Pajamas? Sexy clothes? Or are you naked?" That was an image that wouldn't leave now that he'd pictured it. Kindra, naked, legs crossed, head thrown back, hand on the mouse.

She gasped. "Not naked. Just regular clothes."

"Show me," he urged.

She sat down in the chair. It swiveled a little. She looked at him in question.

"And then you just read?"

Kindra nodded wordlessly.

"So read to me. Out loud." He had chosen the message he wanted. It was up on the screen.

There was a pause, then she turned toward the screen. Mack saw her jaw work as she swallowed hard. Then she spoke in a tremulous voice.

" 'Kindra, I want my hands all over you.' " Her cheeks stained a pretty pink color.

He dropped his hands to her shoulders and spread his fingers out.

She jerked forward.

"Shh. Keep reading."

Her body was rigid, straight in the chair, but after a deep breath, she read, " 'I want to run my fingers down over your nipples and fill my hands with your hot tits.' "

She whispered the last word, succumbing to shyness at the last second.

"What? I didn't catch the last thing you said."

Right. He had heard her, she was sure of it. He was playing with her again. And she liked it. A lot.

She said, marginally louder, " 'Tits.' "

Kindra knew her face was burning. She couldn't believe she was doing this, but at the same time she was excited, pulsing with need and feeling brassy and bold. Mack's hands were trailing down her chest, brushing past her nipples to cup her, squeezing gently. He pulled her tank top up past her breasts.

Her eyes drifted closed.

"What else?"

She refocused on the screen. " 'Then I'll rub your nipples, pinch them until you beg for me to suck them . . .' " She trailed off with a gasp.

Mack was already rubbing and pinching, his hands moving slowly and lazily as if he had nothing better to do but stand there over her and tease her, working her like a radio dial. She panted. She groaned.

Her head fell back. He moved and moved until she couldn't stand it. Twisting in the chair, arching to make him take more, she cried out.

His hands didn't move away or take more, they just kept brushing and squeezing until she was gripping the seat of the chair in agony.

"Mack, please!"

"Please what?"

"Suck them. Please." Shyness came a distant second to greedy passion.

"Since you asked so nicely." His head came over her shoulder, and he pushed her shirt out of the way.

He pulled her into his mouth, and she groaned. Yes, that's what she wanted, and she threw her arm back to allow him better access. Desire shot through her, and she pushed her sandals against the carpet.

The wheels moved the chair a little and sent him off balance.

"Now don't go anywhere," he said as he stood back up.

Kindra reached her arms up, intent on pulling him back, but he moved out of her reach.

"What's next?"

"What?" She realized he meant the e-mail, of course, but needed to hear him say it. Wanted him to guide her.

"You know what I mean. Read, Kindra."

So she did, her inhibitions melting like marshmallows over a campfire. If reading got him to touch her, that's what she would do, because she really, really wanted him to keep touching her. " 'If you're wearing a skirt, my hand will move down past your stomach, cupping you.' "

Her breath hitched. Mack's hand covered her.

"So hot. You're burning right through the denim."

She could burn through steel right now. " 'Then if you're wearing panties, you'll stand up and I'll take them off.' "

Resigned, eager, she got to her feet without him telling her to. She panted as Mack got down on his knees. Hands went up her skirt, slid under her panties around to her ass, and massaged her naked skin. Mack dropped hot hard kisses on the front of her skirt.

Then he pulled her panties down, fast, and a shiver passed through her.

"Step out, then sit back down." His voice was ragged, gruff.

She stood there a moment, catching her breath, aware that her top was still bunched up above her breasts. Mack was still fully dressed, but she didn't feel uncomfortable.

This was more arousing than she could have ever imagined. She felt dizzy, heady with the sensations rushing through her body.

She sat back down, pressing her knees together and

leaning back against the chair. Mack went behind her again, and she could smell the sharp sheen of sweat on him.

"Read."

She found her place in the message.

" 'I'll pull your skirt up, yank your legs apart, then stick my finger inside of you.' " Ohmigod. Mack was dragging her skirt up, spreading her, then in he went, sliding inside her without any hesitation.

She jerked on the chair. "Mack," she murmured on a heavy groan.

"What now?"

She couldn't speak; she couldn't read anymore. Her knees fell farther apart. She wiggled, trying to entice him to action. His finger was just resting inside her.

"I can't do it anymore," she gasped.

He still wasn't moving. His voice in her ear was low and coaxing. "You do it when you're here alone, don't you? I bet you do the reading and the touching. Don't you?"

"Mack," she begged, tilting her head back.

His finger moved so slowly she thought she would scream with frustration. She tried to move herself down farther on him, but he held her still.

"Answer the question, Kindra. Do you touch yourself?"

She saw what he was doing now. He wasn't going to move until she told him. Desperate, she told him the truth. Anything to have him slide into her.

"Yes," she moaned. "I touch myself."

Mack told himself to breathe. He was bent over Kindra, his head tantalizingly close to her tit and she was spread for him. His finger was inside her where she was tight and warm.

And wet. Damn was she wet. For him.

"I thought maybe you did." It was an image that would stay with him for a lifetime, Kindra in her chair with her fingers between her thighs. But tonight he was doing all the touching.

"I'll read this time for you." He focused on the screen. " 'I'll slide in all the way, nice and deep, then back out again. In again, then out. You'll like that, won't you?' "

As he moved his finger to the words, Kindra whimpered.

"Yes, I like it."

Mack liked it too. She was swollen, pulsing, and slick with need. He went on.

" 'You're so hot and wet and ready to be fucked, but you won't get to be fucked, just my finger. Or maybe two . . .' "

Kindra gave a breathy sigh as he pushed another finger alongside the first. It was a hot snug fit.

"Oh, yes," she whispered.

" 'Or maybe not.' " Mack withdrew.

She gave a cry of disappointment that went straight to his cock.

" 'Or maybe I'll touch your clit, rubbing it until you can't sit still.' "

Kindra was already having trouble sitting still. Mack used his weight leaning over to hold her gently in the chair. He didn't want her bucking his finger off her and interrupting her pleasure.

With each stroke, she made a low sound of approval. Her nipple brushed his cheek as she arched her back. He moved faster over her clit, rubbing in a light circle.

" 'Then when you're not expecting it, I'll slide back into you with two fingers, stretching you.' "

Mack went back inside Kindra, closing his own eyes

for a second at the tight feel of her. He could smell her desire now, sweet and tangy, as she leaned back against the chair, her fingers ripping at the fabric seat.

Her skirt was bunched at her waist and he had a nice view of her damp curls, spread for his fingers. It took everything he had to focus back on the computer screen, but he wanted to finish this.

He wanted Kindra to trust him. He wanted her to come before he did, while he was still in all his clothes. He wanted to show her what she had been missing.

What she could have with him.

" 'You're going to come for me, Kindra, with my fingers inside you, stroking and sliding. You'll feel so good, and when you come, I want to hear you scream.' "

Kindra's breath was hard and fast, her muscles starting to twitch. He could feel how close she was. Burying his head in her neck, he kept stroking. Her skin was hot and damp from exertion and she had squeezed her eyes shut.

With his own words, he urged, "Come on, Kindra, come for me, baby."

She did, with a loud cry. Her ass lifted off the chair, but Mack held her down and kept moving. He could feel her orgasm, shaking and throbbing through her, her body closing around his fingers as it pulsed with relief.

"Mack," she cried. "Oh, sh-it!"

He slowed down his rhythm and laughed softly into her shoulder in triumph. Damn, that was the sexiest thing he had ever seen. Or felt. He had given her something he suspected no man ever had, and he felt a rush of tenderness for Kindra that was equally new.

He realized with sudden shock that he was falling for her. Hook, line, and sinker.

It felt right. Everything felt right about Kindra.

Dusting kisses onto her neck and jaw, he withdrew his fingers and marveled that he had made Kindra Hill say "shit" out loud. She was quite a woman.

Kindra took deep breaths and tried to slow down her heart rate. What the heck had just happened? She was pretty sure she'd had an orgasm, but nothing she'd experienced before had ever prepared her for *that*.

That mind-blowing, rip-roaring, pulsing, frenzied feeling.

She wondered if Rob, her ex-boyfriend, could reimburse her for the hours of her life she'd lost lying beneath him bored out of her mind.

Now this, what Mack had done to her, was a very valuable use of her time. Like yoga, only sweatier. She'd never felt so languid and relaxed in her life.

It didn't even bother her to realize she was sitting there with her top pushed up and her skirt around her waist. Not when Mack was whispering such wonderful things in her ear.

"Did you like that?"

"Yes." Yes, a thousand times yes. And unless he was deaf and blind and devoid of all sensation in his skin, he knew she had enjoyed it.

He rubbed his nose and mouth along her jaw. "I'm so glad you liked it. But we're not finished, you know."

Mack seemed to have a talent for saying exactly what she wanted to hear.

She shivered as his breath blew across her hot, sweaty skin. He was blowing onto her breasts, and her nipples hardened.

"What's next?"

He stood up. "Let's check."

Then he was back at the computer again and Kindra adjusted her skirt back over her thighs as she thought about how many e-mails they had found in her trash. A dozen or so. Twelve hours.

Ohmigod. She went warm all over.

Though she couldn't remember exactly, Russ's e-mails were full of all sorts of naughty things, unique positions, and help her, if she wasn't mistaken there was one revolving almost entirely around spanking.

Somehow she didn't think even Mack could get her to enjoy having her ass smacked.

As he scanned the screen, Mack unbuttoned his shirt. It slid down his arms, revealing a bronzed back and shoulders, with rippling biceps that oozed strength and power. They were smooth, gleaming with a slight sheen of sweat, and he tossed his shirt to the floor negligently.

His pants were sinking on his hips.

Then again, maybe if Mack was gentle . . .

As he turned back to her, she yanked her shirt back down.

"Modest?" He looked amused.

"I'm half naked and you're not."

"I took my shirt off. That makes me half naked. So you should take yours off and we'll be even."

"That doesn't count!"

He shrugged. "I guess it doesn't matter. You can leave it on if you want for this next part."

Next part? That sounded frightening and elusive. Like a science experiment.

Gripping the chair, she tried not to panic as Mack walked toward her. So far it had been great, but Kindra was a traditionalist when it came to sex. She was thinking missionary style and what if he was thinking . . . something else?

He stopped in front of her. "What's the matter? Your face has gone ghost white."

"What comes next?"

The reaction took her by surprise. Mack dropped his hands. He looked hurt, of all things.

"Kindra, don't you trust me?"

Oh, shoot, now she felt like a jerk. "Well, yes, but I didn't know . . ."

"Hey." He tipped her chin up so she was forced to meet his eye. "Anything you don't want to do, you say stop and I will. I'd never hurt you."

His mouth stayed open, like he was going to add something, but then he clamped it back shut.

Kindra loosened her hold on the chair. "Okay. I'm sorry. I do trust you, it's just that this is new for me."

Pleasure was new for her. She didn't know how to handle it.

Mack pulled her to her feet and settled his hands on her waist. It felt good there in his embrace. Right.

"Now, we can either stop here for the night, or we can do what I found on your computer." His voice was low and cajoling.

Okay, she had to ask. He knew she was going to ask. Her new breathy voice that she seemed to have adopted overnight came out. "What?"

"Something simple, really. I lie on the bed. You just get on my cock and ride."

Ooohh. Her thighs hummed to life. If only he'd have said so in the first place.

Traditional was so boring. It was time she expanded her sexual horizons. Right now.

"Would you like that?"

Kindra tried to suck back the excess saliva that was suddenly in her mouth. She nodded violently.

He laughed. "Then we need a bed and the condoms."

She had dropped the condoms on the living room

floor when Mack had grabbed her by the front door. As far as the bed went, well, the guest room was next to the office. It was closest and the sheets were fresh.

Plus she didn't think that she wanted Mack in her own bed, where she slept every night. Once this was all over and she went back to her ordinary sexless life, she didn't want to lie there at night alone and remember.

"The guest room is right next door. And I dropped the condoms in the living room. I'll go get them."

She speed-walked into the living room and found the discarded box on the carpet as Mack stood in the doorway of the guest room and watched. As she approached him, he moved backward into the room, his fingers hooked in the belt loops of his pants.

"Now remember, you promised not to laugh."

"I won't." She watched in fascination as Mack unzipped his pants and they dropped to the floor.

He kicked them out of the way, then bent and shed his boxer shorts before she could even admire his hard muscular thighs and calves. He rose back up and put his hands on his hips.

Whoa. No laughing here.

That was not a laughing matter at all.

She gawked. She blushed. She drooled a little. Swallowing was painful.

He smirked. "What do you think?"

Kindra spoke without thinking. The words in her head just flew out of her mouth before she even realized she was speaking. "I think I'm in for the ride of my life."

His eyes went dark with shock.

Her hand went over her mouth, but she didn't regret saying it. Nor could she stop salivating over him. While the rest of Mack was the result of hard hours spent in the gym, his . . . thing was just a wonder of nature.

All the words to name him seemed wrong to Kindra. *Penis* was clinical and the *C* and the *D* words were just never going to come out of her mouth.

Mack strode toward her. "Fuck. Get over here."

Gladly.

He gave her a hard wet kiss, then pulled her tank top over her head. Taking the condoms out of her hand, he sat down on the bed. With a wicked grin, he lay down, arms tucked behind his head.

"If you want it, come and get it."

There was no doubt she wanted it. But she wasn't sure she even knew how to come and get it. The few times she'd been on top in the past, she had felt silly and exposed, and had changed positions again quickly.

But it would be different with Mack. Everything was different with Mack.

Taking a deep breath, she undid her skirt and let it drop to the floor. His grin fell off his face.

Still in the chunky high-heel sandals, she walked toward the bed. She bent over and lifted her ankle on the bed to undo them.

"No," Mack groaned. "Leave them on."

It didn't matter to her. On her knees she crawled across the bed to him, tossing her hair back over her shoulder. Mack was rolling on a condom.

Gingerly, she put one knee on either side of him and sat on his legs.

Yep. Feeling silly. Her hands had nowhere to go, and the upper half of her body felt way too exposed.

"Bend forward a minute," he said, beckoning her with his hand.

Kindra leaned over him, and Mack's tongue came out and flicked across her nipple.

That didn't feel silly. That felt sinfully good.

He sucked and licked until her nipple and the underside of her breast were slick and wet, hard with need.

"Okay," he said in dismissal, lying back down. "You can sit back up now."

"Gee, thanks," she said, her breath hitched.

But Mack had made her forget her awkwardness. Now when she sat back up, she arched her back and gripped Mack's hips. She moved against him to tease them both. His hot hardness was sliding against her and she sucked in her breath.

Teasing was overrated. She needed him now.

Lifting her legs a little, she guided him with her hand, then eased herself down on him.

"Oh, yes!" she blurted out as he filled and stretched her, spreading her legs so he went as deep as she could take.

"Yes," he agreed.

But he didn't move. Kindra's eyes flew open. "Aren't you . . ."

If he just rocked his hips up a little, this would really be something to write home about.

Slowly his head went back and forth on the floral comforter covering her guest bed. "No. I'm just lying here, remember? You've got to ride it."

"What if I can't?" Could she?

Well, shoot. What was the worst that could happen? It wouldn't work and they would just try something else.

And moving against him just had to feel good if sitting still was this satiating.

"You can. I know you can. Come on, Kindra, just lift and fuck. Nothing to it."

Like paint by numbers. She'd always been good at those. Just lift and fuck.

She did.

Oh, yeah.

And again.

Kindra palmed her hands across Mack's hard chest and rode him hard and fast, pleasure gripping every inch of her body. Her eyes were closed, teeth gritted as she moved.

"That's it," he urged. "It's all yours, baby."

All hers. Mack. With a final thrust down, she came hard, pinching his chest as she rode her passion through its pulsing completion.

Collapsing against his chest, she shuddered and pulled in huge lungfuls of air. Mack's hand stroked her back softly, a tender caress that made her heart swell with gratitude.

She knew what he was doing. He was making it good for her and not worrying about his own pleasure. Maybe it was just to prove his original point, that sex in person was better than talking about it, but somehow she thought it was more than that.

Mack was just a nice guy who could tell that she was a sexual novice, and he was trying to make it right for her. That was the only explanation for why she had screamed her way through two orgasms now and he'd had none.

Lying there on his chest, her hot breasts pressed against him, and Mack still buried deep inside her, hard and throbbing, she knew she wanted to pleasure him the way he had her.

She thought she might know how.

There was something that she had noticed men seemed to gravitate toward. Her ex-boyfriend had preferred it. Of course, Rob had thrown hot sauce on his ice cream, so he probably wasn't the best person to set standards by.

But Russ constantly brought it up in his e-mails, with

various themes but still the same main element. Even with such limited experience, it was safe to say that Mack might enjoy what she was thinking of.

She had the delicious thought that she might like it almost as much as Mack.

Chapter Five

Mack let his hand rub lazily across Kindra's smooth back, still aroused but content to just lie there for a minute. It had occurred to him as Kindra had moved on his cock, her face flushed and excited, that he loved her.

That he didn't want this night to end. He wanted to spend each day loving her and showing her how special she was.

Would he make a total ass out of himself if he blabbered to her about his feelings? It would look a little suspicious, with them still joined, to be declaring love. If he were a woman, he wouldn't believe him.

In the morning, when it was time to leave and they were doing that weird "what do we say to each other" thing, he would tell her he was in love with her. That this didn't have to end.

They could be good together. Would be good together.

Kindra moved off him.

He turned on his side to watch her. "Where are you going?"

"Nowhere." She was wiggling away from him and was eyeing the bed carefully.

Mack didn't trust the look on her face. Kindra was unpredictable, he'd found out. If she was going to try and make a break for it, she had another thing coming. He wasn't finished with her yet.

He sat up, ready to grab her if need be. So far she didn't look like she was trying to leave. She was doing a really interesting crawling sort of thing across the comforter.

It gave him a nice view of long pale legs and auburn hair tossing down her back. He grinned at the sandals still on her feet.

"What the hell are you doing?" he asked her finally.

Her lip bit in concentration, she said, "I'm trying to figure something out. I want to do something from another e-mail. I'm not sure it will work, but we can try."

Hell. Kindra was coming up with positions she wanted to try on her own now.

Sexy little thing.

He was about to grab her and flip her onto her back and pump himself into her, when suddenly she went on her knees.

All fours, actually.

And wiggled her tight little ass in front of his face.

His mouth went dry. "What the *hell* are you doing?" he groaned.

Innocent eyes blinked at him over her shoulder. "Won't this work? I thought you could . . . you know, this way."

Oh, shit, fuck, damn.

Instead of answering, Mack got on his knees and grabbed her hips. With one fluid motion he sank into her moist heat.

"Oh!" she gasped. "It does work."

Oh, yeah, it worked all right.

The control Mack had been holding on to with all his

might since he'd walked in the door of Kindra's house evaporated.

Her milky white skin taunting him in front, her hair sliding and bouncing, he rocked into her. Still wet and swollen, she met him thrust for thrust, her muscles squeezing on his cock.

One, two, three, hell, he was gone. He came with a groan, pushing forward so hard, her knees buckled and they collapsed on the bed.

His body jerked and shuddered as it finished its release. Still shaking, he said anxiously, "Are you okay?"

In the future, he needed to be more careful. He could have poked her eye out he'd rammed so hard.

"I'm fabulous," she said in a throaty voice that sounded nothing like the Kindra Hill he knew who rolled her eyes behind her coffee mug in staff meetings.

Of course he'd never been sprawled out on top of her before, with her face smashed down into the mattress. Maybe her voice sounded like that because she couldn't breathe.

He started to pull back.

"No, don't." She turned her head, laying her cheek on the bed, a smile dancing across her face. "Just stay like this for a minute if you can."

He could stay like that all night if she wanted. "I'm too heavy," he said gruffly. "I'm crushing you."

"No, the mattress sinks. You feel good on me. Hard. I can still feel you throbbing inside me."

Damn, there it was again. That inflated chest feeling. Definitely love.

Despite her reassuring words, he shifted a little so he wasn't lying flat against her. Still entwined with her, he stroked her soft hair.

"You're very beautiful," he murmured.

Her cheeks went pink. "You don't have to say that."

"It's true. You must know it too, or you wouldn't try so hard to hide it."

"It's easier that way, you know," she said, her finger playing with the fold of the comforter. "Then no one notices you."

Too bad it hadn't worked. "I noticed you. I've been noticing you since the day I started at MicroDesign."

She scoffed. "Yeah, right. You had to catch me having cybersex before you noticed me."

"No. Catching you having cybersex only showed me proof of what I had already guessed. That you're one funny, sexy lady underneath the boring clothes."

She didn't look convinced, though her eyes were wistful. "I don't believe you."

"Would you believe me if I told you that I know you always drink your coffee out of a mug that has wild-flowers on it, and that you listen to classical music in your office? That every Friday you go out to lunch with Ashley and that you do at least half of Bill's work every week because he's a lazy shit." His voice softened. "That you roll your eyes at every asinine speech Mr. Parker makes, and that when Judy's son died, you brought her dinner for a week."

And maybe he knew Kindra better than even he had suspected.

"Oh," was all she said, her expression a little stunned.

She didn't say anything else and he didn't need her to. He wanted his words to sink in, and they lay silently for another minute.

When his stomach let out a loud growl into the quiet room, they both laughed.

"Sorry, but you know, I rushed dinner. My stomach's reminding me." He reluctantly eased himself out of her.

He gave one last stroke along her back, then, with a

satisfied sigh, pulled the condom off. "Where should I put this?"

Kindra pulled herself to a sitting position, and started unbuckling the sandals from her feet. "In the bathroom right across the hall. Why don't I reheat our dinners while you do that?"

"Uh . . . because we left the boxes in my car." When he had been too preoccupied with getting Kindra into the house and naked to worry about bacteria growth. "I don't think it's a good idea to eat beef that's been sitting out for two hours."

"What a waste." She stretched her arms up over her head, kicking the sandals off the bed to the floor.

Her breasts rose and he admired the graceful curve of her neck and shoulder. "Oh, it was worth it," he told her truthfully.

Even as his stomach disagreed and growled again, rumbling long and loud.

She giggled "I can fix you a ham sandwich."

Damn, that was cute. She'd offered to make him a sandwich. Mack knew it was only lunch meat, but hey, he must mean something to her, right?

"You don't have to do that. Just show me where everything is and I'll fix it."

With a smile, she put her hand on his knee and brushed with her fingertips. "Don't be silly. I don't mind doing it."

A fabulous idea came to him. "Would you mind making the sandwich naked?"

Kindra standing there, bending over to retrieve the ham from the fridge, spreading mustard . . . Now if only she would put the high-heel sandals back on, they would really be on to something.

"Yes, I would mind!" she said, snatching her hand back.

Well, hell, it had been worth a try.

And as if to prove her point, she stood up and pulled her skirt off the floor and wiggled into it. Mack watched her skin disappear with regret, but then consoled himself with the fact that, after eating, he could peel all her clothing back off again.

Five minutes later he met her in the kitchen, having taken care of business and thrown his boxer shorts on. He absolutely refused to put a single stitch of clothing on beyond that.

Kindra's house was small, but it was comfortable and clean. She had decorated with big beige furniture and the kitchen was a soft yellow. It wasn't frilly and fussy the way some women liked. Yet it was so much more personable than his white-walled apartment.

Kindra was putting his sandwich on the table. The sight of her barefoot, in her wrinkled tank top and no bra, her hair loose and mussed, floored him. She looked gorgeous, her lips swollen and her eyes languid and satisfied. A small smile played around her lips.

The room was warm and smelled like bread, and Mack knew right then and there that this was where he wanted to be. Every day.

Kindra smiled at Mack as he came into the kitchen. He was scratching his chest absently and he looked as if he'd taken a baseball between the eyes. It made her a little nervous.

But she reasoned he was probably starving, having essentially skipped his dinner.

Mack went right past the table and to her back door. He pulled up the blind and peered out into the darkness. "Do you have a yard at all?"

It should have been a weird question, but Kindra felt too damn good to care about the why. After the orgasms he had given her, he could ask anything that came to mind, including the balance in her checkbook and whom she'd voted for in the last election, and she wouldn't care. She flipped the light switch that flooded the backyard with a spotlight.

"It's not real big, but it's enough for me. It's surrounded by a wooden fence and I'm working on planting some perennials around the patio."

He peered out and nodded in approval. "Perfect for a dog."

She laughed. "You're the one who wants a poodle named Bitsy, not me."

"I never said that, you said that." Mack abandoned his post at the door and sat down at the table. He patted the seat next to him.

As she sat down, she said, "Yeah, well, I'd like a dog, but not right now. Not by myself. Taking care of a house alone is enough."

Mack didn't say anything, just gave her an odd look, his head tilted and a strange half smile teasing about his lips.

Why was he looking at her like that?

Then she flushed.

Ohmigod, did he think she was hinting? That she wanted a relationship?

She'd rather eat maggots than have him think she was going to now try and latch on to him like a dryer sheet to Velcro. Even though the idea held certain appeal, she had sworn to herself that she would go into this night knowing it was a one time deal.

Mack was out of her league.

He was here to prove a point and get a little free action.

They could handle showing up at work on Monday with things the way they were right now. But if he started thinking that she was going to cling, or if she actually lost her mind and did start to cling, they were going to have a car wreck on their hands. Total disaster.

As he bit his sandwich, Kindra realized that this conversation crap needed to not happen. He was being too nice.

Why couldn't he be like most guys and just take what he wanted and roll over and go to sleep? Why did he have to say sweet things that showed she wasn't just a bedpost notch to him?

Telling her he knew she drank out of a wildflower mug, calling her beautiful. Geez, didn't he know that a woman hears things like that and starts hoping?

"Aren't you eating anything?" he asked, his mouth full.

"No, I'm not hungry." She was sick, actually.

She had gone and fallen for Mack.

Or rather, she'd fallen for Mack a year ago when he had first walked in the door at MicroDesign, but she had known then that she could never hope to catch his eye.

Well, now she had his eye, and other things, and she found her stupid little heart wishing for more still.

That had to stop. She ground her thoughts to a halt right there.

This was it. One night. Nothing more.

And it was all she was going to have. So she might as well kill the conversation and get back to why he was here in the first place.

Sex.

Plain and simple.

Just the thought of which had her skirt firing up like a gas grill.

"That was great," Mack said as he dusted the last crumbs off his mouth. "Thanks, I feel better."

"Good." She stood up, the rustle of her skirt on her

legs reminding her that her panties were still crumpled up on the floor in the office. Which was just as well. She had no intention of putting any underwear back on until Mack left.

"Come here, Mack, I want to show you something."

His contented look gave way to interest.

"Is this like, here, look at the pictures of my trip to London, or like, here, look at another dirty e-mail with me?"

Not having much experience tossing off sultry looks, Kindra wasn't sure if she was doing it right, but she gave it her best effort. Running her fingers through her hair, she said, "I've never been to London."

"Damn, Kindra." He stood up so fast, he knocked his chair over with a crash. "You are so sexy."

It wasn't a declaration of love by far, but it was a heck of a lot more than she'd had on Thursday. She'd take it. She'd take him.

Plus the fact that he was close to panting was downright gratifying. And the way his hands were groping her ass as he followed her down the hall was enough to embolden her.

She could do this. She wanted this.

When she stopped in the doorway of her office, Mack bumped up against her. His hard-on pressed into her and she rubbed herself back against him.

A nice low guttural moan rang from him.

Hands were up her skirt.

Whoa, too fast.

Swatting him away, she stepped into the room. "Just a minute."

"Why?" Mack reached for her again.

Feeling a little heady with power and desire, Kindra said, "Sit in the chair."

His eyebrows raised. "Why?" he repeated.

"Just do it." She pointed at the chair, heart thumping as she waited to see if he would obey her command.

Mack held his hands up in mock surrender and sauntered over to the chair. "Fine, I'll do it."

He dropped into the chair and spread his legs in a masculine slouch. He flung his arm over the back and tried to look nonchalant, but the bulge in his boxers gave him away.

Kindra smiled. Whatever her complicated feelings for Mack were, he certainly made her feel sexy. All woman. Confident in herself.

Avoiding the chair in case he might think to grab her or touch her, Kindra went to her computer. She had a camera to record onto her computer.

They were going to use it. Right now.

Turning it toward the center of the room, the carpet and Mack in the chair popped up on her screen. Adjusting it, she made sure that Mack's complete body was in view.

She was going to record herself having sex with Mack, and when she was alone after tonight, she could watch it. She would ache for Mack and this night together and she would get herself off to it.

No more Russ.

From now on, she'd have Mack. If not in person, then on her computer.

Mack looked frozen in the chair, his eyes wide, his shoulders tense, jaw clenched. "Kindra?"

"Yes?" Two more steps and she would be on the screen with him.

"Did you just turn that camera on?"

"Yes." She stepped up to him and pushed her hands into the pockets of her denim skirt, tugging it down so her naval was exposed. "You don't mind, do you?"

His hand twitched on the back of the chair, his cock strained against his boxers. "Can I watch it with you later?"

She went wet, hot and fast, and the denim of her skirt rubbed against her moistness as desire raced through her. "Yes."

"Then I don't mind."

Mouth dry, Kindra stepped in front of the camera and turned so both their profiles would be recorded. She licked her lips nervously and her breath hitched.

Mack seemed to sense her sudden apprehension. He said, "Take your shirt off."

"Okay." Lifting her arms, Kindra arched her back and pulled the tank top off, letting it tumble out of her hand as she tossed her hair out of her eyes.

"Touch your nipples." He was leaning back again, lips parted, eyes dark and cloudy. His voice was soft and coaxing.

Kindra became painfully aware of the camera. This was supposed to be her show. She had intended to strip for Mack, then give him a lap dance of sorts in the chair. Not do what he wanted, not touch herself.

"Go on," he urged. "I can see how hard and hot they are. They're just begging to be touched."

They were hard and hot. Her nipples were aching, erect and budding. She closed her eyes. She couldn't do this.

Sensing Mack had moved closer, her eyes flew open. He had rolled the chair until he was right in front of her. Desperate, wanting his hands on her, aching with need and feeling too inhibited to touch herself, she rocked forward.

Mack put his hands on her inner thighs. Her skirt went up. His head bent. Fingers parted her. She gripped his shoulders.

Hot breath teased her clit, but he didn't touch her. The need was painful.

"Mack, please."

"I'll take care of this if you touch your tits," he murmured, giving her damp curls a little sharp tug.

When put that way . . . Kindra reached up and cupped her breasts, gasping with pleasure as Mack's tongue found her and stroked lightly.

She threw her head back, and gave a soft moan. He was teasing, tasting with a maddeningly light touch that had her squeezing and rubbing her nipples in desperation. He pulled back completely and gazed up at her.

Her hands didn't stop.

"Oh, yeah, like that. That's good, baby." Then he bent back over and plunged his tongue deep inside her.

Kindra came with a cry, and the only thing that kept her standing was Mack's hands on her legs, holding her still. Her hands dropped and she drew in a shaky breath.

"Mack . . ." As the tight passion settled down to satisfaction, Kindra felt her eyes pricking. She bit her lip. God, she was not going to be a total dip and cry, was she?

She'd rather go bald. At least there were wigs to fix that. Nothing was going to prevent total humiliation if she went emotional and confessed her feelings for Mack.

He was laughing softly, his grip on her legs relaxing. His soft lips pressed her inner thigh. "You're incredible," he murmured.

It was going to happen. She was going to cry. Shoot. Blinking hard, she pushed him back into the chair. Feelings of love rose up in her and threatened to overwhelm her. If she couldn't tell him, she could show him.

And hide her face in the process.

Kindra went down on her knees.

Mack's eyebrows shot up.

He opened his mouth to say something.

Kindra didn't wait to hear. Pulling his erection out from his black boxers, she bent over and took a nice long luscious suck.

Chapter Six

Mack stared at the ceiling and gave a lusty sigh. Damn, he felt good. Never better, in fact. The lack of sleep didn't bother him.

Not when he had spent half the night making love to Kindra. She was incredible. Giving, daring, yet shy. The way she was in bed reflected the complexity of her personality out of bed.

Full of surprises.

Mack rolled over in Kindra's guest bed and watched her sleeping, her auburn hair spilling across her face. She had pulled the blanket up tightly under her chin, and her lush mouth was open as she breathed in and out with a soft whisper.

Settling himself up against her back, Mack stroked her smooth thighs. His body responded instantly, and a huge boner was pressing into her backside in less than thirty seconds.

He couldn't help himself. Kindra did things to him, made him feel a way he never had.

When she woke up, he was going to tell her that he'd fallen in love with her.

No time like the present. Dusting a kiss on her shoulder, he reached around and slid a finger inside her, then back out, teasing her clit.

He felt her body swell and moisten. Her eyes popped open.

"Mack," she murmured, her voice heavy with sleep. "It's too early."

"Then why are you wet?" He sucked her earlobe.

Already her body was rocking against his hand, her breath hitching.

"I'm not," she insisted. "I'm still asleep."

"Then you must be having a damn good dream."

Kindra's fingers clenched the sheet as she moved faster against him.

Mack added a second finger and sent her over the edge. Kindra shuddered and relaxed back on the pillow.

"Mmmm."

"My thoughts exactly." He rubbed his lips across her cheek and pulled his hand back.

"So what are your plans for the day?" He pictured snuggling half the day away, maybe grabbing some lunch and a movie, sharing a shower. Stopping by his apartment for fresh clothes and his toothbrush, then hightailing it back to Kindra's for another night together.

Driving in to work together tomorrow.

Kindra stiffened. "Today? Oh, I have . . . things to do."

"What things?" He didn't like the sound of that. "I could do them with you."

"No, no." Now she scooted away from him and sat up, hugging the sheet around herself. "It's girl stuff."

Confused, a feeling of foreboding creeping over him, Mack said, "What girl things? Like buying tampons or something? That doesn't bother me."

Well, actually it did, but if that meant he could spend

the day with Kindra, he could tolerate the whole heavy versus light flow conversation.

She turned back to him. "Mack . . ."

Foreboding was no longer creeping up. It was flat out biting him on the ass. There was an "I'm sorry" coming here, he just knew it.

"Look, I'm sorry, but I don't think it's a good idea to see each other again."

"What?" Now he sat straight up. What the hell was she talking about? He had just decided they were perfect for each other. She couldn't possibly mean that their one-night stand was a real, honest to-God, one-night stand.

"This was fabulous, really, an amazing night, but that's all it was. You know that."

He didn't know that. God, he felt so cheap, so used. Baffled, he gaped at her.

Gently, she gave him a small smile, clutching the sheet across her chest. "Your twelve hours is up."

His own words thrown back at him. Mack struggled for composure even though his chest felt as if someone had dug their fist in and ripped out his heart.

He'd thought there was something there, that sometimes Kindra had looked at him with tenderness. That the things they'd done were so much more than sex. They'd been intimate, personal.

Obviously he had been completely wrong.

"Do you want some breakfast before you go?"

Her back was exposed, creamy white flesh mocking him, taunting him as she looked at him over her shoulder. Her beauty nearly undid him.

But he'd be damned if he'd grovel or cry. Somehow he'd get out of this with his dignity intact.

"No, thanks." Like he was going to sit there in the

kitchen and eat some freaking eggs while she wished him gone.

"Did I prove my point?" he asked roughly.

Her little pink tongue slipped out and licked her lip. "Oh, yeah, you proved it. This was much, much better than cybersex."

It was something.

Not what he wanted, but something. And at least he could be comforted by the fact that he hadn't blurted out his feelings and suffered extra humiliation as she let him down gently.

Nor would he follow her around like a dog after a bitch in heat, though she did reduce him to panting.

"Good," he said, his jaw clenched. "Tell that guy to get some new lines, will you? That alone will make it better for you."

Then he got up off the bed and strode to the bathroom, not sticking around to hear Kindra's reply. The sudden image of Kindra in her computer chair letting that filthy guy talk nasty to her made him livid. Hot with fury and sick with jealousy.

If he couldn't have her, he sure as hell didn't want anyone to have her, especially not some cyber-Romeo who didn't know sexy from sushi.

Mack closed the bathroom door behind him.

He'd proven his point all right. Proven he was an idiot.

Kindra stared at her in-box. A half-dozen messages from Russ were winking at her. Subject headings like "Where are you?," "Miss you," and "Feeling horny" leapt out.

She had yet to read any of them.

Listening to Russ talk about crotchless panties sud-

denly sounded about as fun as bleaching her mustache.
A waste of a good ten minutes.

This wasn't supposed to happen. She had sent Mack
away that morning, determined to protect her heart at
all costs.

Watching him stomp off, stiff and gruff, had been the
hardest thing she'd done to date, if she didn't count
jumping those hurdles in high school gym class.

But now she was supposed to resume her life.

Go to work. Wear boring clothes. Chat with Russ.
Never have good sex again.

Gee, that sounded appealing.

Without thought, her hand ran the cursor through the
computer menu. She retrieved the video she had made
the night before. Thirty seconds later she and Mack were
on her screen.

His voice was low, commanding. Kindra watched herself, head thrown back, eyes half closed and breath hitching. She caressed her nipples.

Mack spread her thighs.

Kindra live began to pant in unison with her recorded
self.

Oh, Mack. What the heck had she done?

So what if he didn't want a relationship? She could
have done *this* with him again.

Until he got tired of her.

Which would be worse in the end.

No, she had done the right thing.

Mack's tongue plunged into her onscreen.

The doorbell rang. Kindra leapt up, turning off her
monitor. Maybe it was Mack, coming back. Maybe he
wanted to make her change her mind. Or maybe he had
just forgotten his socks or something.

She peered through the living room window as she
ran to the door. Or maybe it was her friends. Shoot.

Reluctantly, she opened the door.

Ashley groaned. "Oh, Kindra, you're wearing track pants again."

"So?" They were perfect it's-Sunday-and-my-life-is-over pants.

Trish pushed past her. "Is he still here? How was it? You did sleep with him, didn't you?"

Kindra had no interest in dishing out details on her night with Mack. "No, he's not still here."

Ashley collapsed on her couch, enormous hoop earrings dangling down over her lime green sweater. "But he was here, right?"

"Yes, we went out to dinner, then came back here." Kindra stuck her hands in her nylon pants and paced across the room. She felt a headache coming on. A real one this time, unlike the one she had faked for Russ.

"Well, change your clothes, then tell us all about it," Ashley urged.

"Why do I have to change my clothes?"

"Because we're going to the movies, remember?" Ashley said. "Did you forget?"

"Yes."

"Must have been some night," Trish snickered. "Details, dear, we want details."

"Are you okay, Kindra?" Violet asked, pushing her glasses up with one finger. "You look like something's wrong."

Everything was wrong. Kindra stopped pacing and pushed her hair out of her eyes. "I'm not okay. I'm in love with Mack!"

Violet's eyes widened. Trish gasped.

Ashley moaned. "Oh, Kindra, how could you?"

"I didn't mean to!" Like she'd set out to make herself miserable by falling in love with an unobtainable paragon.

"That must have been good sex," Trish remarked.

"It was." Better than good. Ecstasy-inducing, mind-bending, earth-shaking, great sex. She sighed.

"But it was more than great sex, it was . . . intimate." Another lusty sigh emerged. "And now that I've let the cat out of the bag, I don't think I can stuff it back in."

"What do you mean?" Violet asked.

She wasn't sure exactly. She just knew she couldn't be the same old Kindra-the-wallflower anymore. She had changed. Mack had brought out parts of herself she had forgotten existed.

"I may not be able to have Mack, but I'm tired of being taken advantage of at work. I'm going to stand up for myself, and get some excitement in my life."

"Does that mean better clothes?" Ashley asked hopefully.

"Will you quit harping on my clothes?" she said in exasperation. "But yes, it means new clothes."

"Cool." Trish swung her backpack purse back on. "Let's skip the movie and go shopping instead."

Ashley stood up and hugged Kindra. "Hey, I'm sorry things didn't work out with Mack, but you never know. Maybe he feels the same way about you."

Hah. And Mack Stone was going to get a pet poodle named Bitsy. Please.

Mack sucked down his third cup of coffee in the last hour and glared at Jim, his coworker. God, Jim was annoying. Of course, everyone was annoying this morning.

After a miserable Sunday afternoon wallowing in self-pity, Mack had spent a sleepless night. He'd woken up Monday morning with a pounding head and an aching heart.

Then to make it all worse, Kindra had strode into work

that morning looking breezy and sensual, confident and happy.

For the first time ever she was wearing her hair down at work. The soft auburn sleekness bounced over her shoulders, and she was wearing very subtle makeup that brought out her green eyes and made her cheekbones look a mile long.

Instead of black, her suit was brown. Warm chocolate that made her skin glow. The cut was feminine, tighter, and shorter than he'd ever seen Kindra in.

She looked fantastic. Gorgeous. Edible.

Damned if he wasn't the only one to notice it either. Half the office staff was sniffing around her. The male half.

Mack stood over Jim's desk, wishing Jim would put his doughnut down so they could solve the problem they were working on. Bright laughter floated over to them. Mack gritted his teeth and turned.

It was Kindra perched on the reception desk, surrounded by three guys. Mack rubbed his forehead. When Kindra had seen him this morning, he had gotten nothing more than a cool hello.

He'd seen her naked. He had been inside her.

But these geeks got her smile, her full attention, and her laugh.

Kindra had a great laugh.

"Damn," Jim said around a mouthful of doughnut. "Something is different about Kindra this morning. Maybe she finally got a little action over the weekend." He snorted in laughter.

Mack turned and glared at Jim. "Watch your damn mouth."

Jim stopped laughing. "What's the matter with you?" Then his eyebrows rose. "Oh, I get it. Kindra was with *you* this weekend, wasn't she?"

Mack didn't answer, but turned back to watch Kindra and her entourage.

Jim said, "I've never seen you look so ticked off. Has the great Mack Stone finally fallen?"

Like a boulder.

Without thinking, he marched himself over to Kindra and interrupted rudely by elbowing past Bob from payroll.

"I need to talk to you."

Kindra flushed. She darted her eyes around and her shoulders tensed. "I'm busy right now."

"I don't care."

Kindra glared at him, held her chin up high, and walked away, her hair swinging.

Mack stood there flabbergasted. She had walked away from him.

A hand touched his arm. He looked down at Ashley, who was tugging him away from the crowd.

"What?" he said, trying to pull his arm away.

"Get a clue, Mack," she whispered. "You can't just embarrass the hell out of Kindra by acting like a total cretin and then expect her to listen to you."

She pointed her finger at him. "Now you listen to me. How do you feel about Kindra?"

Sick with love. He tugged at his tie. "That's none of your business."

"Do you love her?"

He couldn't say yes, but he couldn't say no either. He looked at Ashley in agony.

She nodded in satisfaction. "Good. She loves you too, you know, but she thinks you were in it for the sex."

"I never said that!"

"You never said otherwise," Miss Wisdom pointed out to him.

Mack ran his fingers through his hair. Could it be

true? Did Kindra love him? Hope rose like a hot-air balloon.

But what if she didn't?

"Do you think I should tell her how I feel now?"

"No, I think you should both spend the rest of your lives miserable for being so stupid." She rolled her eyes. "Yes, you should tell her!"

Mack barely even noticed Ashley's sarcasm. If Ashley was wrong about Kindra's feelings, he certainly couldn't feel any lousier than he did right now.

And if she was right . . .

Oh, man. Bliss.

Mack had an idea. He bent and squeezed Ashley by the shoulders. "Thanks, Ashley. I owe you one."

Then he turned and headed to his office, telling himself that Kindra was worth all the embarrassment he would suffer if this didn't work.

Kindra was still in shock an hour later. What exactly had Mack been doing?

Had she wounded his male ego by telling him one night was enough?

Rubbing her temples, she spat hair out of her mouth. Wearing the hair down was supposed to be symbolic, but it was just getting on her nerves. She was constantly pawing it to get it out of her way.

The words on her screen were blurring in front of her. She'd been hiding in her office since she had walked away from Mack, and she couldn't concentrate on anything.

She'd been staring at the same proposal for a solid thirty minutes and the words were dancing tiny tangos with each other.

Frustrated, she clicked to check her e-mail. Anything

to distract her. It was possible there would be another pleading message from Russ begging her not to sever their relationship.

Those had been his exact words after she had e-mailed him the night before telling him she wasn't interested any longer. The word *relationship* made her snort out loud.

Talking about sex in a chat room was not a relationship.

Neither was one night together.

She groaned. This wasn't distracting her from thinking about Mack.

She was a federal disaster area. Hurricane Kindra.

Then her eye landed on her new messages. There was one from Mack Stone.

"Oh, no."

If he talked dirty to her, she was not going to be able to resist.

One eye closed, the other covered by her hand, she clicked to open the e-mail. Then she spread her fingers and held her breath.

The message was short.

Marry me.

Kindra dropped her hands and gripped her desk. "Ohmigod, ohmigod."

Was this some sort of cruel joke from Mack or Russ or some office prankster? Her vision went blurry.

Her stomach lurched like she'd had bad calamari.

The door to her office opened.

Frantic, she bent her head and scrolled down so her screen was blank. Praying it was Ashley, she said, "Yes?" in a bright fake voice.

"Woof."

What the heck was that? Her head snapped up. She turned, blinking hard.

Now she'd seen everything. Truly. Mack was standing in her doorway with a fluffy white poodle sticking out of his computer backpack.

"What are you doing?" she blurted out.

"Hoping like hell I'm not making an ass out of myself."

No comment.

Kindra thumbed back toward her screen, her heart pounding way too fast to be normal. If she passed out, she hoped Mack would think to call 911. "Did you just send me a message?"

"If it said 'Marry me,' then yes, I did."

That's it. She was gone. Tears raced down her face and she struggled not to blubber. "Why?"

"Kindra." He took a step forward. "Because I love you."

"No, you don't." Now why had she just said that? Hadn't she learned anything? If the man of her dreams proposed and said he loved her, she needed to latch on and ask questions later.

"Yes, I do." The fluffy little dog put its paws on his shoulder and panted. "Come on, I have a freaking dog on my back. With pink bows in its hair. Doesn't that tell you anything?"

It told her volumes. That Mack did love her. The pink bows confirmed it. She laughed. "I love you too."

"Whew." He grinned. "You had me worried there. Does that mean you'll marry me? We can live in your house and raise Bitsy together?"

"Yes." But the dog's name had to go.

Kindra stood up and went to Mack. Right into his arms. Where she belonged.

The kiss he gave her was long and passionate, moist lips and groping hands. His hot tongue lapped against hers.

"Oh, baby," he groaned.

Oh, baby was right. Kindra snuggled up against his hard chest and tugged on his cranberry tie. She absolutely loved the way he looked in a tie.

Mack gestured to her computer. "You have to tell cyber-Romeo to take a hike. Then we'll change your e-mail address. Maybe to IbelongtoMack@hotmail.com."

She laughed. "I already did. Yesterday. Told him to take a hike, that is, not changed my address."

His eyes burned. "You know, we should take the dog home before she has an accident down my back."

"Oh, good idea." Kindra was due a long leisurely lunch, since she'd never had one in four years on the job.

Feeling fabulous and daring, she let her hand slide down past his waist. She squeezed him and grinned in satisfaction when he went hard.

He said in a tight voice, "Want to have a nooner?"

Yes, please.

"Sure. Let me grab my purse." Kindra rubbed the little dog's head over Mack's shoulder and said, "She really is cute."

Bitsy barked.

Mack shifted the pack on his back. "You know, I never did get to watch that little video we made. Maybe we could do that first. Did you save it?"

"It's on my hard drive." But Kindra had a better idea.

Her hand back on his pants stroking him, she whispered in his ear, "Let's make another one instead."

Mack watched Kindra walk toward the door, her sweet

little ass swaying as she shot him a "come and get it" look over her shoulder.

Damn, he was one lucky guy.

He followed her, his tongue probably hanging as low as Bitsy's. "Baby, let's go burn up your hard drive."

PRESS ANY KEY

Chapter One

"I don't feel the love in this room."

Jared Kincaid stared at Harold, who was standing in the middle of his office, hands on his leather pants–clad hips.

What Jared felt was not love, but a skull-grinding, breath-robbing headache. Trust him to get hired at a marketing firm where the boss was having an existential midlife crisis.

It had started with Harold's leaving his wife six weeks ago. Now it had graduated to his boss's wearing a gay hairdresser's wardrobe to work every day, preaching to the staff about oneness with self, and eating massive quantities of hummus.

Since Jared's instinct was to tell Harold to take his love and shove it up his leather pants, he remained silent. With a little luck, in a month or two Harold would rediscover his true passion lay in Beamers and Armani suits and they could get back to normal.

A sultry low laugh filled the room. Jared gritted his teeth.

That laugh was a perfect example of why he was

doomed to middle management and a lifetime of dodging trouble. Trouble followed Jared. Everywhere he went.

Trouble usually had long legs and breasts. This trouble had all of that plus blowzy blond hair, a Southern accent, and lush cherry lips that pouted and taunted.

And her name. Who the hell named their kid Candy Appleton? Had her mother envisioned her newborn baby as a future porn star?

Maybe it had been cute when Candy was a little girl, before she'd grown breasts, but now, on that body . . . it was just *perverted*.

Candy, who looked relaxed and sexy as hell in her red suit, kicked the heel of her crossed foot up and down, annoying Jared even further. When she did that, he had a view straight up her thigh nearly to the promised land.

She'd be the type to wear garters, he was sure. Black ones, green ones. Red ones, cream ones.

He shifted in his chair, slouching to hide the fact that he now had a steel boner.

A boner. In the middle of the goddamn day, in the middle of his boss's office.

Trouble. Plain and simple.

Trouble spoke. "Harold, I don't think Jared's ready to feel the love."

He sat up straight. What was that supposed to mean? He could feel the love if he wanted to. If he could ever figure out what the hell Harold was talking about.

Candy tossed him one of those sultry, open-mouth smiles that made him want to tug her full bottom lip into his mouth and suck hard. He dug his fingernails into his thigh.

Harold frowned. "Is that true, Jared? You're not ready to feel the love?"

He was ready to feel up Candy's curves. Did that

count? Jared cleared his throat. "Uhh, what exactly are we talking about here?"

"I'm talking about the fact that we have exactly three weeks to get together the ad campaign for Chunk o' Chocolate, and you and Candy have barely spent an hour on it."

That's because he just about ran away every time Candy came near him. She scared the hell out of him. He had been forced to leave five years of hard work and a 401k plan behind him when he'd left his previous marketing firm, due to an unplanned encounter in the copier room with the big boss's secretary. Unknown to him at the time, that secretary was also the boss's girlfriend.

Work and sex didn't mix. Jared and women didn't mix. Every embarrassing and detrimental incident in his life could be traced back to a woman and his inability to control himself around them.

The buck stopped here. Or his dick, however you wanted to look at it.

He was not going to screw this up. Or screw Candy, no matter how much he wanted to taste those lethal lips.

"We can work on it whenever Candy likes." He avoided looking at her and focused on the bright yellow spot Harold had dyed on the front of his rapidly diminishing hair. It looked like a flashing caution light.

Caution: Middle-aged man approaching baldness.

Candy said, "Maybe you should assign someone else to work with Jared. I don't think he really likes me all that much." Her words were slow, and rolled, like a water drop across his skin.

That's where she was wrong. He liked Candy. Candy was sweet and lickable and belonged in his mouth, where he could swirl it around, sucking and tasting every delectable inch.

Harold clapped his hands together, startling Jared out of his erotic fantasy.

"See, that's what I'm talking about! Jared doesn't like you, and you don't like Jared. I can't have that."

Candy didn't like him? Jared turned to her in amazement. Well, hell, that hurt. It was okay if he was avoiding her, but she wasn't supposed to avoid him.

He was likable. He returned phone calls and held open doors for women. Of course, whenever Candy was around, he usually just grunted and bolted for the nearest exit. He supposed she might take that personally.

But what was he supposed to do? Tell her it wasn't her, it was her hot knockers that had him running like a cat from water? That was sure to go over big.

"I like Candy," he managed to say, not at all sure he wanted to know where Harold was going with this.

Candy laughed again, and he was suddenly aware of his poor word choice.

"Liar," she murmured. "But that shouldn't have anything to do with this client."

"It doesn't."

Harold studied them both and said, "I've noticed the tension between you two, and it's got to stop. It's affecting the rest of the staff. It's altering the feng shui state of the office. There are negative auras camped in my company, and that has got to go."

If Harold pulled out crystals and started chanting, Jared was out of there.

Not that he could afford to quit. As luck would have it, he'd bought himself a pricey condo right before he'd gotten canned from his previous job. The three months pounding the pavement had put a real dent in his assets. Another stint of unemployment and he'd be eating macaroni and cheese out of his car after the bank foreclosed on his mortgage.

"We don't want negative auras." Candy dropped her foot to the ground and smiled at Harold.

It made Jared suspicious. She never looked as if she was being sarcastic, yet he suspected she was. She was intelligent, and her ad work was brilliant, yet that brain was housed in a stripper's body.

He had the feeling that, if left alone, Candy could outmaneuver them all, leaving a string of drooling men in her wake as she deftly climbed her way up the corporate ladder.

Maybe he'd catch a glimpse under her skirt on her way up.

Jesus, he was hopeless.

"So Candy is willing to work on improvement. What about you, Jared? Do I have your word that you'll open your mind to a more natural unity?"

Sure. Why not. He had to say yes. This was his boss, no matter how off-the-wall Harold was acting, and he was still in charge. Jared didn't like macaroni and cheese, so he forced his mouth to open and say, "You have my word, Harold."

Harold beamed. He said, "Yesterday I had the best idea. You're going to love this. There is obviously something holding you and Candy back, something that needs to be resolved." Harold put his finger to his lip. "We could be talking about a betrayal in a past life, I'm not sure."

Jared pressed his hand to his temple. If he'd had a past life, he'd obviously done something really shitty to have earned this torture in his present life.

"What did you have in mind?" Candy leaned forward as she redirected Harold.

"I've signed the two of you up for online couple counseling!"

Jared's head pulsed so violently he could swear he went momentarily blind.

"Oh!" Candy cleared her throat. "Well, that sounds like a great idea."

It wasn't a great idea. It was a stupid, asinine, garbage-can-full-of-crap idea cooked up by his boss who had temporarily lost his mind due to the onset of male pattern baldness.

"We're not a couple, Harold. We don't need counseling." He tugged on the pant leg of his black suit trousers and tried not to panic.

He didn't want some unlicensed Internet shrink telling him he had the hots for his mother or some other such sick shit.

"Yes, you do. There are unresolved issues between you, maybe some domination control problems from your past life, and I want this resolved before we lose Chunk o' Chocolate." Harold pointed to his computer, sitting on his large masculine cherry desk.

"You're all enrolled, ready to go. This is a three-hour session. You are not to leave my office until you've finished the session and given me the printable certificate of completion."

Jared couldn't breathe. Oh my God, Harold was locking him in the plush corner office with Candy for three hours? Alone? With a touchy-feely counseling session to muddle through?

Maybe he could suddenly develop a fever. Or trip and take his eye out on the corner of Harold's desk.

Trouble. Had he pegged her or what?

Candy watched the horror flash across Jared Kincaid's face with interest. He really didn't like her.

She had joked about it, but it was starting to bother her. Everyone liked her, especially men. She had been born a flirt, had always known how to work a smile and a hair flip. It was in her genes, passed down through the women in her family, and instead of fighting it, she had learned to embrace it.

Candy was proud of her femininity, but even more so of her brain. But just because she had that brain didn't mean she wanted to deny she was a woman. She liked wearing heels, and soft flirty dresses when the occasion warranted, and she liked the casual push-pull between men and women.

She liked to flirt, and she was good at it. Candy knew she in no way qualified as a slut, having slept with only two men by the age of twenty-seven. Nor was she a dick-tease as her ex-husband had once accused her. To her mind, you were a tease only if you let a man touch, then taunted him with no. You were a tease only if you promised him sex, then laughed in his face.

Those were nasty games she wasn't interested in playing. But smiles and friendly conversation, that she couldn't resist. And men responded.

All men except for Jared.

She was starting to take it personally.

Jared was saying coldly, "I don't think I can do that, Harold. I don't see the value in that type of exercise."

Ouch. Probably not the best thing for Jared to say. Candy waited, watching Harold's bowling ball–shaped face turn pink.

"I think there is value. And that's all that matters. Don't make me angry, Jared. We're all about love here at Stratford Marketing."

Jared's jaw twitched. Candy pressed her lips together to prevent laughter from spilling out.

She didn't think Jared was all about love. Jared was all about getting his job done and getting the hell out of the office, from what she could tell. He didn't socialize with any of the staff, and he was downright cold to her.

There was a control, a raw edgy dominating control that flickered in his black eyes, and showed in his rigid stance every time she saw him.

It fascinated her.

And he was gorgeous.

It took a lot to draw Candy's interest. Usually men were falling all over her, in a semi-idiotic tongue-wagging sort of way. Maybe that was the reason her eyes were drawn to Jared over and over again.

When he looked at her, she burned. Deep between her thighs where it mattered.

He always looked away with a flicker of disinterest. He never smiled.

Whereas she knew she tended to look as if the wind had blown her into a room, Jared was impeccable in his black suit and merino blue shirt and tie. His black hair never changed, but was short and smooth with a touch of gel that flipped the front up half an inch.

Jared stared at Harold. "So you're saying I have to do this?"

Harold, bless his confused and misguided heart, said firmly with lips pressed together, "That's what I'm saying."

Candy wasn't looking forward to answering probing questions about past lives and intimacy issues either, but she was looking forward to three hours alone with Jared.

Surely in three hours she could make him smile.

Or groan.

Oh, my, where had that thought come from? Appalled at herself, she shifted in her chair and clenched her thighs together. There was enough energy between them to light up the Chicago skyline for three days and nights.

Or heat up Harold's office for three hours.

"Fine." Jared broke eye contact with Harold and leaned back in his chair, unbuttoning his suit jacket. His casual slouch belied the anger apparent on his face.

Candy smiled. "What a great idea, Harold. Jared and I are going to have so much fun getting to know each other."

In more ways than one if she had any say in it.

Harold nodded. "I thought so too. Here." He turned his laptop around to face them. "You're all set to go. See you in three hours."

"Okay." She gave Harold a little finger wave as he headed for the door.

Harold paused. "Be nice to each other."

"I'm always nice," Jared said in a hard low voice that shivered over Candy.

Exactly how nice could she convince him to be?

Candy knew she should be ashamed of herself. But never, ever had she engaged in a casual affair. Nor had a man ever taken so much as one minute to think about satisfying her. They all looked at her and wanted. No one ever cared about what she wanted.

Since the day Jared had walked into the office two months ago, she had been watching, wishing, imagining he would be different.

Jared was making her crazy, making her so achy and desperate that she was liable to start rubbing up against her desk at work if she didn't find some kind of release soon. Would it be so wrong to indulge a little?

If she could break down Jared's mysterious defenses, she would see he was like any other man, out to please himself, and the urgent need would dissipate. Then they could do the Chunk o' Chocolate ad, and she could get back to concentrating on something other than what his chest would look like bare.

"I'm nice too," Candy reassured Harold as he gave them both a doubtful look.

Then the door closed and they were alone.

Jared did nothing. He sat in his chair without moving a muscle and stared out the window.

"Well, no sense in pouting, Jared." She stood up and leaned over Harold's desk, dragging the laptop toward her. "Let's get started."

If she were completely ignorant of her own sexuality, she would have no idea that her backside was in Jared's face. But she was aware of her body, and knew very clearly that bending over meant she was showing a long display of leg. And that her behind with her skirt hugging tight over it was pushed slightly out toward him. She even knew to splay her palms on the desk, lock her elbows, and bend one knee to make the view all the more enticing.

Candy knew how to attract a man's attention. She just didn't know how to keep it focused on her once she had it. Jared, who displayed such iron-clad control, looked as if he would never walk away from a woman until he knew she was satisfied. It would be a matter of pride for him, she suspected. And whoo-whee, was she ready to be satisfied. She wanted a reaction from him.

"Shit," Jared said in a nasty angry whisper.

That was a start.

Candy grinned at the computer screen. "Hmmm? Did you say something?"

He spoke louder. "I said shit. I can't believe I'm letting Harold get away with this."

Candy read the title of the online course in front of them. "Rediscovering Harmony: An Intimate Step-by-Step Guide for Couples in Jeopardy."

Jared snorted.

"We have to type our names in." She starting typing and felt Jared stand up and move beside her.

"You're not really going to do this, are you?"

He filled her space, smothering her with a heady masculine scent of cologne and coffee.

"For my job, I can do Harold's silly little counseling." She flipped her hair out of her eyes. "I don't have anything to hide, and it's not like it means anything."

"True."

There seemed to be a world of meaning in that word and she shifted away from him, her cheeks burning. He was leaning over her to read the screen, his suit jacket brushing against her hip.

"Is Candy your real name?"

It was the first time Jared had ever expressed any interest in her, and she felt her confidence shake a little. Jared might just be too much for her to handle. But she'd never know unless she tried.

"Yes. It's not short for Candace or anything."

He made a noncommittal sound.

She typed JARED KINCAID into the spot for the partner's name. "What's your middle name?"

"Just skip it."

Instead, she typed in HOOVER, then smiled at him. "Am I close?"

"No." He didn't even pull a half smile. "Let's get on to the first question."

Candy nodded. She was eager enough herself. To see exactly how far Jared would be willing to go.

Chapter Two

Jared waited for Candy to click on the first question. They needed to make their way through this stupid counseling as fast as humanly possible. Before he grabbed her, threw her on the desk, and shot all his control to hell with a taste of her.

If they rushed through the questions, he could be out of here in an hour and run to the break room and toss ice cubes down his pants. It was his only hope.

This was all Harold's fault. Or Candy's, for having the nerve to walk around with an ass like that. He could blame Jessie, who had gotten him fired from his last job. Or it could be because he'd never been smart enough to get married and indulge himself with regular sex.

Or maybe he was just a horny idiot.

With a soft spot for pouty doe-eyed women.

Candy leaned over the desk again. "Okay, keep your shirt on."

Jared ground his teeth together.

Candy's lips moved as she read the question silently.

"Well?" He waited for her to enlighten him as to what embarrassing personal details they had to reveal.

"This isn't bad at all, Jared. I think it's supposed to illustrate to couples how little they really know about each other. And to rediscover their interest in one another."

Whatever. Jared sat back down in the chair so Candy's thigh would stop brushing his arm. "So what does it say?"

"Question number one just asks where you're from. You know, where were you born and where did you grow up."

Candy was right. It wasn't as bad as he had suspected. And if Harold wanted to pay him to talk about growing up in Skokie, that was fine with him.

She glanced back at him with a smile, her long legs still straight, her elbow resting on the desk. "Guess where I was born."

He pictured her wandering around a wicker-filled bedroom with louvered windows, wearing a satiny camisole and panties and biting a peach. God, when had he gotten such a vivid imagination? And why did it have to involve Candy in her underwear? "Georgia."

She scoffed. "No, dead wrong. Tennessee."

Oh, there was a difference? "Sorry, I'm not an expert on Southern dialects."

Her little pink tongue slipped out and wet her bottom lip. The full one. The one that demanded he bite it. Jared shifted again, wondering if it was possible to sustain an erection for three hours with no other stimulus than dirty thoughts.

"You're a Yankee through and through, aren't you?"

She made it sound like that was slightly more desirable than an ant infestation in her kitchen.

"I've lived in Chicago all my life."

"Brothers and sisters?" Candy wasn't looking at the computer screen, but was just lounging there draped across the desk, looking mildly curious with a little curving smile gracing the corner of her mouth.

He had no reason to answer. He should suggest they get on with the damn quiz. Instead, he found himself saying, "Three older brothers and one little sister. My parents were insane, apparently."

She threw her head back and laughed, those blond wispy curls tumbling down her back. "Your mother must have loved kids, that's all."

He fought a smile, but couldn't stop it. "I'm not sure that she did. She used to tell us that she was guaranteed a spot in heaven. That God would never deny entrance to a woman with five kids as bad as we were."

She laughed.

"Were you bad, Jared?" Her voice was throaty, her laughter evaporating, but amusement still lingering in her eyes.

For a second, he thought she was flirting with him. And his answer slipped out before he could check it. "Oh, yeah. I was very, very bad."

Her eyes went wide. The full smile came back.

Shit. She was flirting with him. And he was doing it back.

Before she could say something that he would regret, he quickly spoke in what he prayed was a casual, innocent, no-sexual-intent kind of voice. "What about you? Any brothers or sisters down there in Tennessee?"

There was a slight pause, before she said, "I have a younger sister."

Jared tried to picture another woman looking like Candy and couldn't quite conceive it. Candy was one of a kind. Delicious.

"So what's her name? Taffy?" He realized immediately that sounded a lot ruder than he'd intended.

But Candy just laughed. "Actually, her name is Margaret and she's studying the cello at Julliard."

"You've got to be kidding me." *Margaret?*

Jared got a visual of Candy sitting with a cello between her legs. Somehow the image was hard to conjure, though he did feel a pang of envy for the fictional cello and the prized position between Candy's legs. But Candy and orchestral instruments just didn't go together in his mind, no matter what erotic spin he could put on it.

Yet he could see Candy smiling and intelligently directing a room full of ad clients. Damn. Smart and sexy. It was a lethal combination.

"No, I'm not kidding." Candy pulled a strand of hair out of her mouth, one leg still straight, the other bending at the knee, sending her hip out provocatively to the side.

It also dragged her skirt up another solid inch on that side, showing way more than Jared needed to see. Not that he was complaining. It just sent scissors through another thread of his control.

"Margaret and I have different fathers. My mom says my daddy was her true love, a brief burst of passion that left her heartbroken and alone before I was even born."

Candy shrugged. "He left her for another woman when he found out she was pregnant. So two years later she married Margaret's dad because she thought he would stick around and take care of her."

Jared dragged his eyes off Candy's thighs. Leering at her suddenly made him feel no better than the lecher who had run out on her mom. He placed his eyes squarely on her face and vowed not to let his gaze stray. "Did he stick around?"

"Yeah. They're still married and very happy. They really love each other and he never made me feel any different from Margaret even though I wasn't his blood daughter."

She smiled then, and Jared was amazed at the lack of bitterness in her voice. "He adopted me and gave me the last name *Appleton*. I was three by then, so too late to change my first name from Candy. So I've been Candy Appleton ever since."

Then she stood up. Her legs went way, way up as she stretched, reaching her arms over her head while she went up onto the tips of her toes in her high-heel shoes. Her blouse tugged and pulled, straining to escape the waist of her skirt and molding to her breasts. Her suit jacket splayed, held together by one overworked button, and Jared watched in morbid fascination.

He was waiting for the whole thing to blow. The button to fly off, the blouse to slide up, her creamy navel skin bared to him all while she tottered on heels at his mercy.

Then he would take the spot previously reserved for the cello and ease her skirt up.

Jared calculated how much money was left in his checking account and gave himself up for lost.

Chapter Three

Candy hoped like heck she knew what she was doing. Jared looked as if he could chew up nails and tie them into bows with his tongue. She couldn't tell if he was turned on, furious, or both.

And what had possessed her to run on at the mouth about her mother and stepfather? Not that she had an ounce of experience in having casual affairs, but she had to assume you didn't start them out by talking about your family.

Give her another five minutes and she'd be whipping out photos of last Christmas and her cat wearing a Santa hat.

She finished stretching, her legs stiff from bending over the desk, and chewed her lip as she thought over her next move. This shouldn't be so doggone hard. She'd been flirting since the cradle, as her mother frequently liked to remind her. But now when she needed it, all she could think to do was smile, which was lame and appeared to have no impact on Jared whatsoever.

It must be nerves. After all, there was a lot more at stake here than getting good restaurant service. Before she left this office today, she wanted a date with Jared. A date that would end up with them naked and Jared turning that intense concentration squarely on her.

Time to take a deep breath and turn up the heat.

"What's the next question?" Jared said, shrugging out of his suit jacket.

Oh, Lord, he had broad shoulders. She didn't think she'd ever seen him without his jacket on, and it was a sight worth lingering over. She lingered so long he raised an eyebrow.

"The question?"

The quiz. Right. With elephantine effort, she turned around and tried to focus on the computer screen, her cheeks burning.

Jared was turning up the heat, and he didn't even know it.

After quickly typing in their responses to birth place, she went on to three. "Question three. Describe the moment you met."

That was easy. Jared had strolled into the office one Monday morning back in January and she had known lickety split that he would be the one to pull her out of the sexual deep freeze she'd been in since her divorce. He had been wearing a black suit with a burgundy shirt and tie, and he had looked at her, scanned her, and moved on. Dismissed. Dissed.

He had never once deviated in his behavior since.

Jared said nothing. Candy kept her eyes on the screen.

"I guess I'll just type in that we met at work."

"Fine."

Her fingers trembled as she typed, and she blew her hair out of her eyes, ignoring the disappointment she felt. Dang, what did she expect? Jared to say his eyes had met hers over the length of the meeting room table and it had been fate?

There was no doubt in her mind he could not even pinpoint the first time he had seen her.

Jared was desperate. They hadn't even gotten to the hard questions yet and he was in danger of barking and drooling.

The first time he had seen Candy was branded into his mind. He had walked into Stratford Marketing and had gone into the meeting room for an eight A.M. appointment with Harold.

Candy had been there, wearing a cherry red turtleneck sweater that matched her lips. Her blond hair had been pulled back into a twist of some kind and she had on a knee-length white wool skirt and boots. He had felt as if he were staring at a life-sized peppermint, all white and shiny and sweet.

The sight had stunned him, giving him a spontaneous and mortifying erection, and had left his brain and body sizzling like a pound of bacon.

He'd gotten the hell out of that meeting room and thus had started the past eight weeks of dodging her like a bullet. She wouldn't kill him, but she'd send him back to the unemployment lines.

"Next question." He crossed his leg, widely, to accommodate for the throb in his pants, and picked a nice spot on Harold's desk to study. There was a picture of a couple of preteen kids. Gangly. Little Harolds with hair.

"We're cooking now," she said with a perky little smile. "We're already up to question four."

Just what he did not need. She was acting cute. It had been better when she'd been talking about her family. That had at least made her seem real, a live human being with feelings and obviously someone he could not just tangle in Harold's office with and walk away with no regrets or recriminations. But when she did this . . . this bent-over, smiling thing, he forgot everything, including his own name.

"What's the matter?" She sat down in the chair next to him, and pulled the laptop closer to the edge of the desk. "You're scowling and I haven't even read the question yet."

He glanced at his watch. "It doesn't feel like we're accomplishing anything. I think we need to skip a few questions or something."

With a little laugh, she let her fingers fall onto the back of his hand. Her fingers, for God's sake. On his skin. Touching him.

"What's your hurry?"

Now hold on. He turned in his chair, hoping the movement would knock her hand off his. It didn't.

He didn't like that tone in her voice. That let's-see-where-this-goes laugh.

"I thought we were in a hurry. You said you were before."

"Did I?" Her fingers squeezed his hand, her thumb sliding down around his, rubbing back and forth. "If I did then I've changed my mind. Sometimes slow is better than fast, don't you think?"

It was a struggle not to twitch. Or grab her and kiss the Southern smile out of her.

"Slow isn't better with Internet speeds. Or when you're driving on the highway. Or waiting for a paycheck."

Her head tilted. There was a gleam in her eye he just didn't trust.

"But slow is better when you're savoring a good meal. Or taking a stroll by the lake. Or making love."

Ah, hell. He'd been really, really afraid she would say

something like that. Jared went perfectly still, concerned that any sort of movement, of any muscle in his body, might be misinterpreted as an invitation.

He said slowly, carefully, neither smiling nor frowning, "But we aren't doing any of those things."

Candy pulled her hand back. He was not reassured by the action since it was accompanied by her leaning way forward and undoing that loyal button on her jacket.

Those wonderful full lips parted with a little moist sound and she said, "We're not doing any of them . . . yet."

Jared swallowed. Hard. Instinct told him to ignore the comment, to change the subject, to spill a cup of coffee on Harold's computer and get out while he still could.

That's not what he did, of course. He had to know. Just had to. "Are you interested in doing any of those things?"

Candy had him. She had done it. She had gotten a reaction from Jared, and it was a very positive one, if the flare to his nostrils was any indication.

"I'm interested in one or two. How about you?"

He nodded. "A walk by the lake sounds nice."

She sat straight up. Was he serious? "It's March and forty degrees outside! One strong wind and we would be coated in icy lake water."

"It was your idea. And I wasn't aware we were talking about doing any of those things together."

His posture didn't change and his expression was the same neutral gaze, unblinking and in control. It took all she had not to just get up and crawl out of Harold's office in humiliation. But if she was any judge of men, which given her ex-husband was questionable at best, there was lust brewing in Jared's eyes.

Way in the back, but there nonetheless. Plus the nostril flare.

It was enough to keep her in her seat. "Well, I certainly wouldn't want to do any of those things alone. Would you?"

Candy smiled at him and shrugged out of her jacket, struggling with the sleeves. She ended up wiggling back and forth tugging on the jacket, trying to keep her blouse sleeve in place, until Jared took hold of both sleeves and stripped her of the jacket before she could even take a breath.

"Thanks."

"You're welcome. And I don't like to . . . eat alone either."

Have mercy. Having spent the last two years wondering why she couldn't get the least bit aroused, Candy now had her answer. She had been waiting for Jared. And all he needed to do was breathe and she found herself with damp panties.

"Question four." Her voice shattered on a mouselike squeak and Candy cleared her throat. "Where do you most like your partner to touch you?"

Candy leaned forward and looked closer at the screen. Was that really what it said or had her personal thoughts done a wishful Freudian voice-over?

Jared said, "What the hell kind of question is that?"

One on the couples' guide to harmony, apparently. Candy had read the question right.

"Harold can't possibly expect us to answer that. And we've never even touched each other, so it's completely invalid."

"Unless we just answer where we'd like, ah, someone to touch us." Candy shocked herself right out of the chair. She bounced up and paced around the backside of her chair, hiding behind Jared.

Of all the tacky, inappropriate, over-the-top things to

say. He was going to give her a quarter to go buy a clue. He wasn't interested, and throwing herself at him was just embarrassing them both.

She knew it. It was coming. Where was a whale's mouth to dive into when you needed one?

Jared swiveled around to face her and said, "Well, that's easy enough for a man to answer. I think we all want to be touched in the same place. And I'm not talking about our feet."

She was sure he wasn't.

Before she could think of a response that didn't make her sound like a priss or a total slut, but a nice "I'm interested" in-between, Jared spoke again.

His hand was slung over the back of the chair, and his shirt strained across his muscular chest. "So, if *someone* was going to touch me, that's where I would want it to be."

Candy forced herself to stop pacing. "Why don't you type that in on the assessment then?"

Jared let out a laugh. It was the first time she had ever heard him amused enough to laugh. It was a deep rich sound that washed over her and sent her goosepimply.

"I'll do that." He grabbed the laptop and typed with both hands, fast and efficiently. "What should I put for your answer? Where would you want to be touched, Candy?"

Everywhere. Times three.

"Weeell." She drawled the word out, hoping time would give her courage. She knew what she wanted, it was just a matter of saying it out loud.

Squeezing her fists shut tight, Candy tossed back her hair and went for broke. "My breasts."

Jared wasn't looking at her, but she saw his fingers pause over the keyboard. His voice was low, persuasive.

"Would you say specifically your nipples, or all of your breasts, Candy? And touched with hands, or with a tongue? I want to be as accurate as possible you know, for the counseling."

Candy gripped the back of the chair to prevent falling down in a dead faint. Lord, the man was sexy even on the back of his head. "Both. Everything."

The fingers resumed. "Got it."

Then Jared scrolled down the screen. "Let's see about question five."

Candy had never been a drinker, but she felt the sudden need for a splash of bourbon. Or a barrel of bourbon. She had started this, aided by Harold's ridiculous intimacy quest, and she needed to see it through. Her crotch demanded it.

"I'm ready."

"What is the difference between sex, love, and romance?" Jared snorted. "Oh, this one's easy."

"Really?" Leaning against her chair Candy said, "So what's your answer?"

Jared didn't even look up at her as he typed. "Sex you do, love you feel, and romance you say."

Well he just had it all figured out. Candy protested, "That's not true. You can do love, too, by showing someone you love them with a gift or a thoughtful gesture. You can say you love someone. You can show romance with a candlelit dinner and you can feel romantic. Sex you most certainly can feel, and talking and romance are all involved in sex as well. They're all interconnected but very different."

As anyone could see.

Jared glanced at her with a pained expression. "You're right. I was wrong."

His answer startled a laugh out of her. "What?"

"Isn't that what you want me to say? We could argue, but I figure this just saves us time."

"No, I don't want you to just agree with me. I want to hear your opinion. I want to discuss it, have an exchange of ideas, and possibly learn something new from your knowledge."

He looked doubtful. "No woman has ever wanted to hear what I have to say. Not really."

Candy looked down at him, taking in his gorgeous dark eyes and black hair. The way his cheekbones were so strong and sensual, narrowing down into a proud chin and thin lips. She had a sudden insight. Women probably treated Jared the way men treated her.

Like an object. Like an arm ornament.

The rush of understanding made her blurt out, "I want to hear what you have to say. Whether I agree or not."

His eyes swept over her, and she stood still, defiant, daring him to shut her down. Let him frown at her now and she wouldn't mind so much.

He didn't frown. He paused, pursed his lips together, then shook his head slightly. Finally he said, "I'll keep that in mind."

It was enough for her.

He added, "But we're sticking with my original answer because yours is too hard to type in."

Candy laughed and leaned forward. She was edging closer to him, hoping to innocently glance at the screen over his shoulder. Which would force her to brush against him, of course.

"Oh, look, there's a bonus section between questions five and six. It's a tip on keeping the romance alive." Jared shook his head. "Jesus, what the hell was Harold thinking? Didn't he even look at this thing?"

"I doubt it." Candy put her hands on the back of his

chair to steady herself and bent over his shoulder. If she turned to the right, their lips would be a smidgen apart. But for now, she looked straight at the screen.

"What's the tip?"

Jared turned. His breath hit her cheek. "Looking for some advice?"

She shrugged and the movement caused her breasts to brush against his back and shoulder. "You never know. It could be something good."

"It says you should massage your partner. Starting at the feet and working your way up, with special emphasis on erogenous zones."

Candy thought about Jared's hand massaging up her legs, zeroing in on her inner thighs, and settling in for a long, hot haul.

"They also suggest the use of edible massage oils, with flavors like chocolate and raspberry."

Oh, Lord. The idea of him licking chocolate sauce off her nipple contributed to her increasingly damp panties problem. If she spent much more time with Jared she was going to have to start carrying a spare pair.

Candy turned. Jared was watching her. His lips were close enough to touch. To lick. To kiss.

She whispered, "It sounds sticky."

The smell of coffee rushed over her as he breathed, a little harder and faster than was normal. Candy pulled her bottom lip into her mouth and tugged.

He said, "It sounds delicious."

"If you're hungry."

"Oh, I'm hungry, Candy. It's lunchtime, you know." Jared's eyes dropped to her lips.

He was going to kiss her, he was going to kiss her, he was going to . . . turn back to the computer.

Dang it. Where was a jar of chocolate massage oil when she needed it?

She was going to have to start carrying that around in her purse along with the spare panties.

Chapter Four

Holy hell, he had almost kissed her. Had he learned nothing from Jessie and the clandestine copy room kiss? Work and sex didn't mix. Ever.

Even when you were locked in a cozy room with the office babe and she was standing so close a gnat would have trouble squeezing between you.

Especially not when you were discussing the titillating effects of chocolate sauce during a massage.

And certainly not when the same office babe kept lobbing off personal remarks that made you feel as if she might actually listen to you if you spoke.

Candy was revealing herself to be hiding as many layers as an onion. As Jared stared at the computer screen in front of him, he wondered how one woman could be intelligent, kind, funny, and so damn gorgeous all at the same time? If he wasn't careful, he might actually find himself tumbling into some serious *like*.

If she could cook too, he was toast. Crispy burnt toast, without a job.

"What's the next question?" she said.

Shit, who cared? He had bigger problems here than

Harold's dumb-ass counseling. Like the massive append-age throbbing in agony in his pants.

He read the question anyway, painfully aware there was no relief in sight for his poor neglected dick. "Number six. Do you like the city or country better?"

Knowing he should be grateful for the lack of refer-ence to smearing food sauce on each other's bodies, he answered the question quickly. "City."

As he typed, Candy said, "Country."

Jared didn't risk a look in her direction, since she was still hovering over him. But he couldn't stop him-self from saying, "A country girl, huh? I'm not surprised with that twang of yours."

Candy stood up. "I do not have a twang. You can't even tell I'm from the South."

Right. Candy had Southern Belle stamped on each and every curve of her body, and she would probably even moan in pleasure with a cute little accent. "You're not a 'Hee-Haw' episode, that's for sure, but there is no way you could pass for a native Chicagoan."

He chanced a look over at her. Her hands were on her hips. "Are you insulting me?"

"Not at all."

She looked ready to argue, but he staved her off by reading the next question. "Number seven. What's your favorite way to spend an evening together?"

Did that mean before they got naked, or after?

Candy had relaxed back against his chair, her hip nestled snug against the side, the twang comment ap-parently forgotten. "Well, I would want a nice romantic dinner, at home. Good wine, some jazz playing in the back-ground, and a video we could watch together. We would talk about our day, the movie, everything, and then, uh, proceed from there."

It sounded very ordinary. It sounded like exactly what he wanted.

The thought startled him. His relationships had never been particularly romantic. He didn't seem to inspire those feelings in women. Usually the only conversation involved their coaxing and pleading that he do things that he knew were bound to get him into deep shit. Like copy room kisses.

At about seventeen he'd given up on expecting anything that resembled friendship with a woman. The only women he could ever claim to have had an honest-to-God conversation with were a former fifty-year-old coworker, and his friend Kim, whom he'd known since they were nine. He was guessing it wasn't a coincidence that Kim also happened to be a lesbian.

Even his weekly chats on the phone with his mother involved more platitudes and discussion over his laundry and the weather than anything real.

"What about you?" Candy asked him.

He thought about lying, or saying something quelling, but instead he said, "The same. Only add a fireplace to it."

The reward was a glorious smile that spread from one end of Candy's golden face to the other. "Really?"

The pleasure that little word brought him had him shifting from discomfort, and it had nothing to do with his still-very-much-there erection. It was worse than he could ever have imagined.

He had tumbled already.

He actually liked her.

Which meant he was so screwed.

"Really," he confirmed, then rushed on. "So, question eight. Here we go. Why did you choose your current career?"

Easy enough from his point of view. Because it paid reasonably well, he was good at it, and involved nothing gruesome, like slinging trash or probing body cavities.

Candy shifted so that her opposite hip jutted out. "Well, it's sort of complicated. I had to pick a career that was equal parts men and women because if I was a woman in an all-male field, I wouldn't be taken seriously." She glanced at him. "The name, you know."

The name, the hair, the legs, the accent. Just for starters.

"Yet I can't work with all women either. Women seem to exclude me and aren't friendly. I've never been able to figure it out, but it seems like the harder I try, the more they pull back."

Try jealousy. Candy would draw male attention no matter what she did, and women would react to that, he was sure. In the negative.

"So, I decided marketing had a good male-female mix and I like the challenge of anticipating the client's needs."

Well, his answer sounded stupid now. Good thing he hadn't said it out loud.

"I enjoy my job, but I still don't have many friends here. I can't seem to break into the inner circle." She shook her head sadly, all trace of flirtation and the business-woman gone. Candy just looked hurt and vulnerable.

"No one really likes me."

His brain begged him not to say it. His heart and other body parts didn't listen. "I like you."

Candy crossed her arms over her chest and laughed, a nervous startled sound. "No, you don't. You avoid me like I have something catchy. That's why we're in Harold's office, remember?"

He stood up and turned to her, moving into her space

before she could dart away. His hands fell on each of hers. Her eyes went wide as he spoke.

"Maybe that's because I liked you too much."

Then those lips that had been taunting his every waking moment, and a good portion of his sleeping ones as well, lifted and rounded into a perfect O. He took advantage of her surprise by leaning forward.

A second later his lips were on hers. It should have been short and sweet, just a light touch then retreat. The second he tasted her lips, all tangy and plump, there was no chance of that.

She was tense, her hands gripping his sleeves, but her mouth fell open for him on a soft sigh. Without warning his tongue decided to take a detour by her tonsils, and hot pulsing need gripped him below the belt.

Someone moaned. He hoped like hell it wasn't him.

Candy held on to Jared for dear life and struggled to stay upright. Have mercy. It felt like he was *eating* her mouth, licking and sucking and tugging.

It was too much; she couldn't keep up with the hard, fast movements of his tongue and mouth. The only thing she could do was let him consume her, hang on, and groan her pleasure.

She had the moaning thing down pat, whenever there was actually time to take a breath. Mostly she was fighting for air and working hard not to wobble in her heels.

His hands rose up her arms to her face and cupped her cheeks. It wasn't tender, it was fierce, dominating, his strength holding her still while he moved over her mouth.

Confusion mixed with passion, and Candy squeezed his arms harder. This wasn't what she had expected. She had envisioned tight control from Jared, emotion firmly out of the picture as he kissed her with skill and charm.

After her ex-husband and his selfish lovemaking, she had vowed to find someone different, who would focus on her needs, not his. She had thought Jared would be that man.

But Jared was anything but reserved, and her reaction was anything but what she had expected. She was enjoying herself. It was arousing to know that she had sent Jared skittering over the edge, dropping his control somewhere back about question six.

Jared stepped away, taking his heat and masculine scent with him. "Jesus."

Candy forced her eyes open, and dragged in a shuddery breath. Wiping her wet mouth with her thumb and index finger, she watched him, wondering if he would stammer or apologize.

She should have known better. Jared was no stutterer.

"See, I told you I like you." He straightened his tie, but kept his eyes trained on her.

Candy felt her cheeks burn. She had to admit, that was a much better answer than a muttered apology would have been. None of this was working out the way she had planned it. Her original idea had been to have Jared ask her out, then seduction would ensue.

This was wilder, more uncontrolled, almost *dirty*. They had been making out in their boss's office. And she liked it.

"Maybe you do," she agreed. Then with an acting ability she hadn't known she possessed, she sauntered past him, catching her arm on his as she approached Harold's desk.

Jared sucked in his breath. Candy didn't look back.

She bent over in front of Harold's desk again and propped her chin up with her hand. "So, how long have you . . . liked me? As a friend."

Jared pried his eyes off Candy's legs and wondered

what game she was playing now. His feelings of friendship had nothing to do with that kiss. That kiss was based on two months' worth of stored-up lust.

Friendship had just come into the picture in the last half hour, and he had to assume he'd just about blown that with his grab-her-and-mash-her kiss.

He found he actually regretted the idea that he might have shattered the growing rapport between them. Maybe if he retreated now, he could salvage some kind of friendship between them.

Dropping into the chair so he wouldn't be tempted to touch her, he cleared his throat. "We haven't really talked to each other a whole lot, but I respect the work you do. You're very efficient, always on time, and your presentations are professional and thought provoking."

He sounded as if he were giving her a yearly productivity review. But better that than saying what he really thought.

Which was that she had an adorable smile and said funny things that made his heart squeeze. Not to mention she had a body that made him wish he were a sponge so he could rub all over it. Wet.

She made a noise with her teeth. "That's not what I mean. I'm talking about *liking* me."

He was drowning in this conversation. Since he had promised to behave himself, he would not repeat a single one of the R-rated ideas running through his head, all focusing on how much he could like her.

Instead he said, "That's what I was talking about too."

There was a pause, and her finger hovered in front of the screen. "Look, question nine fits right in with what we're talking about."

What were they talking about? Because hell if he knew.

"What do you like the most about your partner?" Candy was still propped up on her hand, leaning over the desk.

Her legs were straight, her curvy little behind back in front of his face, way too close for comfort. Her hair was tumbling over her shoulders, and she had pulled her lip into her mouth and was making little sucking noises with it.

Then, for some unknown reason that probably involved nefarious plans to torture him, she spread her legs. Just widened them a bit so that her feet were planted a foot apart. Her skirt inched up under the strain.

It could be she was getting more comfortable. Or it could be that she knew the effect spreading her thighs would have on him.

He was an arm's length from her. He studied the smoothness of her stocking-covered legs. They were perfect. Narrow, yet muscular, they climbed up to her skirt, double doses of torture.

One lean forward, one hand out, and he could be touching that thigh. He could be sliding up that skirt, not stopping until he hit paydirt. If she wore garters as he suspected, there would be no stockings protecting her panties from him.

And there was nothing to stop him from pushing aside whatever scrap of lace she was wearing and touching deep inside Candy.

"This is a fun question," she chirped on cheerfully, unaware he was battling with the forces of good and evil.

Evil was pulling ahead by a nose, which was quickly lengthening into a mile.

"I like a lot of things about you, Jared. You're a hard worker, you don't gossip, you dress really well, and you're intelligent."

He barely heard her. He was moving. Leaning forward, edging closer and closer to her, until he could smell her scent.

She was wearing a light floral perfume, mixed with something berry, probably a lotion she'd rubbed on after her shower. It pulled him closer, drawing him in, his breath hitching in anticipation. He was there, just behind her, straining to control himself.

He was not going to touch. He wasn't. He was just taking a better look.

Candy's knee bent a little. Her skirt lifted. And he saw it. The edge of her stocking, and the little hook that connected it to the garter. Above the hook was a strap of lace, contrasting against the flash of golden peach skin next to it.

His breath caught and he tilted his head. His own legs were spread, and he was resting his hands between his knees as he bent down a little lower until he found what he was looking for.

A narrow, dark view up her skirt. His eyes trailed past the garter, past the creamy thigh above it to her panties. They were black lace, of course, and shifted a little to the right so that he had a clear shot of the curls covering her soft mound on one side.

"Jared?"

"Hmmm?" He licked his lips. His hands itched and jerked restlessly. There was no possible way he could stop looking. She was so beautiful and lushly feminine, and he wanted her the way he had never wanted another woman.

Candy twisted a little. "Where are you? What are you doing?"

He couldn't see her face as she wiggled around. Swallowing hard, he kept his eyes trained right on her inner thighs. Unable to force a lie past his aching lips, he said in a low voice, "I'm looking up your skirt."

"What?" Candy jerked forward, robbing him of his view. She hit the desk, then whirled around, half leaning, bending her legs in at the knees.

He didn't say anything. There was really nothing good to say in a moment like this. An apology would probably be in order.

But hell, he could not truthfully regret one second. And she would know he was lying. The drool at the corner of his mouth would give him away.

Candy clutched her hand to her chest. She gaped at him. Then slowly, the tension eased out of her. Her hand fell back to her side and her eyes went wide.

The knees unbent. Her voice was fascinated. "Did . . . did you like what you saw?"

He sat back in his chair so hard it wobbled. "Oh, yeah."

A delighted smile crossed her face. "What else do you like about me? You never did answer."

Candy didn't look angry with him. She looked intrigued. It made him even harder, if that were possible.

As he watched her, all blond and gorgeous, leaning against the desk with a speculative and pleased gleam in her eye, Jared found himself saying things he had never imagined he would ever say to a woman.

"I like your smile, and your laugh. And I like how you talk, like your sentences don't know when to stop. You're smart, sweet, and funny."

To him, it sounded like the biggest load of crap he'd ever uttered in his life, even though it was all true. But Candy seemed to like it, if the softening expression on her face and the fluttering hand at her breast were any indication.

A little embarrassed, he added gruffly, "Anything else you want to know?"

"Yeah. Why hasn't some woman snapped you up and run off with you?"

"I haven't met a woman yet who thought she wanted to live with me."

It had never bothered him either, not until now. The thought of his overpriced roomy condo didn't please him for the first time since he had bought it.

"Where do you live?" she asked, crossing her legs and leaning back against the desk.

"I bought a place in the South Loop area." If the chair had wheels he could shift it back away from Candy, but it was heavy and firmly in place. "What question are we on?"

The desire to get out of the room was back, tenfold. Another half an hour of this and he was going to be on his knees begging her to put him out of his misery.

"Oh." She shook her head. "I don't remember."

She turned back around and he promised God he would call his mother every Sunday from now until she died if Candy just wouldn't bend over.

Candy stayed standing, but her backside was still tempting him, so he sat on his hands to keep them in place. He thrust his legs out to try and adjust the growing problem in his pants.

"Oh, we have to skip this next question."

"Why?" Not that he cared or even needed to know.

Candy half turned and her hip jutted out toward him. His hands broke free and went screaming in her direction. He stopped them as they were seconds away from landing on her thighs just above the knees.

"It asks when was the first time we had sex and where."

She smiled at him, a naughty knowing smile that sent his blood pressure to dangerous levels.

He knew the answer to that question.

They were going to have sex. Now. In the boss's office.

Chapter Five

Candy watched strange things happen to Jared's face. His eyes darkened, his breathing went shallow, and he looked as if he was in pain.

One glance below his waist told her why. His erection was more than obvious. It had popped up like a *Star Wars* light saber.

A thrill raced through her that she had caused that. Jared was turned on by her. And whew, was she turned on by him.

"There's another bonus romance tip after that question," she told him, not bothering to wait for an answer since Jared looked beyond speech.

"Skip it," he said, his voice harsh and raw.

"No, it could be fun." She clicked on the screen. "It's actually a video."

Still a little giddy from the realization that Jared liked her smile, she stepped back away from the desk as the video clip loaded.

Her heel landed on Jared's ankle, and she stumbled, fighting for balance. Shoot, she was going to fall down in an ungracious heap right in front of him.

Flailing her arms about like a misguided chicken, she felt Jared's big hands land on her waist. Then down she went, landing on his lap with a solid thump. Right on his erection.

Lord, that thing was big. It was poking her square in the behind.

"Thanks," she said breathlessly, knowing full well it wasn't her graceless stumble that had her gasping for air.

An indistinguishable sound came from Jared's mouth right behind her ear. Candy wiggled forward, intent on standing up, when the video caught her attention.

It was a couple naked in a bathtub, industriously lathering each other up. "Oh!" she said as desire kicked her in the gut.

She went still on Jared's lap, afraid to move, unsure what he wanted her to do. She knew what she wanted, and Jared's lower half clearly wanted the same thing, but given the tension in his body, she wasn't sure his brain agreed.

Her legs dangled between his, and she crossed her arms across her chest with painstakingly slow movements, determined not to wiggle. She could smell him, that heavy masculine scent of aftershave. She could hear him breathing. Feel the tight hardness of his muscles beneath her.

His chest brushed against her back.

"What the hell?" Jared said, his hands on her waist tightening.

Those fingers of his were right at her waistband. One shift and he would be touching her skin where her blouse had pulled out of her skirt.

Leaning forward a little, Candy read the caption alongside the image. "A great way to relax and rediscover romance is with a long sensual bubble bath. Take the time

to explore each other's bodies with the added aphro-
disiac of warm water and satiny bath gels."

The pair onscreen did look relaxed. The woman was
facing the man, sitting on his lap, and they were kissing,
tongues entwined, and her wet breasts pushed up
against his chest. The bubbles of the bath covered the
major body parts, but it still served its purpose.

Making her crazy, wishing she could be wet and slippery with Jared.

The woman rocked up and down, making bubbly waves
around them while Harold's office filled with the sound
of their panting.

"They seem to be enjoying themselves," she said, unable to drag her eyes away.

Jared's hands convulsed on her waist. She could swear
that his erection was actually throbbing against her,
making her want to turn around and beg that he push
inside her. She wanted what that woman was getting.

"Candy, stand up."

"What?" Disappointment rushed through her, and her
mouth was wet and heavy with desire. "Why?"

"Because this isn't right." He gave her a not-so-gentle
shove. "It's wrong. We're in Harold's office."

Despite her disappointment, the panic in his voice
amused her. And his words thrilled her. She had known
Jared would be different. Instead of just taking what he
could get, he was holding back for the sake of decency.

Office propriety.

Which she had been about to toss out the window.

Candy suspected that Jared was waiting for someone
too, just the way that she was. He was waiting for the
one woman who would see beyond the body and the
clothes and show interest in the man.

That woman was her, she decided. Whether it was for

one day, one night, or something more, she didn't know. But she wanted Jared, needed to feel him inside her. If not today, then soon. Very soon.

With great reluctance, she let him shove her forward until she was back on her feet. She turned and rested her knees against his, pushing her hair back off her face.

She had to ask. Wanted him to say it. "Do you want me, Jared?"

He nodded without hesitation. "Yes. I do. Since the day I met you."

She shuddered, her body pulsing with need. "That's something else I like about you, you know. I like that you *like* me, but haven't done anything about it."

Pressing forward, she spread her legs until one was on either side of his. "I want you to do something about it. Now."

He didn't say anything. He didn't do anything. He just sat there, clenching his hands tightly on the arm of the chair, his jaw taut, his eyes tortured.

"Unless you want to hear question eleven instead."

Candy wanted another kiss from him, and plans for a date. Until she got one of the two, she'd stand here in front of him all day and read the random and vague questions of Harold's couple counseling.

Glancing over her shoulder, she said, "Question eleven. What's your favorite smell?"

She was about to go into the scent of freshly cut grass, baking apple pies, and the ocean, when Jared spoke first.

"Sex and Candy. That's what I want to smell."

Have mercy.

Shocked, she whirled around to face him again, sure she'd heard him wrong. She clearly hadn't. The expression of lust raging on his face showed her that he knew exactly what he had said. And meant it.

She went wet, wishing she weren't standing with her legs so far apart. The hot, thrilling ache was unbearable.

She took back that very wish a split second later when Jared reached forward and placed a wide warm hand on each of her knees. Then he shoved the skirt all the way up to her waist, leaving her naked but for her panties a foot in front of his face.

His breath tickled her, and she arched her back, gripping the desk so she wouldn't fall down. Her legs shook a little, and the only sound in the room was their combined ragged breathing.

Leaning in to hover in front of her panties, Jared closed his eyes and breathed in deeply. "Mmmm. I can smell it already."

Candy knew she should be mortified, blushing eight shades of purple and leaping away from him. But the only thing she felt was desire, rushing hot and strong through every inch of her. She felt intensely feminine, in control, and powerful in a way she'd never experienced before.

As his nose brushed across her panties, Candy's fingers found their way to his shoulders. She gripped his shirt, digging in with greedy and desperate need, tossing her head back on a soft moan. Jared took his time, languidly studying her, his thumbs tracing patterns above her knees on her stockings. Once or twice his breath hitched, but otherwise he was perfectly in control.

She was about to lose hers and whimper. Or beg. Or press forward so that his mouth would bump her right where she wanted him the most.

Then he spoke again, eyes still roving over her, fingers light and in no hurry. "Can I taste you, too?"

Are there bears in the woods?

"Oh, yes. Please."

Candy's eagerness came close to undoing him. Instead, he took a deep breath and moved his hands up Candy's thighs, past the line of her stocking onto her smooth bare flesh. She was hot to the touch, the way his own body felt, and he couldn't muzzle a groan from jerking out.

Damn, she was beautiful. Curvy and pink and his for the taking. Right now. The peek up her skirt he'd had earlier hadn't done her justice. Now, laid all out before him, she looked and smelled delicious.

The floral of her perfume had melted with the musky scent of her desire, leaving him dry-mouthed and hornier than hell.

With one finger, he dragged the loose black lace away from her and over to the side, holding it in place there against her inner thigh muscle. Little sounds of encouragement rained down on his head, and her fingers dug into his shoulders, pinching his skin.

With another finger and thumb, Jared gently spread her folds apart, brushing her blond curls aside.

This time, he was the one who moaned. Damn, she looked so good. And wet. She was more than ready.

He brushed the tip of his tongue across her, closing his eyes against the heat and tangy taste. Somewhere, in the back of his mind, he had been imagining this for weeks. It was better than he could have ever dreamed.

As was the lurch Candy gave, and the high-pitched cry that flew out of her mouth. He didn't look up, just gave another long slow lick. This time her pleasure was muffled, and he guessed she'd remembered exactly where they were, and how thin Harold's wood door was.

He moved again, faster, rhythmically crossing over her, sliding his tongue inside her, and pulling back again. He felt surrounded by her, enclosed by her thighs and her breasts hovering over his head. Her fingers pulled his shirt so hard it had jerked out of his pants as he tasted her, smelled her, loved her.

His tongue went deeper, his fingers pulled her panties harder to the side, and with his other hand he cupped her ass. Her panties had slid into the crevice between her cheeks, and he tugged them back out slowly. He allowed his finger to explore along the path where the underwear had been, sliding along from behind until his finger had met up his tongue, both pressing into her.

Candy bucked and writhed, way too close to ripping off an orgasm without him.

Wrenching his mouth and hand away, he took a deep breath and laughed softly at her startled curse. Getting to his feet, he licked the moisture of Candy's body off his lips and smiled at her.

"I just remembered something."

"What?" She panted, her eyes glazed. Candy was holding on to the desk for support now that he had stood and taken his shoulders up out of her immediate reach.

"You said you like to be touched on your breasts. I should be doing that instead."

Frustration was evident in the way she shook her head and said, "I liked what you were doing just fine."

Jared put a hand on each breast and caressed her nipples through her blouse.

Candy's eyes fluttered shut. "Or this is good too."

He had to agree. Faster than he would have thought possible, he had the buttons on her white blouse undone and was reaching inside to cup her breasts.

She was wearing white lace, a startling contrast to the black panties. As he rolled her nipple beneath his finger, he said, "You rebel. Your bra and panties don't match."

Eyes half closed, she muttered, "I put the panties on first. Then realized I couldn't wear a black bra with a white blouse."

"So you're not a rebel?" he teased, kicking her legs farther apart so he could wedge his thigh in between hers.

"Doesn't sex in my boss's office make me a rebel?"

Jared pressed against Candy, annoyed to find her skirt had fallen back down to cover her. Her words fascinated him. It seemed obvious that's where they were heading, but to hear her say it out loud was a huge turn-on.

"Is that what we're doing? Having sex?"

"Sort of."

Dragging her bra down to expose her full breast, Jared pulled the pink nipple into his mouth and sucked softly. "Nice and sweet."

Candy's hands landed on his head and she tugged on his hair.

He pulled back half an inch. "What should we do to make it more than sort-of sex?"

Then he trailed his tongue along the side of her breast as it popped over the edge of the lace bra. He forced himself to go slow, to stay in control, to not just rip every inch of her clothing off the way he wanted to and sink into her softness.

A hand slithered down and caressed him through his pants, sending a jolt reverberating through every cell in his body. "Candy?"

"This is where you wanted to be touched, right?"

He nodded dumbly.

"Then I'll touch you. And when I'm finished, we can make it full sex by having you inside me."

Yes. Yes, yes, and hell yes.

"If that's what you want . . ."

"To touch you? Or you inside me?" Her hand stilled. Damn, she was killing him. He said, "Both."

"Yes, that's what I want. Here. Now."

He was about to agree that was the best goddamn idea he'd ever heard in his life, when she grabbed his belt buckle and undid it before he could even open his mouth. Nimble fingers unbuttoned and unzipped him.

"Very efficient," he murmured.

Candy grinned. "Efficiency in the workplace leads to greater productivity."

He laughed. Then sputtered off into a moan when her hand went inside his pants and wrapped around him.

She squeezed.

He panted.

Caressing up the length of him, her eyes went wide. "Ooh, it's so big."

And he didn't even pay her to say that.

From another woman, that would have sounded insincere, but not when Candy said it. No one could fake the kind of honest pleasure on her face, or the way her eyes struggled to stay open.

The idea that he could trust Candy flitted through his mind, before he lost all rational thought.

"Does this feel good?"

Her speed had increased, and she was rubbing up and down with light feathery strokes. *Good* was a hilarious understatement.

Any better than this and he was going to be done before he started. "Yes, but . . ."

Her hand slipped down to cup his testicles.

"Candy, I . . ."

Shit, now she had both hands on him.

"What, Jared?"

He forced himself to speak. "I have a condom in my wallet. Let me get it out."

She stilled.

He panicked. If she said no, he was going to cry like a baby.

Her hands left his pants and pressed against his chest. Then she kissed his cheek, her full warm lips just brushing across his skin.

No woman but his mother had ever kissed his cheek.

A weird tenderness came over him, quieting his urgent desire and leaving him waiting for Candy to tell him his next move.

If she had changed her mind, he respected that.

"Which pocket is your wallet in?"

But her not changing her mind was better.

"Left." He started to reach around for it, but she stopped him.

"No, I'll get it." Then she was rummaging around in his pocket, feeling here, feeling there, the teasing light touches making him nuts.

Finally she held the wallet up, smiling, looking confident and sure. "Which compartment?"

"I don't know." It was somewhere in there collecting dust.

He watched her riffle through the wallet, stopping to look at his driver's license.

"Checking to make sure I'm who I say I am?" he asked, amused.

"I wanted to see how old you are. Thirty-one if my math's right. And I couldn't resist looking at your picture. You look perfect, like you always do."

It should have been a compliment, but the wrinkling

of her nose made it sound like a bad thing. "You don't like that?"

"I do. I love the way you're put together all the time, but Lord, Jared, it's hard to stand next to you." She found the condom and pulled it out. "I'm so scattered-looking all the time, I can't compete with you."

Scattered-looking? Is that what she called it? He would have thought *blond bombshell* was a better way to phrase it.

"I love the way you look." He smoothed her hair back from her face. "That curvy body and your brains, together they're lethal. You're gorgeous, Candy. Now give me the condom."

Candy stared at Jared in disbelief and something that felt suspiciously like hope. She knew when men were lying, when they were feeding her what she wanted to hear. Half the conversations in her life were based on empty compliments meant to coax her into bed.

Jared was telling the truth. He thought she was smart.

If she wasn't already planning to have sex with him, she would have just for that alone.

Ripping the foil package open, she said, "I've got it."

His eyes darkened. "Okay. But before you do that . . ."

Hands were suddenly up her skirt. Before she could blink, her panties were down at her knees, then sinking to the floor. Jared's hand lingered on her bare behind for a minute before retreating.

Her mouth was hot and thick with saliva and she reached for him impatiently, rolling on the condom with trembling fingers. She hadn't been kidding about the big thing. Jared was no slouch in the size department and she distracted herself by running her hands across him again, giving his hot skin a squeeze.

The condom stuck, and it took her three times to unroll it, but she finally got it on and flipped her hair back out of her eyes.

Jared surprised her with a kiss, a long wet, lingering kiss that robbed her of the last of her reserve. As his hands held her head, and he rocked against her with his penis, she moaned, "Now. Please."

He pushed her skirt out of the way and without warning his finger sank inside her. A shudder ripped through her.

"You're still nice and wet. Ready for me?"

Since the minute they'd walked into this office. "Oh, yes."

Jared backed her up a foot until she was leaning against Harold's desk, the surface cool on her backside. Then nudging her legs apart, he entered her with one quick thrust.

He filled every inch of her, stretching her, and Candy repeated, "Oh, yes!"

They stood there for long seconds, Jared's head bent down and Candy's nails digging into his arms. She could feel the length of him pulsing inside her, making her want more than this tight teasing.

Jared must have had the same idea. He moved. Slow. In and out until Candy's arms dropped to her sides and she let her head loll back. She didn't thrust her hips to meet him, but just settled back and let him rock into her. It was languid and deep, and Jared leaned forward and dashed his tongue across her nipple.

She barely felt the cold hard surface of the desk pressing into her backside, and hooked a leg around Jared's knee so she wouldn't fall as he started to move faster.

Relaxed went to gripping in a split second as his hands

snaked around to grab her ass and push harder, in rough urgent mating. She bit her lip to hold back the violent cries she wanted to scream, and their labored pants mixed together as Jared moved them closer to fulfillment.

It seemed as if she should tell him to slow down, as if they should savor this first time together, but her body wasn't having any of it. Her hips start driving forward, meeting Jared's thrusts with a little slapping sound of skin and zippers.

It was that sound that made her come. Along with the look on Jared's face as his own orgasm overcame him. Candy clung to the desk and felt Jared's shudders mingle with hers as they rode out their pleasure.

The orgasm was tight and hard, pulling at her almost painfully, and she let out a cry as it slowed and passed, shivers racing up her spine.

Candy couldn't move, stunned by her explosive reaction to Jared. The man was good.

He leaned against her, breathing hard, nearly toppling her backward onto the desk with his weight.

"I'm falling!" she cried out, scrambling for a grip, her hand knocking the computer hard.

Strong arms prevented her fall.

"Sorry."

Jared stepped back, pulling out of her, and Candy closed her eyes for a second at the loss. She liked him against her, big and strong, in pursuit of her, and was sorry to be past that. But he continued to lean toward her, placing a soft kiss on her jaw. This was a good look on him too, this triumphant relaxed expression he was wearing.

He smoothed her skirt back down into place, a smile twitching at the corner of his mouth. "Damn, I can't believe we just did it in Harold's office."

She grinned back. "Oh, I can believe it. The dent in my butt proves it."

Alarm crossed his face, making Candy feel like gooey chocolate. "Are you okay, babe?"

She nodded, trying to decide if *babe* could be classified as a term of endearment or not. "I'm fine."

"We must be crazy." Jared placed another soft kiss on her forehead and gestured to his pants. "And what the hell am I supposed to do with this condom now? Toss it in Harold's wastebasket?"

Good question. She eyed the condom dubiously as he pried it off. "You'll have to put it in your pocket, I guess."

The horror that crossed his face made her giggle.

"And carry it around all day?"

"No, just until you get to your office, then you can throw it in the wastebasket there."

"The cleaning lady will think I'm a pervert."

Candy began doing the buttons on her blouse back up. "Well, then just wrap it in tissues." She plucked six tissues out of the box on the edge of Harold's desk. "Here you go."

Jared took them and wrapped up the condom, grimacing the whole time. "The price of spontaneity, I guess."

He still had her pinned against the desk, so she tried to slide around him as he tucked the mummified condom into his pocket.

Before she could get by him, Jared grabbed her arm and trapped her leg with his. "Where are you going?"

"To get my panties off the floor."

She expected him to grin, but he didn't. Holding her tight, he said, "Can I see you tonight?"

Candy smiled, unable to contain herself. Not only had he asked her out, but he actually looked as if he cared what her answer would be.

"Yes. Now let me get my panties before we manage to get ourselves caught."

Then a knock rattled the door and they heard Harold call out, "How's it going in there?"

Chapter Six

Jared said, "Holy shit." He zipped his pants and moved away from Candy, tripping on the edge of the chair next to him. "We didn't even lock the door."

He was dead. Harold had wanted him to sort out his differences with Candy, not have sex with her. On company time.

The doorknob was turning. One glance at Candy showed her frozen in horror, her hair every which way, and her blouse buttoned wrong, leaving a big gaping hole in her middle, flashing pink skin.

Neither one of them was wearing their jacket, and the entire room had the sweet smell of sex in the air. He didn't even want to think about the condom in his pocket.

In an attempt to stave off the inevitable, he called out, "Uh, we're doing great. Just give us five more minutes, Harold."

Candy's black lace underwear was still lying on the floor.

"Get your panties," he whispered.

She started and bent over just as Harold stopped opening the door. "Oh, you're not finished?"

"Not quite." Jared pulled his suit jacket back on and ran his hand through his hair to smooth it down.

Candy shoved the panties into her waistband.

"Fine, but let me know when you're done."

Harold whistled as he shut the door and walked off back down the hall. The sick feeling in Jared's gut lessened a notch. "Shit, that was close."

Candy pulled her panties back out. "Watch the door while I put these on."

Visions of her with one foot in her underwear and one foot out with Harold throwing the door open popped into his head. "Just leave them off and put them in your jacket pocket."

She looked at him as if he'd announced he was going to start wearing dresses.

"Yuck! I can't walk around the rest of the day wearing stockings and a garter belt, but no panties. It would be uncomfortable and I'd feel like everyone knew." Kicking her heels off, Candy quickly slipped into the panties and shimmied them up her legs.

Jared thought about her sitting in her office with no panties on under her skirt, her soft backside pressing into the chair. Her curls rubbing against her skirt. And nobody would know but him. He went hard again just thinking about it.

Candy stepped back into her heels then put on her jacket. "We need to finish the counseling session, you know, before Harold comes back."

Right. That's why they were there in the first place. Somehow or other that had managed to slip his mind.

"Candy, the screen's blank."

She whirled around. "What? Oh, my gosh, we unplugged it."

Between pounding against the desk and flailing arms,

he wasn't surprised. "Why wasn't Harold using his battery? How stupid is that?"

Candy plugged the computer back in and rebooted it. Jared was distracted by her hot little ass bending over and wiggling in the air as she stuck the plug in the socket.

He said, "Maybe this is better. We can get out of the rest of those dumb-ass questions. We'll tell Harold it crashed."

She looked doubtful, but he pulled her into his arms and kissed her with plenty of tongue until she relaxed.

"Mmm," she said.

"You took the words right out of my mouth." He stopped her as she tried to tug loose and head for the door.

"Seven tonight? I'll pick you up." He wasn't letting her out of this office without a commitment to see him again.

"Okay."

"You go out first. I'll run Harold to ground and tell him we've solved our problems and his karma is at peak levels."

She grinned as they paused in front of the door. "I like your karma."

"There's plenty more where that came from." And because he couldn't resist, he squeezed her ass and molded her skirt to her, one finger sliding down between her legs.

Her eyes fluttered shut. "Oh, stop it, Jared."

"Sorry." Not.

Jared opened the door, and when she stepped out, Candy found herself face to face with Harold. "Oh! Harold."

Oh, Lord, she must look guilty as sin.

And Harold was studying them *way* too closely.

"Everything okay?"

"Wonderful. Great." She cleared her throat and ran her fingers through her hair, guessing it looked like a blond feather duster. "Wow, what a great idea, Harold. That counseling just broke through all kinds of barriers and really brought Jared and me to a . . . new level of understanding."

She broke off her babbling when she heard Jared cough over a laugh.

Harold still looked puzzled, but he smiled. "So you finished the session?"

Jared spoke. "Actually, we were two questions from finishing when your laptop crashed, Harold." He shrugged. "Just one of those things, so we didn't get our certificate of completion."

Candy tried to maneuver around Harold, being careful not to touch his leather pants.

"What? No certificate?" Harold pouted, which was so not attractive on a fifty-year-old bald man. "Then how do I know you actually did the counseling? For all I know, you've spent the last two hours playing checkers online."

More like naked Twister. Candy couldn't think of a single doggone thing to say and starting inching down the hall, noticing there were quite a few curious heads poking out of offices.

"I can guarantee you that we were not playing checkers," Jared said in a serious voice. "And you'll see the results of your counseling when we hand you Chunk o' Chocolate completed next week. We're going to work on it tonight."

"Tonight? You're working late?" Harold's ears perked up, presumably at the idea of employees working overtime without compensation.

"Yes. We'll work on it all night if we have to."

A gurgling sound left Candy's mouth before she could stop it.

"Are you okay, Candy?" Harold's eyes swung toward her.

She didn't dare look at Jared. She blinked at Harold and grabbed her neck. "No, actually, I have something stuck in my throat. Excuse me, I'm going to go get a drink."

Without waiting for an answer, she got the heck out of there, rushing down the hall on wobbly ankles. First stop was the ladies' room.

Jan from payroll was walking down the hall with a stack of mail in her hand. She fell into step beside Candy.

"How was Harold's kooky Internet counseling?" Jan asked in a whisper.

Since Jan had been one of the few Stratford Marketing women who had been nice to her, Candy couldn't blow her off the way she really wanted to.

She gave Jan a weak smile. "It wasn't as kooky as I thought it would be."

Jan flipped her dark hair over her shoulder and grinned. "But at least you got to do it with a hottie like Jared Kincaid. With my luck, Harold would stick me in counseling with the office geek."

Oh, Lord, Candy was blushing. She could feel the heat stain spreading across her cheeks. "You just treat it like any other work assignment."

Yeah, right. If you were a hooker, maybe.

"What's Jared like? Is he really the cool customer he looks to be?"

Cool wasn't the word she would use.

"He was very . . . accommodating." Candy choked on the word as she came to a halt outside the ladies' room. "Excuse me, Jan. I have to use the rest room."

Jan stopped next to her. "Well, while you're in there,

you might want to fix your blouse. It seems to have gotten crooked during your counseling session."

She winked and started off down the hall.

Candy glanced down in horror. A good deal of her stomach was flashing through the *Titanic*-sized hole in the middle of her blouse.

And Harold hadn't even seemed to notice.

Maybe his eyes were going the same way as his hair.

Yanking her blouse halves together, she pushed open the door and wondered how long until the last employee would leave the building for the day.

She just might want to hide in the rest room until then.

Jared didn't know what the hell he was doing.

Everything had seemed a lot easier when he and Candy had been seminaked and moaning in Harold's office earlier.

Now things were complicated.

Candy had avoided him the rest of the day, and he had been unable to work because of all the confusing feelings tumbling around inside him. Feelings that were about as welcome as the stomach flu.

Feelings that had him standing outside her door sweating in his wool coat like it was July.

As he rang the doorbell to her apartment, he wondered exactly why Candy had agreed to meet him tonight. He also wondered exactly why he had agreed to meet Candy tonight. He didn't know what he wanted any more than he knew what she wanted.

Aside from sex, that is. If she even wanted any more of that. And just why in the hell did he care so much?

Candy opened the door and smiled shyly at him. "Hi."

Oh, damn, she was wearing jeans that hugged every inch of her hips and rounded ass. A red turtleneck sweater stretched optimistically across her breasts and pulled northward toward her belly button when she reached up to run a hand through her hair.

The flash of skin left him dazed and hard. And possessive. He didn't want anyone else to see Candy's skin but him.

That sweater was the same one she'd been wearing the day they met, and it made her face glow golden. She'd put some kind of shiny wet-looking stuff on her lips and he wanted to eat it off, one little nibble at a time.

After an embarrassing pause, he managed to say, "Hi. You look great."

Oh, now there was an original compliment.

"Thanks. Do you want to come in or did you have plans to go somewhere?" Candy tucked her hands behind her back and rocked on the balls of her feet in sexy little black boots.

"Actually, we should get going. I made dinner plans."

Alarm crossed her face. "I'm not dressed for dinner."

"Don't worry, this place is casual." And blissfully close. His place was only twenty minutes from Candy's.

"Oh, okay. Let me get my coat. Come on in." She turned and disappeared into her apartment. "Do I need the Chunk o' Chocolate file? Or do you have copies?"

Naïve girl. She actually thought they were going to do work? He'd been called a lot of things over the years, but never stupid. Any man asinine enough to discuss how to market chocolate when he had Candy Appleton alone in his condo was . . . not Jared.

"I have copies." In his desk back at the office.

Jared stepped into her living room and was immediately assaulted by an excess of floral patterns. Jesus,

Candy had a whole meadow growing in there, various rioting prints covering a sofa, a loveseat, and an overstuffed chair.

Violent red poppies danced across her curtains, and every table was littered with little things that he wouldn't even claim to know the name of. Things like little tiny wicker chairs with plants growing out of their seats, and wooden cats. The coffee table held a bowl full of lemons on it, and a round ball of orange fur that was probably a live cat was sleeping next to it.

He pictured those poppy curtains hanging in his apartment and shuddered. Not that he wanted Candy to live with him or anything. But love did not extend to ugly drapes.

The L word brought him up short. What the hell was he thinking? He did not *love* her. He was interested in her. He wanted to get to know her. He had great admiration for her brain and her breasts, but that had nothing whatsoever to do with love.

Did it?

Candy stuffed her arms into a very fluffy camel-colored coat, with huge quantities of white fur pluming around her face.

He didn't even know her.

She smiled. "I'm ready," she said in a breathless siren voice.

He did know she was trouble. But sometimes getting into trouble was so much fun.

"Is something wrong, Jared?"

"No, not at all. Why do you ask?"

She shrugged and the fur nearly swallowed her face. "You just look a little serious. I was worried that maybe you're embarrassed because we diddled around in Harold's office."

Diddled? He was pretty sure he'd just been insulted.

"Diddling is not what I would call it. And I'm not embarrassed. I don't get embarrassed. Especially not when I enjoyed being with you and would do it again in a heartbeat." He was conscious his voice was rising, but shit, he couldn't help it.

Diddled, for God's sake.

Candy reached out, put her warm little hand on his cheek, and stroked with her thumb. "I'd do it again too."

His anger vanished along with the last of his futile resistance. "Good," he said gruffly.

Candy was starting to figure out that Jared was a whole lot of masculine bluster. Beneath the cool stare and the cutting words he sometimes tossed off, he had feelings.

Twenty minutes later when she walked into his condo, she realized those feelings included being really doggone romantic.

He had recreated her idea of a perfect evening, right down to his own addition of a fire popping warmly in the fireplace.

Oh, Lord. If she hadn't been on the edge before—taking in the table set for two, the chilling wine, and the scented candles burning did her in for sure. It felt almost like she was falling in love with Jared.

Which was insane, since she was supposed to be using him just for the purpose of having some romping good sex. But the stupid man had gone and actually listened to what she had said when she'd been talking. She wasn't sure any man besides her stepfather had ever actually heard a single word she'd said outside of work-related topics.

Dean, her ex-husband, sure in the heck never had.

"Oh, Jared, you didn't have to go to so much trouble." But she was sure glad he had.

"It wasn't any trouble."

For a man who claimed not to get embarrassed, he was doing a pretty good imitation of just that.

It just made him all the more gorgeous.

Jared was wearing casual black pants and a sky blue shirt, which made his blue eyes even lighter against his dark hair. He had a smooth, understated style, always looking good but never veering into the female world of primping.

He picked up a remote control and turned the stereo on. Jazz music started playing softly. Her legs threatened to give way. He'd even remembered the jazz.

When he held her chair out for her, she looked at the pasta sitting in a covered bowl ready to be served. If he had cooked food that was edible, she might just never want to leave. "Did you cook this?"

He snorted. "Hell, no. I don't cook. I ordered it from an Italian restaurant around the corner."

Then he sat down across from her. He sounded oddly eager when he said, "Do you cook?"

"Not unless you call PB and J sandwiches cooking."

"I can make omelets," he said.

She was impressed. Scrambled was the most she could manage. "I can boil hot dogs and heat up canned corn."

They both laughed while he poured the wine and served them pasta and bread. She took a steaming bite and silently thanked the unknown chef. Having spent a good portion of her lunch hour holed up in the ladies' room, she was now starving.

After a few bites, Candy said, "We're not going to get to any work on Chunk o' Chocolate, are we?"

Jared looked up from his plate. "We'll get to it." He grinned. "Sometime before it's due on Harold's desk."

She was afraid he would say that. Or really damn pleased was probably the more honest answer.

"Jared, we should at least try and work on it." Candy tried to sound firm, but she knew she was failing miserably.

He kept smiling. Geez, she loved his smile. He didn't ever look so relaxed at work, and she felt a giddy pleasure that she could bring that grin to his face.

"Alright, let's think up some slogans while we eat." Jared took a sip of his wine. "What rhymes with chunk?"

"Monk. Punk. Funk." She leaned back in her chair and nibbled on her bread. "So, how about a monk at a disco eating chocolate?"

He shot her a withering look.

She giggled. "Hunk rhymes too."

"We're talking about the ad, Candy, not me."

His deadpan expression made her laugh out loud. "Hunky and modest, huh?"

"I'm a pretty good catch, aren't I?" His serious expression cracked a little, his lip twitching up in a smile.

"I know you are. Didn't I ask why no one's caught you yet?"

"Maybe I've been waiting for the right woman to figure out how to catch me."

A fishing net? Handcuffs? With fantastic sex?

Candy wished she knew, because she was starting to think she'd like to snag Jared for herself.

"So say a woman wanted to catch you. What would be the best way to do that?" She tried to keep her voice light, but a quiver crept into it.

Jared put his fork down and gave her a searching look that made her want to squirm. He said, "I think by just being herself, and letting me be myself."

Then he shrugged. "It sounds like an after-school

special, but it's true. I don't want games, I want a partner, a friend."

He raised his wineglass in mock salute, and his voice lightened. "Sounds pretty stupid, doesn't it?"

"No." Candy shook her head rapidly. "No, it doesn't. I . . . I was married once."

Jared's eyes bulged. "You were?"

"Yeah." She tried to smile, but couldn't quite force it. "Dean was my boyfriend in high school. It was never a good relationship, not even then. We broke up when I went to college, but when I came back home, he came on strong, said all the right things."

Yet to this day she couldn't imagine what she had been thinking when she had married him. "As soon as we were married, I knew it was a mistake, but I didn't want to admit that."

Jared was gripping his glass tightly. "What did he do to you?"

Startled, she said, "Nothing. I mean, he didn't abuse me or anything horrible like that. We just had nothing in common; we didn't talk. He was violently jealous of guys looking at me, and it just got worse. He had to control everything with our money, where I was going, what I was doing. He didn't want me wearing makeup or nice clothes."

No, Dean had never hit her, but he had made her life miserable, and had stripped her of her dignity. He had humiliated her in front of people she cared about. "He said it was my fault men looked at me, that I was a flirt, a tease."

"Jesus, Candy. How long were you with him?"

It wasn't pity in Jared's voice, just honest concern. It made her feel better about blurting out her past business to him.

"Three years." Years that she had accepted were gone and she couldn't get back.

"That's a long time to live like that."

"It is. But I got away as soon as I was ready, and thank goodness we never had any children together."

"Are you divorced then?"

His hand had snaked across the table and was holding hers, stroking with a light touch.

"Oh, heck yeah. He tried to fight it, but the judge was friends with my stepdad and he wasn't having any of Dean's crap. Judge Anderson pushed it through nice and fast, and I moved to Knoxville. But it still felt too close to Dean, so I picked up and came to Chicago. My roommate from college lives here."

She waited for the apology that was sure to come. The pity or even the recrimination. If Jared thought there was an ounce of truth to Dean's accusations of her being a dick-tease, she would either die from mortification or impale him with a salad fork.

He didn't do what she expected at all.

Instead, he squeezed her hand hard and said matter-of-factly, "Your ex sounds like a big pussy."

"Jared!" Good gravy, she couldn't believe he'd said that. She'd never heard him sound so brutal and angry before.

But then Dean inspired those feelings in her too.

"Well, he is." Jared was unrepentant. "Any real man would be proud to have you as his wife. He'd want you to dress up and look all sexy, so he could stroll into a room and let every guy there know that he had managed to marry a hot woman like you."

Candy flushed with pleasure.

"So I think your ex had issues about his manhood. That's the only explanation for treating you like that."

Candy had issues with Dean's manhood now too, since Jared had managed to make her moan squished up against a mahogany office desk. Dean had never inspired anything more than a pleasant sigh from her, and that was on his best days.

"He wanted to own you, didn't he?" Jared had pushed his chair back, but hadn't let go of her hand.

Candy's arm was stretched clear across the table, but she never even noticed the awkward position. Jared's words sliced something deep inside, touching a raw spot she hadn't known even existed anymore.

"What do you mean?" She thought she knew precisely what he meant.

"That your ex wanted a pretty wife on his arm, like a cool car or a great stereo system. Then when he had you, he worried about losing you to someone else who might want you."

Maybe she had suspected that all along, but she had never discussed it with anyone. To have Jared guess what might be the truth was a new humiliation. "Probably," she choked out.

Then she spoke in a rush. "Listen, Jared, I don't . . . I'm not . . . my ex wasn't right about the tease thing. I . . ."

Crud. Candy trailed off, mortified beyond words. She had sashayed into Harold's office and wiggled her rear in Jared's face. There was no reason for him to think anything other than that she was a flirt who got around.

"Come here." Jared patted his knee as if he were Santa and she were a naughty little girl who needed reassurance.

Common sense told her not to do it. But of course she did.

And Santa had never had thighs that muscular.

Nor had Santa ever asked her about her sex life. Jared did.

He asked baldly, "When was the last time you were *with* a man? Before today, that is."

She swallowed hard and studied the buttons on his shirt. "It was Dean. Three months before I left him two years ago."

"So you haven't slept with any man since your divorce?"

"No, I've dated, but just casually."

"Until today."

"Yes."

He frowned. "I screwed up then, Candy. I shouldn't have lost control like that."

His eyes dropped to her lips. A finger stroked her chin briefly. "You deserve better than that."

Candy was shocked that he could even think for one minute that it had been less than perfect. It had been wild, yes, and the opposite of what she had thought she wanted, but it had been the most erotic experience of her life.

So far. She was hoping they could expand on her portfolio here soon.

"Jared. It was just right. See, I had to know that I could let myself go like that. I was starting to think there was something wrong with me because every man I've dated since the divorce made me feel about as sexy as a fish carcass."

Jared's mouth fell open. "That's not very sexy."

She giggled. "No. But I wanted it to be different with you. And it was."

Jared's hands rested against the small of her back and he had managed to slip under her sweater to touch her skin. "So I made you feel sexy?"

"Oh, yes."

His lips brushed her neck. "Do I make you feel sexy now?"

"Yes."

"I can make you feel sexier."

Jared moved up her sides, causing a shiver to pass through her. "But what about Chunk o' Chocolate?"

Candy's eyes fell closed as Jared reached her breasts and slowly made his way around to the front to caress her nipples.

"Chocolate is a replacement for sex. You don't need it." His tongue teased her, slipping into her ear then back out.

She tried to laugh, but it sounded like a wheezing moan. It felt right sitting in his lap, his erection pressing against her and his hot breath pushing down her neck.

Jared murmured, "I'll never try to possess you. I'll never do anything you don't want. I'll listen."

Candy put her hands on Jared's shoulders and knew that she'd gone and done the stupid. She had fallen in love with Jared, and there wasn't a thing she could do about it now.

Her brain, which she had been touting all these years as something to everyone who thought her a ditz, had decided to abandon her. Her body was betraying her by quivering like a Jell-O mold under Jared's touch, leaving her with the damp panty problem all over again.

Which left her heart on its own to tumble straight forward into idiocy.

It was her heart that was responsible for her blurting out, "I don't want this day to end."

Jared's mouth stilled at the corner of hers. "It doesn't have to. Spend the night with me."

It wasn't a good idea. It was a bad, you're going to wake up and be really damn sorry, idea, but Candy didn't give a rat's patootie.

She kissed him, savoring the taste of the wine on his lips. "I didn't bring my PJs."

Jared's eyebrows raised. "Candy, you do not need your PJs."

"They're cute," she teased him. "Pink with white kitties on them."

"You're cuter naked." His hands were on the bottom of her sweater, ready to shuck it off her.

She gripped his shirt. "You've never seen me naked. Not really."

"All the more reason to hurry." He tugged her sweater, yanking it up to her breasts. "Lift your arms."

Jared's voice was hard and urgent. Candy did as he requested and said, "Okay, but I get the top."

He stopped tugging on her sweater. "Top what? I don't have any bunk beds, sugar."

Candy's arms were still in the air, and the neck of her turtleneck sweater was inside out over her face. "On top of you."

She wiggled, red fuzz clinging to her lips and her eyelashes matting. "Now get this sweater off me. I can't breathe or see anything."

Jared pulled until her head popped through, her hair flattened into her eyes. She waved her arms around in the air. "My hands are still stuck."

But Jared was too busy unhooking her front-clasp bra to help her out. When his mouth closed around her nipple and drew her toward him, Candy found she didn't give a darn if she was tangled up in cable knit.

Flinging her sweater-trapped arms over his head, she arched her back and let him at them.

Chapter Seven

Jared sucked on Candy until she was squirming and calling his name. Her arms were still trapped behind his head, her cherry sweater rubbing against his neck, and it kept her from moving very far.

A hand on her back and one on her breast and she was stuck firmly in place, despite her wiggling around on his lap. He was enjoying her growing desperation. It was close to matching his.

Pulling back, he stared at her rosy nipple, shiny from his mouth and firm like a plump grape. He couldn't resist a little nip.

Candy jerked forward. Somehow she managed to yank her arms free and he felt the sweater trail down his back. She pushed her hair back off her face and slid her bra down off each shoulder and onto the floor.

Then she sat back, taking her nipples out of his reach, making an enticing picture as she arched her back topless. It took him two seconds of gazing at her naked breasts to beg, "Take your jeans off."

"I still get the top, remember?" she warned as she shimmied back and stood up.

Even if he had forgotten, his boner would have reminded him. He nodded. "Oh, hell, yeah, I remember."

She smiled and he just about came on the spot. If he
had been falling for her before, he was gone now that
he had heard about her shit-for-brains ex-husband.

He had liked her before. He had respected her. Now
he admired her too. Despite her overt femininity, Candy
was a strong woman.

The woman for him.

Candy undid the button on her jeans, then the zipper, with all the speed of an anemic turtle, a mischie-
vous grin on her face.

"Hurry up," he said, no shame whatsoever. "Or I'm
going to rip them off you."

"You would not." Her hand stopped moving altogether.

"Do you want to find out?"

She laughed. "No, not really."

Turning to the side, she pushed the jeans down over
her hips, her hands gliding along the rounded curve of
her ass. His mouth went dry.

She had on different panties than earlier. These were
fire-engine red. Rip-them-off-me red.

To think when he'd stepped into Harold's office
today he had thought he would be able to resist her.
He'd never stood a chance.

Candy held on to his table while she kicked off her
boots and stepped out of the jeans. She turned to him,
wearing nothing but those satiny panties. Her tongue
slipped out and moistened her lips.

Jesus. He was so goddamn lucky.

"Much better than girly cat pajamas," he managed to
say.

She smiled. Two steps and she was in front of him.

He wrapped his arm around her back and closed the remaining inches between them. Running his mouth along her salty skin, he sucked lightly just below her rib cage.

"Good enough to eat," he murmured.

Candy climbed onto his lap, straddling him. "You're overdressed for the part."

"So are you."

"I'm only wearing panties."

"That's too much."

He was distracted by the tantalizing view of her flushed breasts directly in front of his mouth. Forgetting about stripping off her panties for now, he focused on the obvious.

With his tongue.

Back and forth, over and around, slicking her nipple, nibbling and pulling on the taut skin. She smelled like spring, fresh and alive, and he held on to the small of her back, keeping her close to him.

Candy tried to move away from him. "No, stop. I can't take it."

Jared moved to her other breast and gave it the same extended treatment. "Yes, you can. You can take it all."

"I can't." Her ass rubbed against his thighs and she tried to rock up on his cock with the front of her panties.

He shifted out of the way of her touch, his finger working the other nipple he didn't have his mouth around.

Candy moaned. "Jared, I don't want to come yet. You're going to make me come."

That was the plan.

She went up on her knees, hitting his bare arm with her inner thighs as she struggled to get her breasts away from him. Jared felt the cool dampness of her desire on his skin.

That got him to pull back and look down into his lap. The middle of her red satin panties was dark with moisture, and the stain was spreading.

Man, she was sexy.

He brought his thumb over her mound, tracing the damp spot on her panties. "You're a little wet, aren't you?"

She wiggled around as if she could somehow shift his finger inside her panties. "I'm *really* wet."

He laughed softly, but Candy didn't. She reached out and ripped his shirt apart, sending buttons in three directions. He was so shocked he hit his back against the bars of the wooden chair he was sitting on. He stared at her in a horny stupor.

"I've always wanted to try that," she said, shoving his sleeves down his arms to puddle at his wrists.

"You did it like an old pro."

Candy didn't answer, just ran her fingers across his bare chest, scraping her nails. Her eyes were trained on him.

"You're such a hottie," she said finally, her searching hands moving up to his shoulders to stroke and caress.

Jared had never been called a hottie before. Coming from anyone else, he would have taken serious exception. From Candy, it pleased the hell out of him.

He couldn't wait another damn minute. He wanted to taste her again. Grabbing the back of her head, he pulled her forward until their lips met in a wild grinding kiss, full of slippery lips and pushy tongues.

Hands in her panties, he squeezed her firm ass, dipping his thumbs to brush on the underside of each cheek.

Candy pinched his nipples, driving him nuts, while

she moved up and down on him, the movements as raw and lacking in finesse as their continued kiss.

Jared rocked the chair back, wanting Candy to slide forward in his lap. She did, her breasts landing against his chest as she squeezed her thighs around his legs.

It felt as if he were winging through time and space, rocking with passion, caught somewhere between reality and ecstasy.

He pulled her lip into his mouth to suck hard. And a minute later he really was sailing through the air.

Candy jerked at the jolt that kicked her in the gut when Jared tugged on her lip. She threw her arms forward and wound up knocking Jared's knees with her calves.

Mouths still wrapped around each other, Candy heard him make a startled sound before they both went over with an obnoxious crash as the chair slammed into the floor.

Candy blinked and caught her breath as she landed hard on Jared. He was flat on his back, staring up at her as if he had no idea what had just happened.

"Are you okay?"

He nodded. "You?"

His hand returned to fondling her bottom, so she knew he wasn't injured. "I'm great. Better than great."

"Good."

He touched her chin, guiding her down to him for a kiss. It was a soft gesture, tender, and Candy gave up trying to pretend that she wasn't head over heels for Jared. He was still serious, strong, and sexy as hell, but he also looked almost sweet.

The kiss was sweet as well, but it shifted quickly. It expanded, quickened, Jared's whiskers rubbing her chin raw. She didn't care, she just wanted to feel him, taste him. Her breasts were brushing against his chest, making her ache for more.

Before she could beg for that, Jared said, "Let me get my pants off. Then you can take the top."

"Condom?" she said as she detached herself from his lap. She sat on the floor as he rolled off the chair and got rid of his pants.

"Got it." Jared pulled a whole box out of his pants pocket.

Candy fought the urge to lick her lips. That was a lot of condoms. Maybe Jared had more in mind than just tonight.

He righted the chair and sat back in it, the condom already rolled on. "Come have a seat."

Still on the floor, Candy bent her knees up and slid her panties down, leaving them carelessly where they fell. She stood up and stopped in front of Jared, placing her hands on his shoulders to brace herself.

Closing her eyes halfway, she moved her legs on either side of the chair. Then let out a startled cry when Jared's finger found its way inside her.

"Just making sure you're still ready."

"I'm ready." She meant to move back out his reach, but somehow her body rocked the wrong way. Forward. Onto his finger.

He gave a soft laugh. "If you like one so much, you'll like two even better."

Another finger slid alongside the first, fitting her snugly as he went deep inside her. When his other hand reached out and stroked her clitoris, Candy cried out.

"Of course, if you like this, you'll like the real thing even better."

She nodded. He withdrew his fingers.

Candy used her hand to guide him, then sank down

onto the length of Jared, biting her lip as she did. Pausing a moment, she swallowed hard, enjoying the curse that flew out of Jared's mouth.

But when she tried to ride him, she discovered a problem. "I can't move on you like this. There's nothing to push off of."

Her feet were trapped behind his knees.

But Jared nibbled on her shoulder. "No problem. I can move."

His first thrust was slow and gentle, but within seconds, he had dissolved into hard, urgent movements, which left her gasping. Each thrust sent her up into the air and she clung to him, pinching his skin and digging in with her nails.

The angle sent him deep into her, robbing her of her breath. Her nipples hit his chest, and the light brush of his hard ab muscles against her clitoris was a cruel tease.

Jared stopped without warning.

"What?" she moaned, trying again in vain to pull herself up and down on him.

He didn't say anything, just stood up with her still on him in an impressive muscular move. He rocked once into her, then lowered her to her feet.

"Standing up?" she asked with a grin, waiting for him to start moving again. She wasn't tall enough to work this angle either.

He didn't grin back. His eyes were dark, searching. "Actually I want you to turn around. Will you let me do that?"

She saw what he was doing. Jared was asking her to trust him. To understand that he wasn't like her ex. She knew that already and she wanted him to know she trusted him with everything. Even her heart.

Candy pulled back until he was no longer inside her. "Yes, I'll let you do that."

Then she turned around and splayed her hands on the dining room table, bending over a little.

"You're incredible," Jared murmured before easing himself into her vagina from behind.

He wasn't so bad either. Candy closed her eyes as he went in and out, thrusting harder. She pushed her hips back to meet him and felt her orgasm building up inside her. She was tight and on the edge already when his finger snaked around and rubbed her clitoris.

"Jared."

His answer was a push so hard and deep that she lost her grip on the table and stumbled forward. Her hand landed in a plateful of pasta, now cold. It stayed there while she cried out her orgasm, shuddering and arching her back.

"Candy." Jared removed his finger from her as he came, holding on to her hips and pulsing into her.

His orgasm blended with the final waves of hers, and she closed her eyes to feel him. All of him, filling her from deep inside.

Candy squeezed her inner muscles and was rewarded with another shudder from Jared before he leaned heavily against her back. His weight felt good, solid, steady.

Her racing heart quieted down and she pried her eyes open. Dragging a breath in, she looked in front of her and giggled.

"What?" His breath tickled her hot skin under her shoulder blade.

She held her right hand up. "I fell in the dinner."

"Whoops." Then he leaned over and pulled her fingers into his mouth, running each finger up and down thoroughly.

A burst of fresh desire hit her between the thighs. She was fully aware that Jared had hardened again inside her.

"Mmm. Tastes good."

Then he pulled out of her and dropped her hand.

"Tease," she said as she leaned on the table and watched him remove the condom. She had no interest in moving right now, even if it meant her behind was in the air. She felt too good to move.

"You won't be calling me a tease in a minute when I get another condom on."

"What do you need another condom for? I thought we might do some work on Chunk o' Chocolate."

"Screw Chunk o' Chocolate," he said over his shoulder as he went down the hall to the bathroom. "The only thing I'm going to do with chocolate is melt it and lick it off your body."

There was an idea. Candy wondered where the nearest store was that carried those flavored massage oils the online counseling had recommended.

As she pondered the delights of licking chocolate off Jared, she finally looked around the condo. During their short-lived dinner, she hadn't looked anywhere but at him. Now she could see it was a nice place.

He decorated the way he dressed. Simple, classic. With a touch of rugged. Most of his furniture was in burgundy, and his dining room table was a rich mahogany, while the walls were stark white.

"You like that position, don't you?" he asked as he came back, strutting a bit like a rooster in her opinion.

"What do you mean?" She forced her uncooperative muscles to move, and finally stood up.

"You spent half the day in Harold's office bent over just like that. Only you were wearing clothes then."

"I was starting to wonder if you had even noticed I was shaking my tail at you," she said, stretching her arms over her head. "I kept dangling bait, and you wouldn't take it."

"Is that what you were doing?" His hands landed on her breasts and massaged. "But why were you baiting me?"

"I thought if you and I . . . well, that I would enjoy it. And I have."

"Then enjoy it again."

Before she could even moan out a yes, Jared had picked her up in his arms and tossed her a little to get a better grip.

"Oh! Well, aren't you the man."

His left hand was under her bottom and his right wrapped around her back, holding her without strain. Lord, she knew she wasn't that light, but he made it look effortless.

"Your man," he said, and rubbed his nose along the side of her face.

The words were spoken lightly, but Candy heard something there that was not her imagination. It was there in Jared's eyes, and in the soft touch of his nose and lips along her cheek.

He sounded as intrigued as she was by their new relationship.

The bedroom wasn't far. Jared laid her down in the middle of the big bed and laced his fingers with hers.

"This time let's take turns being on top. Who should go first?"

Candy thought about getting a good grip on the sheet and really working Jared. She didn't bother to mask her enthusiasm for the idea. "Me."

A second later she thought to add, "Please."

Jared laughed. He rolled over onto his back and reached for her. "Since you asked so nice."

Chapter Eight

They were lying in bed a couple of hours later, Candy safely tucked in the crook of Jared's arm. He stared at the ceiling, yawning in contentment.

"Do you think this is what Harold had in mind?"

Candy stirred a little. "I really don't think so. But you know, we should go back and finish the counseling. Otherwise Harold might find us out."

Jared wasn't exactly shaking in his boots. "So what? As long as we get Chunk o's ad done, then why would he care?"

"It will take five minutes. We'll do it on your PC here at home."

Five minutes? Please. Once they started answering those questions, they'd wind up right back in bed again. "Let's just look at Internet porn instead," he joked.

"Jared!"

She sat up and gave him a stern look. "And by the way, I bared my soul to you about my ex-husband."

"You bared a lot of things." His hand drifted to her behind.

"I'm serious. I told you everything, and you didn't

tell me anything. When was the last time you were with a woman?"

He hated these kinds of questions. They were designed purely to get men in trouble with women. Next she'd be asking him if she looked fat.

"Why does it matter? I'm with you now."

The tight press of her lips together showed him that wasn't the answer she had wanted. "I still want to know."

"You were my first time. I was a virgin." He started to grin, then stopped when her face flushed pink. And not from embarrassment.

"See, Candy, this is why I told you I just tell women what they want to hear. Everything I say is wrong." Annoyed, he pulled away from her and put his hands under his head.

"Just tell me what you want me to say and I'll say it."

"What you say is not wrong. I'm sorry." She tried to snuggle back into his arms. "I'm just jealous, that's all."

Jealous was good. As long as it was the mild, healthy kind, not the intense, bunny-boiling kind of jealousy.

"You've got nothing to be jealous of. Most of my relationships have been casual." He relaxed again, enjoying the press of Candy's breasts against his side.

"And Jessie was a mistake. I never should have gotten involved with a coworker, and getting hot and heavy in the office was downright stupid."

The minute the words were out, he realized something about that didn't sound quite right. Candy thought so too, since she stiffened against him.

Before he could babble some kind of apology/explanation, Candy spoke. "You had sex with a coworker in the office?"

The warm bed had suddenly turned Alaskan cold. "No, no, we didn't have *sex*."

"Sort-of sex?"

"Yes. No! It was just some kissing and you know . . . groping and stuff." Holy hell, he was making this worse.

She jerked away from him and sat up. "So do you limit yourself to just one office fling per job, or should I look forward to watching you screw your way through Stratford Marketing?"

There was no way to answer that question without finding his nuts jammed in a meat grinder.

But he gave it a shot, wishing he were wearing a protective cup. "I don't have office affairs. It was a five-minute mistake with Jessie, and I don't consider you a fling anyway."

She gasped. "Oh!"

Tears rose in her eyes as she gathered the sheet around her, jumped off the bed, and prepared to flee. Oh my stars. She didn't even rate as a fling, that's how little she meant to Jared.

Trying to rationalize her way out of a broken heart, she told herself that she'd gotten what she had wanted. A night of passion that had proved there was nothing wrong with her. She was just as capable of multiple orgasms as the next girl.

But somehow that didn't make her feel any better.

Jared said, "Where are you going? I'm trying to tell you how I feel."

"I don't care." She jerked back as he stepped in front of her, blocking the bedroom door.

He was big, imposing. Naked.

"You're not going anywhere until you hear what I have to say."

"I do not want to hear you describe to me what a great one-night stand I was. Thanks, but no thanks." She'd crawl between his legs to get out if she had to.

Astonishment crossed his face. "Is that what you think I'm going to say?"

Brushing tears away, she struggled for composure. If he sent her bawling, she'd never forgive him. "Well, you just told me I don't qualify as a fling, so I guess that makes me a one-night stand."

His jaw snapped shut. He reached for her. Candy sidestepped away from his touch.

"Oh, babe. That's not what I meant. I meant you're more than a fling. You're important to me. You're my future. I . . . I think I could fall in love with you."

Good gravy. Why didn't he just say so in the first place?

Candy said, "Oh."

Followed by a sniffly, "Really? Are you sure?"

"Yeah. I want us to be together if that's what you want."

This time when he reached for her, she let him wrap his arms around her and squeeze. She laid her head on his chest and sighed. "That's what I want, because I think I could fall in love with you too."

"I've never cared about a woman the way I care about you. I'll try not to screw this up, Candy."

She looked up into his sincere dark eyes. "I don't think we'll screw this up. We'll just take it slow."

"And if there's ever a problem, we can always go back for more online intimacy counseling." She gave him a grin.

Jared had a vision of Candy spread across the desk in his home office, while he counseled her intimately. He dropped back and tugged her hand.

"I think we should go do it now. Proactive counseling, before there's a problem." All it took was a little yank with one finger and her sheet plunged to the carpet.

"Oh, you think so?"

"I do." He nodded down the hall. "The computer's right this way. It will help us to get to know each other *really* well."

There were still a few spots on her he hadn't explored with his tongue.

Candy smiled, that full, open-mouth smile that he loved so much. "I want to know everything about you. We only got to question eleven before."

He tried to look sincere. "Babe, you can ask me anything, or touch anything that you'd like."

She laughed. "How generous of you."

He had her moving down the hall with him. Almost there. "I hope you weren't planning on going to bed early tonight."

"No. Why?"

He paused in the doorway of his home office, glad he had furnished it with a wide couch. "Because we're not leaving this room until all the questions have been answered to my satisfaction."

Her eyes went wide with lust. "If I answer the questions slowly and thoroughly, will you give me a certificate of completion when we're done?"

He'd give her more than that.

As he leaned forward to kiss her, he said, "Oh, yeah. Signed and notarized."

A sassy grin crossed her face as she put her fingers on his lips to stop him from kissing her. "Do I have to do all the videos and romance tips too?"

He pictured Candy covered in chocolate sauce while he licked it off her inner thighs. "I insist that you do all the extras, yes."

She dropped her fingers down to his leg and licked his lower lip. "So what are we waiting for?"

Hell if he knew.

Jared scooped her up again while she shrieked in surprise. His arms full of warm and willing woman, he kicked open the door to his office and moved inside.

Now he was going to show her that sex, love, and romance were best when done all at the same time.

Naked.

USER FRIENDLY

Chapter One

"I've been hacked!" Halley Connors stared at her computer screen in shock. She prayed she was having some sort of hallucinogenic episode brought on by lack of sex, or from the dangerously high level of caffeine in her bloodstream.

Normally the picture on her website showed her wielding a tray of hors d'oeuvres for her catering business. Today the tray was gone. So was her dress.

"What?" Her assistant, Nora, came up behind her.

Halley couldn't answer. She was sick. No, this picture was sick. She hadn't been this grossed out since walking in on her parents horizontal on the kitchen table when she was sixteen.

"You're naked!" Nora exclaimed.

Very. And that body wasn't even hers. She'd never seen those breasts in her life.

And what was that blob between her legs? She peered closer. It was a cherub with wings, leaning forward and . . . "Eew! That's disgusting!"

"That's Cupid," Nora said in awe.

"Ohmigod, call Evan." Halley grimaced at the screen

and hoped like hell Evan, her webmaster and best friend, would know how to fix this. "We've got to get this off."

Nora hustled off to her desk and started dialing while Halley's shock was replaced by fear. This could ruin her business, send it straight into the catering toilet where many a good company had landed due to the occasional cockroach or salmonella outbreak. Those were inherent risks in the business and well understood.

But this was unfathomable. She was naked with a perverted cherub between her legs. Even one day of an image like this on her website could have disastrous effects on her bottom line. It had to go, and pronto.

"Evan's not answering."

Halley groaned, a mental image running through her head of one of her conservative clients like Mrs. Brockmorten catching a glimpse of this debauchery. A sweat broke out.

"Who else can we call?"

"We have a couple of backup firms we could call, but do you have the passwords to allow access to your site?"

"Passwords?" Was that something she was supposed to know? "Uh . . . Evan takes care of all that stuff."

And she had been spending as little time as possible with Evan for months, having come to the shocking realization that she wanted his body. Best friends weren't supposed to lust after each other, and he would probably laugh hysterically or blanch in horror if she told him, so she had taken the easy way out.

Total avoidance.

Her naked image grinned at her. She looked really happy with that Cupid down there. She shuddered. Geez, she was going to have to find Evan. Without her knowing the passwords, he was the only one who could restore her catering dignity. Not to mention her clothes.

With that lowering thought, she flipped off her computer with a trembling hand and headed for the door. "If anyone calls about this, explain we've been the victim of a hacker."

"Okay." Nora looked at her wide-eyed, her red hair tumbling around her face. "Where are you going?"

"To Evan's. He's probably sleeping and not answering his phone." Since Evan had starting doing consulting and web design work, he had taken to working in the evenings and sleeping until noon or so.

Which meant he would be sleepy, adorable, and pissed off at her for waking him up. Which was good. If she was fending off angry barbs, she wouldn't be thinking about how perverted she was to be wanting to see him naked.

The mere thought of him without clothes set her nipples standing on end in a double-gun salute. Crossing her arms over her chest, she frowned in annoyance. It should be *illegal* to react like that when thinking about someone you had known for years, who trusted you not to act like a girl and get delusions of relationship grandeur.

Forcing her mind off Evan and her nipples' reaction to him, she left the office wondering who could have done this to her. She was a really nice person, dammit. She treated her employees well, never succumbed to road rage, and gave mittens to the homeless shelter. It wouldn't qualify her for a halo, but she didn't think she was doing too badly.

Halley didn't see how someone could be so deliberately cruel, and by the time she found herself pounding on Evan's door ten minutes later, she was on the verge of noisy tears. All her years of hard work in the catering business could disappear faster than it took Cupid to shoot his arrow.

Not that she wanted to be reminded of the naughty

Cupid between the legs that weren't even hers. But frankly, right now not much could make her forget him.

The door opened.

She forgot Cupid.

Evan Barrett blinked at her, his chocolate eyes heavy with sleep and his caramel hair tousled. He wasn't wearing a shirt, showing off his summer tan and broad shoulders. His hand lazily scratched his chest.

Halley's mouth went dry. Her eyes lowered to his hunter green boxer shorts, which weren't pulled up nearly as far as they could be, revealing that soft tuft of chestnut hair that went down to that fabulous . . .

Damn. He was gorgeous. And while technically not naked, he was close enough to set her, uh, skin on fire.

"Halley?" He squinted and leaned forward a little, as if the lighting was bad.

God, what was she wearing? She realized she hadn't seen Evan in a few weeks, and she had just stormed over here without even doing a makeup check. Glancing down, she gave a sigh of relief. All right. Khaki Capri pants and an aqua blue tank top. Not the stuff of fantasies, but not cellulite-displaying running shorts either.

Then she concluded her mental inventory by reminding herself that until six months ago when she had lost her mind and starting panting after him, she would have thought nothing of letting Evan see her wearing bulky flannel pajamas and a serious case of bed head.

Little reality check. She could be wearing a toga and it wouldn't be relevant to the situation at hand. Which was her catering-in-the-nude website.

Her anger returned, plus a little irritation just because Evan looked so good. If he wasn't so damn cute, none of these confusing feelings would ever have surfaced and their relationship could have stayed on solid, nonnaked footing.

Evan looked confused. "Am I dreaming?"

"What? No, you're not dreaming." And she knew she wasn't either, because if she were, he would be all over her like a cat on tuna right now.

His eyes raked over her, sharpening as the sleep receded. "Damn, that's weird. This is exactly like the sex dream I've been having lately. I open the door, and you're standing there . . . only you're usually wearing a bikini and high heels."

Her jaw dropped. Was he serious? A *sex* dream? About her? Of course he wasn't serious. He was joking, something he did a lot with her. Which was what friends should do. Not lust after each other in secret.

In fact, a lot of his teasing was sexual in nature, but until recently she had never even noticed. But now it had the effect of a furnace turned on full blast. Sweat popped up in unpleasant places.

She tried to smile and forced a rusty laugh past her lips. "Sounds like a nightmare to me."

He shook his head, a slow sexy smile crossing his face. "Not the way I had it playing out."

Her eyes rolled so far back in her head she practically fell over. It wasn't funny as far as she was concerned. Because she really wanted him to mean it. And he didn't.

"Dreams are often better than reality."

Evan laughed and ruffled the top of her hair like she was his favorite terrier. "I've missed you lately. Where have you been hiding?"

At work, far, far away from him and his lethal grin. Away from Evan, she could pretend her feelings were the result of not having had a date in two years. Standing in front of him, she knew better. She had inexplicably developed the hots for her best friend.

"Business is crazy. You know what this time of year is like." She breezed past him into his apartment.

Evan grinned, pushing his hair out of his eyes as he followed her. "So if you're not here to act out my recurring sex dream, what can I do for you? And just in case you were worried, I don't mind that you woke me up. It wasn't a late night last night—I stayed home alone."

Halley hid a grimace behind her hand, pretending to scratch her lip. Yuck. She hadn't even stopped to think about the fact that Evan might not be answering his phone because he was with someone. Having walked in on that twice in the past, she was glad she had been spared that kind of vomit-inducing scene today.

Not that she had seen Evan with a woman lately. In fact, it had been months since he had mentioned dating anyone. *What a shame.* It was wrong to be thrilled at that thought, but there it was.

"I wasn't worried about it," she shrugged. "Because I had to see you."

"Missed me, huh?" he teased.

If he only knew. She whirled around to face him, hands on hips.

"I've been hacked," she said in an outraged voice. "Can you believe it?"

The corner of Evan's mouth pulled up. "That sounds like a personal problem to me, sweet stuff."

The amusement in his voice didn't bother her nearly as much as the silly nickname he used, with no idea whatsoever what it did to her. He'd been calling her that for almost ten years, and now unexplainably, it had the effect of a blowtorch between her thighs.

Which was not what she needed to be thinking about.

"I'm serious." She forced herself to visualize Cupid between her legs, and felt appropriately horrified again. "My website has been hacked and you've got to fix it before clients start seeing it."

Evan flopped down onto the couch with his legs spread and said, "What did they do to it?"

Halley paced back and forth and cleared her throat. "Well, um, it's kind of hard to explain." Like dryer sheets. She'd never been able to figure out how those things worked.

Evan pushed his unkempt hair out of his eyes. "In my dream, this is the part where you walk in and stand in front of me, and I pull on the bikini strings . . ."

Evan's voice was low, charming, and luscious across her body as she walked over to him.

If only he knew how horny that made her, he wouldn't find it so funny anymore. More likely he'd leap out of his window to get away from her.

Halley cleared her throat for emphasis, ignoring the way his boxer shorts pulled up tautly and showed her a fabulous glimpse of his assets. One false move on his part, and she would be seeing a whole lot more.

Giving what she hoped was a casual grin, she said, "I told you to enjoy the dream then. What's behind those strings is a lot better in fiction than in reality." In real life, she wasn't exactly giving Pamela Anderson a run for her money.

Evan patted the seat on the couch next to him, which she totally ignored. Standing was much safer.

Evan said, "I hate it when you're down on your body." He raised his eyebrows up and down. "You've got great tits, sweet stuff."

That was so close to what she wanted to hear, yet so damn far.

"Well, I haven't made it into the Great Tits Hall of Fame yet," she joked, then could have kicked herself. She shouldn't be extending a conversation that dealt with body parts.

Evan threw his arms over the back of the couch and laughed. Then he shrugged on a grin, causing his chest to ripple in an attractive distraction that made Halley feel like a virgin at a Chippendales strip show.

Inspired. Eager. Amazed.

Then he ruined it by talking. "That's because the nominating committee hasn't seen you right now. Geez, are you cold or just happy to see me?"

Considering it was August and he had no air-conditioning, she would give him only one guess.

"Alright, very funny." Fighting the urge to cover her enthusiastic nipples with her hands, she strode off in the direction of his bedroom, where he kept his computer. "I'd say leave my chest out of the conversation but it's bound to pop up again once you see my website."

Not that she was jealous or anything of those huge melon-dwarfing breasts the hacker had stuck under her chin. Okay, so she was jealous, but only a little. At least she could do gymnastics or ballet if the urge ever struck her. *Let's see a D-cup woman do that.*

Halley shuddered as she walked into Evan's bedroom. The queen-size bed wasn't made. Gazing at those crumpled, still-warm sheets made her flustered. And aroused.

Evan let out a yawn next to her. Good to see he was as affected by her as she was by him.

She forced herself to turn away from the bed and walk to Evan's computer area. At least a third of his room was consumed by all kinds of computer equipment, wires, and other things she had no clue what to call.

"What did you say the problem was exactly?"

Uhh. "Someone tampered with the website."

"Well, it can't be too bad. I designed the site myself, you know, and it's completely protected from hackers."

He sat down at his computer desk and turned the machine on.

As it booted up, Halley came to stand behind him, careful not to get too close. She braced herself for the image that was going to pop up any second now. She wasn't sure having Evan fix it was worth the humiliation of having him see it. Then again, it was either Evan or potentially hundreds of customers.

Closing her eyes, she gulped and waited for Evan's hysterical laughter to fill the room.

Chapter Two

Holy hell. Evan was speechless as he took in the sight of Halley smiling prettily on the home page of her website. Totally naked from head to toe.

Tampered was a hell of an understatement.

Halley was right. She had been hacked.

"Those bastards!"

"I know!" Halley's hands landed on his shoulders.

If he hadn't been so distracted, he might have enjoyed that little skin-to-skin contact, but he was too pissed off right now to appreciate it. "What a total kick in the balls. I cannot believe they got through my firewalls. This site was hack-proof!"

Halley's nails dug a little too deep. He winced and shifted away from her.

"That's not the point, Evan. The point is I'm naked!"

Was she ever. Jesus. Halley's ugly beige dress had disappeared and her smile seemed to have gone from professional to suggestive.

He liked it. Now if he could only get her to smile at him like that, instead of the perpetual "best buds" grin she always gave him.

"I don't think they got your best side, sweetheart," he

said when he'd retrieved his voice from his throat, where it had been lodged like a beer nut.

She slapped his shoulder. "That's not even me!"

"I know." Did she think he was stupid? He knew every inch of her body, from her bouncy blond hair to her oddly chubby little toes. And everything in between.

He turned to look at Halley. She hadn't changed much in the ten years they'd been friends. Her hair was a little shorter these days, almost to her ears, and her clothes had toned down in style and color, but she was still the same Halley.

His best bud. That for quite a while now he had been wishing could be more. He had never seen Halley naked, but he had made a study out of her in clothes, and knew every curve of her delicious body.

There were plenty of occasions on which Halley really hadn't been wearing that many clothes in front of him, like trips to the beach and the pool, and those awe-inspiring times when she had opened the door to him in her PJs, no bra under those tight little stretchy tops.

With that kind of data stored in his memory banks, it was no wonder he was suddenly dreaming about her in triple-X.

Today Halley was a little pale, but that could be because she was looking at her head slapped on porn. He wondered how pale she would be if he told her he wanted to be more than friends. Way more than friends.

Not that he had any intention of telling her. That was a surefire way to screw up the best friendship he'd ever had. Sometimes he couldn't control himself and he blurted out comments that were way too revealing, like the recurring dream he'd been having. But Halley always assumed he was joking. Or she wanted to believe he was joking.

"Of course I know that's not you. Your body doesn't

look anything like that." Halley's body was perfect. Breasts that would fit into his hands, a narrow waist, firm, sleek thighs, and an ass that could stop traffic.

Not that he'd noticed or anything.

And the hard-on he was now sporting in his boxer shorts was pure coincidence. A morning erection, twenty minutes late.

"You don't know what my body looks like," Halley said in shocked tones, as if he'd admitted to looking under the bathroom stall.

"Yes, I do. I've seen you in a bathing suit, and this body is not your body." This body, with the overgrown breasts and scrawny legs, did nothing for him. Halley's body made him want to drop to the ground and beg.

He turned and tried really hard not to look at her breasts. He failed miserably, and winced at her nipples jutting out in her tank top, her chest heaving up and down in indignation. If she had any idea the torture he endured in the name of friendship.

Innocently unaware of his lecherous thoughts, Halley said, "It doesn't matter whose body it is. Can you get rid of it?"

"Sure, I can fix it. No problem."

He dragged his gaze away from her firm breasts. With supreme effort, he turned back to the screen and eye-balled the image there again. It was then he noticed the little figure between her legs. Or whoever's legs they were.

"Jesus, Halley, this is the trademark of the Three Commandos, well-known hackers and online legends."

"How can you tell?"

"They always put a cartoon figure in their work. Cherubs, demons, devils, usually revolving around the themes of heaven and hell. And see? There's a C on each wing, and one on his bow. The Three Cs." Evan found himself excited in spite of the circumstances. He had a chance to dig into the Three Commandos' handiwork, and see if he was up to the job of restoring Halley's site to its prehacked state.

Since he had gotten burnout and left software development three years earlier, he had been doing consulting work. It was low stress, paid great, and left him plenty of free time for relaxing and playing in a baseball league. But he missed stuff like this. The challenge of the computer, figuring out its inner workings and how man had manipulated those.

The Three Cs had thrown down a challenge to him. To figure out how they had managed to so obviously and effectively corrupt the site he had built for Halley. It just might require enough brain capacity to keep his mind off Halley for an hour or two.

"So why did they pick on me?" Halley wailed, obviously not concerned about the mysterious guts of a PC.

"Did you serve them bad fish, maybe?"

"I don't serve bad *anything.*"

He didn't doubt it. Halley personally oversaw everything about her business. Despite her horror, he grinned at the screen in total appreciation for the art of the Three Commandos. They had style, you had to give them that.

"Sweet stuff, whatever you did, it earned a cherub going down on you."

Halley flushed. Her cheeks were vivid pink and her mouth dropped. "I didn't do anything, and that's not me," she stubbornly insisted.

"I know it's not you. We've been over this. I'll fix it, so don't get your panties in a bunch." There he was. Doing it again. Mentioning underwear when that was the last thing in the world he should be discussing with Halley.

Inevitably, the image of her in nothing but panties rose in his mind. His cock throbbed and he shifted in his chair, hoping Halley didn't happen to glance down into his lap. The Leaning Tower of Penis might be a little hard to explain.

Halley whacked him on the back. Not a light teasing pat. Or a seductive brush. But a whomp. Right between the shoulder blades. "Let's see how you would feel if you were naked on the Internet."

He tossed her a grin, almost grateful she'd lobbed him hard enough to knock a few teeth loose. Maybe if she whacked him on the head next, he'd recover his sanity. "But you just said that's not you."

"Technicality!" She dug her hands into her hair and twisted her fingers around until her hair was in a makeshift bun. Her shirt rose way up past her belly button, flashing him with smooth pale skin.

God, he loved her. He had loved her almost as long as he had known her. It was a love that had grown out of friendship, and was deep and solid and forever. In the last couple of years that love had extended to the physical, as in he'd love to get his hands on her body.

Sometime before he died or she married some putz.

Evan stared at her and contemplated reaching forward and licking her stomach, dipping his tongue into her belly button. He was abnormally horny today, which was probably the result of not dating for the last six months. For years, he had avoided his feelings for Halley by marathon dating, but lately, he just couldn't even fake his way through it anymore.

Halley waved her hand back and forth in front of his face. "Hello? Did you fall back asleep? Can you fix my site *today*, or do you know someone we can call who can do it if you can't?"

That distracted him from studying the smooth skin

of her abdomen as his ego suffered the insult. How could she even doubt he could fix it? He could fix it with one hand tied behind his back. He could fix it submerged in water. He could fix it even if Halley was sucking his cock.

Well, maybe not that one. Painful hot throbbing filled his boxers. He wouldn't be doing anything else but enjoying, if Halley ever took it upon herself to suck him.

Not that she would ever even dream of doing that with him, the man she thought of like a brother. But that didn't stop him from fantasizing a little. Right now.

"Well?"

Huh? He had forgotten what she'd asked him.

"Oh, yeah, of course I can fix it. It might take me a couple of hours to bypass all the firewalls the hackers might have erected but that won't be a big deal."

"Can you put it back exactly the way it was?"

"Not a problem." The only problem was that she needed to move away from him or he would never be able to concentrate.

Halley needed to get away from Evan. The feel of him, the sound of his voice, the sleepy morning smell that surrounded him, was driving her crazy.

Not batty like her Aunt Ginny. But wild kind of crazy. Really achy kind of crazy.

She hadn't been with a guy since that fiasco she had called a relationship with Lewis, the human plunger.

Given the heat in her Capri pants, it seemed a safe bet that two years was too long to go without a little woohoo.

"Can I borrow your phone?" She backed up slowly, one, two. There, that was better. She couldn't smell him anymore. "I want to call my office and let them know what's going on."

"Sure." His voice was already distracted as he peered

at the computer screen. He started moving the mouse, clicking on things in rapid succession.

Halley was relieved to leave her problem in capable hands and retreat to his kitchen, which still had last night's dinner dishes in it. Dinner looked to have been Cheetos and a frozen burrito.

She shuddered. His eating habits were abysmal, and in the last few years she had taken to cooking for him a couple of times a week. But since she had been avoiding him, he had obviously resorted to barrel scraping.

She could cook something for him in ten minutes that was a thousand times better than a frozen burrito. A nice fluffy omelet would be ideal, she thought as she picked up the phone and dialed her office.

Nora picked up.

"Hi, it's me. How are things going there?" She held her breath waiting for the answer.

"Well." Nora hesitated.

Halley's stomach did a hokey-pokey imitation, shaking and churning. "Tell me."

"Okay. We've had sixteen calls requesting nude catering jobs. Three callers wanted to know if you could serve penis-shaped hors d'oeuvres, one thought he could order a prostitute complete with her own Cupid sex toy, and you remember Mr. Benjamin, that sweet old man whose eightieth birthday we catered last month? He wants a refund since we didn't serve nude at his party." Nora took a deep breath. "And I caught three of our servers printing fifty copies of the home page with your picture on it."

"Oh, no!" Halley sagged against the counter. She was ruined. Completely and utterly ruined. She might as well pack up and go back to the trailer park she had grown up in.

As a total failure.

Nora said in bewilderment, "Who would have thought so many people in suburban Pittsburgh want naked catering?"

That was a question for philosophers and Jerry Springer.

"Evan says he can fix it, so just try and stay calm. You're doing great." Which was more than she could say for herself since she had the urge to collapse on the kitchen floor in a fit of the screaming meemies.

"I shredded the copies the servers printed, but there's nothing to stop them from making more. You might want to reprimand them, it was—"

Halley quickly cut her off. "No, that's okay." She really had no interest in which of her male employees had found it necessary to put on paper fifty copies of her naked body.

Which was not her naked body at all. Geez, that was the worst part of the whole thing. They had given her one of those figures that looked as if it was three or four different bodies welded together. Huge breasts, hourglass waist, curvy behind, and chicken legs.

Naked Catering Barbie. Complete with tray.

Besides, she had a hard time visualizing calling three men into her office and telling them to stop printing out nudie shots of her on company time with expensive office supplies. It sort of shot her advantage as their intimidating boss.

"One last thing," Nora said, her tentative voice betraying the casual words.

"What?" Halley paced back and forth in Evan's kitchen, skirting his overflowing trash can. Whatever Nora had to say, it couldn't get any worse.

She was ready.

"The church charity group called."

Oh, no. This was going to be worse.

"And?"

"They're canceling us for their five-hundred-seat event."

What would Evan do if she suddenly starting screaming "bloody hell" at the top of her lungs?

That charity dinner was five hundred times nineteen ninety-five a plate, which meant she was out a hell of a lot of money.

"They didn't even want to talk to me?" Maybe if she threw in free wine . . .

Nora said, "I tried to talk them out of canceling, I told them it was a hack job, but they didn't care."

She squeezed her eyes closed. "That's okay."

Her life was over, but it wasn't Nora's fault. Nora was clearly upset and Halley didn't want her to feel she was to blame. The Three Commandos were the ones to blame, and they were smarmy illusive Internet surfers, hacking their way through decent hardworking people's lives.

"I'll call you later." She hung up and ran a mental list of all the events they had coming up during the busy August and September wedding season. If even a fourth of them canceled, she was going to suffer from excess inventory, an unnecessarily large staff, and decreased income.

On a shaky sigh, she let the tears break free and roll down her cheek.

"Holy crap, you're not going to believe this." Evan came strolling into the kitchen, a grin dancing across his face.

Halley turned to hide her tears, but the smile collapsing into concern showed her he had already seen them.

He stopped dead and said, "Hey, what's wrong?"

Stupid man. What did he think was wrong? That she'd missed the JCPenney white sale?

"I have perfume in my eye."

"Perfume? In your eye?" He was coming closer to her, frowning as if he was doing some serious thinking.

"Yes. Perfume. In my eye." She bent over the sink and pretended to be rubbing around in her eye, trying to swipe away any remaining signs of her wimpy breakdown. His hands landed on her upper arms as he came up behind her.

Touching was bad. It was very, very bad. Touching meant that he was close to her and that with one little shift back, she could be flush against him, her curves melding into his hardness, his breath rushing past her ear. She could press her backside along his pants and feel him swell with arousal.

Wait a minute. He wouldn't swell with arousal. He would be shocked and horrified at her unfriendly behavior, and she would lose the best friend she'd ever had.

"Let me see."

He was right there. On top of her, cutting off her air and sending her into full-fledged panic. If he would just call her sport or give her a noogie, she'd be fine, but this sweet soft concern was more than she could handle.

"I've got it." Her voice wobbled a little.

Those strong hands forced her to turn around. She blinked like a myopic deer caught in the headlights. Turning her head a little, she tried to lean back away from him, not wanting to smell him or feel him, so she wouldn't embarrass herself by begging for a kiss.

"You're crying," he murmured, his thumb reaching up and wiping the last wet streaks from her cheeks.

"No, it's watering because I have an eyelash in it."

"I thought you said it was perfume."

Was he writing this stuff down? Geez. She glared at him. "Evan, I'm fine."

Then he kissed her nose. A sweet gentle dusting.

A funny little sigh came out of her mouth.

"I'm sorry about your site, you don't deserve that."

His lips brushed across hers, a soft caress that made her feel warm and gooey.

"What are you doing?" she whispered as his arms came around her back and drew her up against his hard, very uncovered chest.

"Comforting you."

It was working. She was so comforted her bones seemed to have dissolved like Alka-Seltzer in water. His thumbs rubbed her waist, his hip pressed against hers, and his mouth came toward hers again.

Evan had kissed her before in the past, and she was sure this wasn't any different. Light brushes for hello and goodbye, a full-mouth kiss when she'd graduated from college. Hugs when her grandmother had died. It was no big deal at all . . . no different.

Except this time his tongue was in her mouth.

Yowsa, that felt good.

It had started out the same, but now it was sweeter, deeper. Wet. A kiss that required open mouths, gripping hands, and rapid breathing.

Slow and steady, he dipped and tasted her, and Halley clung to his chest, too stunned to do anything but lie across him like a limp noodle. This was the last thing in the universe she had expected Evan to do, and even though it felt so damn good, she hesitated.

Evan's hands were in her hair, and he tilted his head to gain better access to her. Halley wondered briefly if

this was how he comforted all his friends. Then she reminded herself she was his only female friend, and she
didn't really care why he was kissing her, just that he
was.

Her mom always said don't look a gift horse in the
mouth. She had never known what in the hell that really meant, but she thought in this case it gave her permission to make out with Evan.

So she threw her arms around him and kissed him
back for all she was worth.

Their mouths slid and pressed together, tongues in-
tertwining in wet passion as they moved from soft to
deep to reckless. It was the fullest, most meaningful kiss
she'd ever had in her twenty-eight years, and when Evan's
hands cupped her behind, she moaned into his mouth.
Oooh, that was nice.

And it made her press against his penis, which was
hard and ready to go. No need to wait for the sixty-
second inflate time. Evan must have already pulled the
ripcord.

Light little kisses fell on her mouth, hard enough to
feel him and taste him, light enough to make her want
more, deeper and fuller. A whimper dragged out of her.
He kissed her jaw, and licked a wet trail down her neck
as she tossed her head back.

Worry over her catering business was long gone.
Only to be replaced by a new tension—tight, burning
sexual tension rising from the center of her body.

"I have an idea," he murmured.

She was getting one too. One that involved no clothes
and she and Evan doing the dirty here on the kitchen
floor.

She shivered as he breathed into her ear, anticipating a suggestive overture from Evan. A confession of

deep desire and longing, a demand that she make love
to him. A sensual coaxing that she was the best friend
he'd ever had and could be so much more . . .

Evan said, "Let's do a little hacking of our own."

Chapter Three

Hacking? Evan wanted to hack her. Huh. Was that a computer geek's way of saying sex?

Halley didn't think it sounded all that great. Hacking away at her, *I got hacked last night, you make me so hot and hacky* . . . no, it was pretty much a bucket of cold water as far as she was concerned.

Maybe this was why they'd never gone beyond friendship.

"What do you mean?" She licked her lips and leaned back in his arms as he continued to rub the most delicious circles across her backside, his thighs moving to enclose hers while his tongue made swirlies on her neck.

Maybe she could put up with hacking, after all.

"Revenge. I'm talking about revenge on the Three Commandos."

What? Wrong. That's not what he was supposed to say. If she had time, she would write a handbook on things men should not say while getting a woman all hot and bothered.

After mentioning an ex-girlfriend or a change in sexual orientation, revenge would be at the top of the list.

"Revenge?" She tried to pull back. This was weird, with a capital W. God, what the hell had she been doing anyway?

His tongue dipped into her ear as he held her tight.

Getting horny, that's what she had been doing.

Was still doing, despite the potential disaster factor being huge. She quivered in his arms, breathing hard as he nuzzled into her neck, sucking lightly, pulling her skin forward with his hot mouth.

Evan didn't seem to be struggling with this baffling change in their relationship. In fact, he was acting as if he had his hands on her ass on a regular basis.

Halley wondered if it was possible to have fallen asleep standing up.

His thumbs drifted up from her waist and brushed across each of her nipples, a tentative quest for permission.

"Oh," she groaned, arching her head back, inviting him to pursue touching her.

"Is this comforting?" he murmured, his head bending in front of her as he slid down her chest with his moist mouth.

Evan dragged her tank top down to expose the tops of her breasts, and she could see his pink tongue heading for the nearest curve.

"I do feel better," she said truthfully. She was also feeling hot, damp, and achy with tight need that snaked around her insides.

Two years' worth of hormones flooded up and out as if the Hoover Dam had been attacked with a sledge-hammer.

Evan seemed to be experiencing similar feelings. Halley could feel his hardness pressing into her as he rocked forward with the full length of his penis. With a desperate ferocity that startled her, Halley dropped her hands to his waist and helped him grind.

It may be wrong, but it sure felt good.

Evan groaned, a little throaty aching moan that gave her a burst of triumphant pleasure. He was stroking the length of his erection between her legs, pulling in and out, as Halley wrapped her thighs around him and clenched.

She could hear his breath grow shallow as he thrust with a quick rhythm, and his moans were stifled in her neck as he buried his head. There was no thought of anything but the throbbing strokes of intimacy between them, strokes that mocked the movements of him actually plunging inside her moist body.

Eyes half closed, she gripped his shoulders and wondered that even with his boxer shorts and her pants, she could feel the heat between them. Panting and beyond rational, she thrust her hips to meet him, causing another full moan to rip from Evan.

Then he misjudged and nudged her a little on her inner thigh.

Wait a minute. Her eyes flew open. Something didn't feel right. This felt too real.

She glanced down and saw smooth golden skin before Evan pushed forward and buried himself between her covered thighs. She wasn't supposed to be seeing skin.

That lion was out of his cage.

His boxers had sprung a leak.

"Evan." She tried to maneuver backward out of his way, but another thrust made her groan and freeze where she was. Oh, my.

She whispered on a ragged breath, "You've fallen out of your shorts."

And he was so glad he had. Evan gripped Halley by the waist and rocked against her. Even though every inch of her was still covered by clothing, he was on the verge of coming. On the edge, about to jump off.

Just to feel her, to smell her, to taste the saltiness of her skin, had him ditching common sense at the door. He was driving himself between her thighs, her soft flesh clenching around him, the rustle of her pants causing hot friction on his cock.

He was fighting for control, but it was slipping away from him. He had wanted Halley for so long now, and she had looked so vulnerable to him, fighting back tears. Needy. Evan knew how hard she worked on her business and she didn't deserve to lose it. Staring into those big shiny blue eyes, he had been overcome by the urge to kiss her and make it all better.

Granted, he'd done a little more than that, but Jesus, he was only human.

"My mistake," he said, staring into her bewildered and glazed eyes.

"Evan." She broke eye contact and shuddered. "You have to stop."

He had already slowed down to soft pulsing strokes, and he really didn't want to stop, but he was damn surprised she'd let him get away with as much as he had. Not that he'd planned on sliding between her legs, but when he had burst through the slit in his shorts, he'd gone with it.

But he stopped now, and pulled back with a smothered groan. Yeah, he could stop. Sure, no problem. He took a painful step backward and ran his fingers through his hair.

This wasn't exactly how he had planned to tell her that his feelings extended just a little beyond friendship. He stood there a minute and tried to think of something to say that didn't sound idiotic or perverted. He wasn't having much luck.

Halley gaped at him. "Well, don't just stand there. Put it away."

That horrified tone in her voice didn't help his speech-making capabilities. Neither did looking down and seeing his cock, sort of rising there between them.

This was embarrassing. But he really didn't think he could put it away. If he put his hand on himself, there was no telling what might happen, and he didn't think it would fit back in his boxers right now anyway. Like trying to stuff a bull into a cat carrier.

"Just give me a minute." Or twelve or thirteen.

"Evan!" She adjusted her tank top and flushed pink. "I can't just stand here when you're . . . hanging out."

Hanging was the wrong word. *Rearing up* was a better way to phrase it. He felt the start of annoyance. She was acting as if he had shown her a box full of worms and tried to make her touch them. "It's not like you haven't seen one before."

"Yeah, but I haven't seen yours."

Actually, she had once when she'd walked in on him changing, but Evan didn't think now was the time to point that out. Instead, he asked her seriously, "Why do you think that is?"

Halley had responded way more enthusiastically to his kiss than he ever would have imagined, which was exactly why they had ended up standing here like this. She had kissed him back so hard and hot that the next thing he'd known, they had been grinding into each other.

Her lips pursed together, and she fanned herself. "Because friends don't show each other body parts."

Evan grinned, feeling relieved despite the grimace on her face. For years he had been afraid that Halley thought of him like a big platonic buddy. That kiss told him differently, and that was all he needed to know. "Maybe we should change that."

To appease her, he moved his cock and gave it a painful shove back into his shorts, where it made a nice tent, stretching the fabric as far as it could go.

"Button the little button."

Now she was pushing it. "No, those things are a pain in the ass. If I button it, then I'm fumbling around trying to unbutton it. When you're in a public rest room, it looks like you're playing with yourself."

She rolled her eyes. "Just keep it where it belongs then."

He grinned, giving her a cocky tilt of his head and a hands-out gesture of acquiescence. "Sweet stuff, I can't think of any better place where it belongs than—"

She cut him off, looking more flustered than angry. "That's not funny."

She moved back, away from his reaching arms, and tripped over his garbage can. "Eew. Your apartment's disgusting, by the way. Don't you ever clean?"

Nothing was alive, as far as he knew. That was good enough for him. "Sure, I clean. I cleaned everything top to bottom in May."

"It's August."

And her point was?

"Listen, can we get back to why I'm here?" She tucked her blond hair behind her ears.

"You're the one talking about my cleaning schedule."

"Why . . . why did you just do that?"

"Do what?"

"Kiss me and everything," she whispered, turning a pretty little pink color.

"I told you. I was comforting you." He smiled slowly

at her, watching her eyes go wide and her mouth drop open. He suddenly felt really damn good about his options with Halley. "Did it help?"

She nodded, obviously too stunned by his prowess to speak.

This was it. He could move in for round two. Now that his cover as a sexual pal was blown, he might as well take advantage of the situation. He took a step forward, eager to touch her again. "Should I comfort you some more?"

Her head flew back and forth in a vicious shake. Okay, that wasn't good. Maybe her speechlessness was terror that he might touch her again.

"No, I have to get back to work. Now." Halley twisted her earring in her ear and darted her eyes, avoiding his gaze.

Evan sighed. For five years he had been keeping a tight lid on his emotions, and in one morning, he had lost control and gone at her like a sex-starved lunatic. Which he was.

"Halley, I'm sorry if I made you uncomfortable or anything. I was just trying to make you feel better." He mentally groaned. Crap, that sounded awful. Like he just whipped out his dick whenever anyone was upset.

She blinked. "Oh, well, I do. Feel better. Thanks."

Halley turned and left the kitchen, heading for his front door at a fast clip.

"Give me a couple of hours and I'll have your site fixed."

Her head bobbed up and down, but she didn't look back at him. "Thanks, I really appreciate it."

"No problem." He stood silent, in agony, trying to formulate a better apology. He wouldn't be able to stand it if he lost Halley as a friend. She meant everything to him.

Rubbing her palms on her brown pants, Halley stopped and turned in the front doorway. She opened her mouth, then closed it, probably just to torture him.

"What did you mean about revenge?" she asked.

Something that had seemed like a fun, friendly kind of thing to do together. Before he'd buried himself in her thighs and blown their friendship forever.

"A friend of mine knows who the Three Commandos are. He's going to e-mail me the URL for their website. I thought we could do a little hacking of our own. Fix his website up the way they did yours."

On any other day, one where he hadn't kissed her senseless, Halley would have said yes. He just knew it. But that frown on her face showed him how much he had risked and lost by listening to his libido.

"I really have to get back to the office. Maybe . . . later."

No surprise there. She wanted to get away from him and he couldn't blame her. But it would have been fun to screw around with those guys with Halley next to him, giggling and coming up with evil reverse-hacking suggestions.

His heart ached painfully. He missed her already and she hadn't even left.

Hey, he would just have to do the hacking on his own then. He couldn't stand those cocky shits who ran around the Internet messing with people's heads and/or their websites. Halley didn't deserve to have her business screwed with just for some geeks' jollies, and it was the least Evan could do in the way of an apology.

"I'll call you when I get the site fixed," he said.

"Great," she said with a nervous smile. Then she edged out the door backward as if she were afraid he might make a grab for her and fondle her silly.

"Bye, Evan." With a wave, she took off running, the

sound of her sandals slapping down the stairs echoing in his miserable heart.

"Yeah. Bye, Halley."

Kicking his nasty, festering, overflowing garbage can, he sent a half-filled fountain drink skittering across the floor. As it leaked three-day-old Coke on the vinyl, he stomped out of the kitchen and down the hall to his bedroom.

The only reason Halley had come to him, her old friend Evan, was to cover up her tits on her website, not to be tortured with his clumsy seduction attempts. He should just fix the site and be done with it.

Or he could stare at the screen all day and fantasize that Halley really was naked in front of him, and he was the cherub.

Evan blinked at the image still on his computer and swore out loud.

Damn, he was hungry.

Comforting her. Evan had been comforting her.

As she ate her lunch, Halley tried to force Evan's kiss out of her mind. She would have had more luck lifting a semitruck with her finger. It was all she could think about.

Evan had been comforting her, and she had leapt on to him like a nympho in a sex video. Admittedly, he had responded—after all, she'd felt that thing between her legs *and* had seen it in all its glory. Impressive glory that it was.

But Evan was a man. And it was hardly surprising that he would get an erection when she was dirty dancing on him. She had long ago determined that men's penises acted independently of the rest of their body, including their brain and heart.

That was why she had gotten the hell out of there. If she had pushed it, pulled out the breasts and a few other tricks, she probably could have convinced Evan to sleep with her.

Which was comparable to throwing ten years of great friendship down the toilet.

Geez, maybe she needed to go home and rent *When Harry Met Sally* to remind herself that sex between friends was a major no-no.

Of course, Harry and Sally had gotten together in the end.

Halley threw down her sprouts and avocado sandwich on her desk and grimaced. Brushing crumbs off her fingertips, she glanced at the pile of messages Nora had left on her desk. She didn't want to look at them, knowing they were nothing but bad news. In the two hours since she'd been back, the phone had been ringing constantly.

Her sandwich churned in her stomach, and she was left with the horrible feeling that if the absolute worst happened, and she lost her business, she would be left with nothing. No business, no Evan.

That thought had her flinging down her paper napkin and standing up. She had worked damn hard to make this business successful. Maybe she had screwed things up with Evan, but she couldn't just sit still and let Bite of Heaven crumble down around her. This was a minor setback, that's all. With a little damage control, everything would be fine.

"Nora," she called as she stepped out of her office.

The hum of a half-dozen employees talking ground to a halt as she entered the reception area. Eyes avoided hers. Horace, one of her younger drivers, boldly ogled her, running his gaze up and down.

Anger raced through her. She was about to reprimand him when Horace shook his head in confusion.

"That doesn't make any sense."

Caught off guard, she asked, "What doesn't?"

"That's not even you in the picture. I can tell by looking at your—"

So much for the thirty-dollar water bra she had bought. Halley cut him off. "Alright, I got it! And of course it's not me."

Like she would ever pose for nude photos in the first place.

The faces staring back at her were a mix of confusion and pity. It made her feel sick. Taking a slow, even breath, she said, "The problem is being dealt with. Let's all just go about our business, shall we?" And stop mulling over her breasts.

There were nods, half smiles, and a reluctant pulling of various bodies off desks where they had been leaning. Talking about her. Probably about how boring she was, and how unlikely it was that her naked picture would ever be splashed on the Internet.

Not that she cared. She didn't want her picture on the Internet. So what if she was boring and flat-chested and so starved for sexual attention that she had to throw herself at her best friend? Big deal. She was successful. She had scratched and clawed her way out of Hazen, West Virginia, and had made something out of herself. Something she could be proud of.

A workaholic who hadn't had sex in two years.

Argh. That wasn't helping.

Nora left the others and approached Halley where she stood clenching her fists and glaring, feeling like a bull just itching to charge. At what, she didn't know. The Three Commandos would be the logical choice.

Nora took her hand and pulled her aside. "Listen, Halley, did you read those messages I put on your desk?"

Since Nora looked ready to pop a pacifier in her mouth and cuddle her in a blankie, Halley guessed they weren't filled with uplifting news.

"No, I haven't gotten to them."

Nora squeezed her hand. "Well, it's just as well that I tell you myself then."

That was promising. "More cancellations?"

Nora tucked her red hair behind her ear and shook her head, giving Halley another maternal look even though she was nearly five years younger than her. "No, actually, things have been quiet on that front, thank goodness. Just more requests for nude catering jobs."

Great. Just great. "I hope you declined."

"Of course!" Nora bit her lip. "But the part you're really not going to like is that your dad called."

"My *dad*?" Ohmigod, her father never called her. Her dad worked twelve hours a day, but there was still barely enough money to put food on the table. Calling long distance to Halley was out of the question.

"Did someone die?" Her heart dropped to her shoes, and she wondered if something was wrong with her mom or with one of her three younger sisters.

Nora shook her head. "No! But he saw the picture on the web."

"*What?* How is that possible?" Her parents didn't have a computer. As far as she knew, her dad had never even seen one. There wasn't a real pressing need for a town of coal miners to surf the web.

Nora whispered, looking distinctly uncomfortable, "I guess your cousin Jake was bored, fooling around, and came across it. When he told your dad last night, your dad insisted Jake show him."

Halley shook her head to clear it. All she did was flip hair in her mouth. "You got all that from my dad?" Her dad wasn't known for long, drawn-out conversations.

"No, your mom got on and told me after your dad couldn't string anything together after 'Where the hell is Halley?' "

Halley clutched her head in pain. "Oh, crap, this is awful. My parents think I have a nude catering business."

They were sweet, hardworking, churchgoing folk. She was surprised her father hadn't already had a heart attack.

"Well, I told them it was a mistake."

But did they know that wasn't her body? Yuck, yuck, and triple yuck.

"Thanks." Halley forced her head up and patted Nora on the arm. Hopefully with a phone call, she could assure her parents she wasn't running a prostitution ring or stripping online.

Something Nora had said popped into her head. "Wait a minute? My dad saw this last night?"

"That's what he said."

"I wonder how long it's been up there like that, then?" She couldn't remember the last time she'd checked the site prior to that morning.

"A week."

Halley spun around. Horace was listening to them with no sign of embarrassment.

"A week?" She was back in bull mode, clenching fists and leaning forward. All she needed was the nose ring and the red cloth target. "But we just started getting calls today."

Horace shifted on the balls of his feet, and coughed into his hand. "It started a week ago with just the tray disappearing, then your top, then your skirt. Last night was when the angel showed up."

She stared at him in horror. "Why didn't you say anything?" *You total jackass.*

He shrugged. "I wanted to see what would happen next."

Unemployment was what was happening next. "Horace, you're fired!"

With the audacity to look startled, Horace said, "Hey! Whoa, don't overreact."

That was not overreacting. Overreacting would be grabbing his nuts with her hand and squeezing the hell out of them.

She had been doing a week-long striptease on her website and no one had bothered to mention it to her.

That was it.

Nobody turned her into an online stripper and got away with it. Time to take Evan up on his idea to get revenge on the Three Commandos.

It was petty and juvenile and wouldn't solve her problems, but the Three Cs were just begging to get knocked down a peg or two.

Besides, she needed to talk to Evan, and clear the air about her dog-in-heat imitation earlier. But first she was going to tell him to hack away, with her permission.

It would be her pleasure.

Chapter Four

Evan stared at Halley on the screen, restored to her previous state of conservative dress and tray holding.

He should be feeling smug, pleased with himself. It had taken him only two hours and thirty-seven minutes to fix Halley's website.

Naked was better, he concluded. Not that weird impostor body, but Halley's real body, soft and curvy and peach colored. That would be way more interesting than the goofy brown dress she was wearing in the original, now-restored, shot.

It wasn't what he should be thinking about, but he couldn't stop the image from assaulting him. Nor could he stop doing a mental instant replay of the kiss he and Halley had exchanged.

A better apology was in order. But he didn't want to apologize. He wanted to lock her up in his bedroom and keep her so sexually satisfied she'd never think to leave him again.

The idea had merit. But it was probably illegal.

But if Halley were willing . . .

Of course, that wasn't going to happen.

Evan stood up and stretched his arms up over his

head. While he had dragged on khaki shorts over his boxers at some point, he had never bothered with a shirt. It was sticky in his apartment since the AC had crashed and his landlord had yet to fix it.

The heat was causing a thin sheen of sweat to roll across his chest and forehead, making him itch. He wandered toward the kitchen, realizing he had never eaten breakfast or lunch and he was now starving. But when Evan got into something like breaking through the hackers' trail, he lost sight of mundane tasks like eating.

Now that he was done, his appetite returned with a vengeance. Despite the funny odor kicking up out of his garbage receptacle in the kitchen. Wrinkling his nose, he bagged it up and hustled it out to the dumpster, squinting as the bright sun hit him in the eyes.

Back inside, he sprayed a little disinfectant and felt better about the whole thing. The kitchen was almost clean now. Halley would be proud of him.

He was eating a bowl of corn flakes with a spotty banana when someone pounded on his door. Furiously.

Could it be? No, she wouldn't come back. Would she? Evan ditched the corn flakes after one last big bite and nearly tripped over his bare feet to get to the door. If this was Halley, if this was his second chance, he was going to pull out all the stops and charm her right out of her tank top.

No, no, he was going to apologize and keep his damn hands to himself. Scout's honor.

He pulled the door open.

Only Evan had never been a Boy Scout.

Halley looked like a hot fudge sundae on a spoon. And he wanted to lick every inch of her.

"Back so soon?"

Halley's hands were on her hips, causing her tank top to shift and bunch in various delicious places. Her lipstick had been bitten off, and her foot tapped up and down restlessly. A desperate passionate sort of gleam radiated from her green eyes, and Evan wasn't idiot enough to think that passion was for him.

Halley looked pissed off and ready to take names.

"Okay, here's the deal." Halley placed her hand on his chest and gave him a healthy shove to push him out of her way as she charged into the apartment like Xena, Warrior Caterer.

He had no idea what she was going to say, but he knew, just knew, it wasn't going to be what he wanted her to say. Which was, *Rip my clothes off me, sport.*

Halley's lip quivered. "That picture of me has been there a week, Evan. A week! A client canceled on me, my employees are printing pictures of me, and my dad saw it. My dad!"

Her glassy eyes were huge.

No, not what he wanted to hear. And shit, she was having a breakdown in front of him. For Halley to lose control was more than a little alarming, it was damn scary.

Evan put his hands on her arms and rubbed in a gentle and hopefully soothing manner. "Shh, sweet stuff, it's alright. I fixed the site. Everything is normal again."

"Thank you." She sniffled, then gave him a ferocious stare, clamping down on her lips to stop the trembling. "But now I want revenge. Just like you said. I want the Three Commandos to hang."

Evan was stunned into momentary silence. Was this a good thing or a bad thing? Maybe releasing all that anxiety would be a great relief for Halley. Or it might send her over the edge into a place that required antidepressants.

A little unsure, he said, "I thought you said that you were busy."

She shrugged, and he released her arms. The tears

and trembling had stopped, and she looked in control of herself again. "My inventory spreadsheets can wait."

Evan studied her carefully, wishing she wouldn't use words like *spread*. She seemed to have forgotten that a few hours earlier he had tried to do just that to her.

Aside from the hysterical reaction to her website, she was acting normally toward him. Did that mean he was forgiven for trying to jump her bones?

"Listen, are we okay? You and me."

Halley's cheeks went pink and she blew her hair out of her eyes. "Why wouldn't we be? Oh, you mean because of earlier. *That.*"

Yes, that. Her embarrassment was obvious, and he couldn't stand that. The thing he loved about his friendship with Halley was how comfortable they were with each other. That was exactly what he didn't want to lose, and why he had never confessed his feelings for her.

He said, "Look, maybe we should just forget it, forget that anything ever happened."

He brushed the uncooperative hair out of her eye in a very platonic fashion and gave her a slow smile, meant to reassure her that he would stick to business. "We'll just get straight to the hacking."

Halley swore to God, if he only knew what he was doing to her. Now that she'd put a twisted perverted spin on the word *hack,* every time he said it, she shivered right down to her toes in orgasmic anticipation.

But at least he was letting her off the hook. They were going to forget her overenthusiastic response to his kiss and go on like normal. "Okay, good, great, yeah, definitely. We'll forget all about it."

Since when had his eyes turned that exact shade of hot chocolate before you added the marshmallows? Forcing herself to focus on the more important thing here—

her career—she said, "So let's get hacking. I want to do something really bad."

It wouldn't bring back the clients or restore her dignity, but it might make her feel less like she'd swallowed a peach pit.

Evan's jaw clenched. Halley became aware that he was only a foot in front of her and that he still wasn't wearing a shirt. Her fingers jerked in eagerness to touch.

"Really bad?" His voice sounded funny, as if she had stepped on his foot in heels.

Somehow that sounded faintly suggestive. Of course, she suspected he could be talking about sewage and somehow she would find a way to be turned on. It was pathetic.

"Yes. Bad. Really bad." Halley wanted to kick herself. She sounded like the Dustin Hoffman character in *Rainman*.

"Okay." He shrugged, giving her a wicked grin. "So, like what? Doctor their website so they're wearing dresses?"

That was appropriately horrible. She liked it. "Do you know who they are?"

"Yeah. My friend Kirk knows one of them. They're three twenty-something computer geeks who do web design. One of them was fired from Microsoft, and they're all college dropouts." Evan shrugged. "You know the kind. Almost too smart to be normal. A couple of people told me the same thing, that they're hackers on the side, mostly for fun, for the challenge of besting security."

Evan frowned as he spoke, and started down the hall.

"You're mad because they hacked *your* site, aren't you?" she asked, wiping her sweaty palms on her pants and following Evan into his bedroom.

"Hell, yeah, I'm mad. Besides, they got you naked. If anyone's going to get you naked, it should be me."

Halley froze. What the heck was that supposed to mean? Evan wasn't facing her, but his voice sounded light, as if he was joking, but *still*. She thought about his behavior that morning, and his . . . tongue sliding into her. Maybe she wasn't the only one with a sudden case of lust.

He had been a long time without a date, longer than anytime since she'd known him. Maybe she had been a convenient sexual release.

She didn't bother to answer him, since she had no clue what to say.

His bed still wasn't made. She was tempted to do it herself, just to get the view of those wrinkled sheets out of her sight, but that would mean leaning over the bed. Smelling his masculine scent on the sheets and being far too close to a vertical position were dangerous.

Evan had the website up in a minute. Halley studied the three men over Evan's shoulder. They looked a little on the geeky side, one wearing glasses and all three in need of a wardrobe consultant, given the overabundance of plaid. But they also looked a little brazen, as if they knew the world would dismiss them on appearances, but they had gotten the last laugh.

"I've never seen any of them in my life, so I don't why they did this to me. And why do three men have a personal web page together? That freaks me out."

"Who knows?" Evan shrugged, his hand moving the mouse around. "So what do you think? Floral dresses for them?"

"Just for the one with glasses." Halley narrowed her eyes as she took in the cocky stance of the taller one on the left with dark hair, as they posed in front of a brick building. "For him, I think you should make him naked. Skinny, hairy, and naked."

Evan laughed in surprise. "Are you serious?"

"Very." Let them see how it felt.

He turned and gave her a searching look, before breaking out into a grin that made her forget all about revenge. "Then I have a better idea."

"What?"

"Let's give them breasts."

Halley felt her jaw drop open. Oh, Evan was much better at this than she was. "Can you do that?" The bizarre image of naked men with breasts popped into her head, and she quickly banished it again. Funny, yes, but definitely freaky.

"Sure." Now Evan was the one looking a touch arrogant as he shrugged. "We just need to find the breasts. I'll download Pamela Anderson or something."

Halley hesitated. "No, her breasts get too much airtime as it is." Not that she was jealous or anything. "Someone else."

"I know who." Evan leaned back in his chair.

Now she was jealous. She didn't want Evan to make suggestions on other women's breasts. She didn't want to know that some movie star or pinup could inspire that lusty gleam in his eye.

She opened her mouth to tell him to forget it, that she had changed her mind.

He spoke first. "How about you, Halley?"

"Me?" She took a step back in horror. Did he mean with her clothes on or off?

"Yes, you." He looked up and grinned. "You've got perfect breasts, sweet stuff, and think of the irony of putting your chest on those guys. It's hilarious."

Well, she wasn't laughing. More like choking on her own tongue.

"No way. I'm just not going to take my shirt off in front of you." There would be no possible way she could do that without flinging herself into his arms.

He scoffed as he stood up. He started toward her. "Oh, come on. I've seen plenty of breasts before, including yours once when you dropped your towel by accident after your shower. It's no big deal."

Not to him. But it was to her. She could not fake nonchalance wearing no shirt in front of him. Taking another step back, she said, "No, I'm not doing it."

Halley stopped moving, frozen to the spot an inch in front of Evan's bed. She was trapped and he was right in front of her. He took her hands, squeezed, slid up her arms, continuing on and on.

"Come on. I've slept in the same bed with you when you were wearing nothing but a T-shirt and panties. You've thrown up on me. I can take a picture of your breasts without it being a big deal."

She wished he hadn't brought up the whole throw-up thing. A few too many shots on her twenty-third birthday and she had lost her dinner of sweet and sour pork down the front of Evan's shirt. Not one of her sexier moments.

The whole thing was depressing. It just served to emphasize how little he thought of her as a woman if he could stand there while she stripped her shirt off and be totally unaffected.

Or would he? Neither of them could claim he had been immune to her earlier. No one could fake a hard-on like that.

Suddenly she wanted to do it. She wanted to strip off her shirt for Evan and see that he could take her picture without any further interest whatsoever.

It was playing with fire, she knew. But they had already crossed some strange line with that wax-melting kiss, and she needed to know. She needed to see that it was forgettable, that Evan had only reacted to her and had no real desire for her.

If he could stand there and watch her half naked and not want her, then hopefully it would be the bucket of cold water needed to douse this fire between her legs.

Breath hitching, she stepped to the side out of Evan's reach and yanked her tank top up over her head. "Fine. If it doesn't bother you, it doesn't bother me. Use mine."

Evan's head swam as every drop of blood in his body rushed south to create the largest, most agonizing hard-on ever known to man. *Damn.*

Halley's chest rose and fell as she defiantly dropped her arms to her sides. Creamy pale flesh taunted him everywhere he looked. Her breasts were straining to escape a pale blue sheer bra.

The hard pinkness of her nipples was clearly visible through the barely there fabric. Evan couldn't move, couldn't think.

While he sure as hell had wanted her to strip, he hadn't for one minute thought she actually would.

In fact, he had never meant to suggest it out loud in the first place. And he hadn't meant to persuade her as vehemently as he had.

But she had done it. And all he could do was drink her in and wonder how easily that sheer stuff on her bra might rip between his greedy fingers.

"Where's your digital camera so we can take a picture?" Halley wet her lips, her fingers hovering over the front clasp on the bra.

Not only was he going to get to see her breasts, he was going to have documentation of it. On film. *Double damn.*

Where the hell was his camera? Moving quickly, he plundered drawer after drawer of his desk, tossing a dictionary and his palm pilot on the floor, scattering pens left and right.

Trying to hide his urgency, he said softly, "Don't move, sweet stuff. I need to find the camera."

Desperate that any delay and Halley might change her mind, he whirled around. The closet. That's were it was. The door slammed against the wall as he threw it open, and as he fumbled around on the shelf, a barrage of sweaters tumbled down onto his head. Followed by a tennis racket, which he just managed to dodge.

Camera finally in hand, he turned around in triumph.

Halley's fingers played with the clasp on her bra. She stood very still, her chin tilted up a little and her eyes wide. Her hesitation was clear.

Evan went equally still, slowing down his jerky movements and giving her a tilted reassuring smile. "Great Tits Hall of Fame, remember?"

She gave a nervous laugh. "I feel stupid."

"No." He took a step forward. "Not stupid. Beautiful."

Hair tumbled in her eyes as she shook her head.

"Yes, you are."

Then he reached her. Tucking one hand tightly over the camera and letting it fall to his side, he reached out with the other hand and gave her nipple a light caress through the raspy sheer bra. She let out a startled yelp.

Shit, he couldn't believe he'd just done that. He pulled his hand back.

"Evan?" Her eyes were heavy, half closed, and her arms were trapped between his body and hers. "You didn't forget about what happened before, did you?"

"No." He leaned closer to her, inhaling her scent of citrus and something else he couldn't define, something earthy and subtle.

"I didn't either."

"Halley, I have to tell you that if you take your bra

off, I'm going to touch you." He meant to put his hand deep into his pocket, but instead he dropped it to her waist.

Her breath sucked in hard. "You are? But I thought we were best friends, that's all."

They were. That should be all. But it wasn't enough. "I can't help it. I want you. Bad."

Prying her cold fingers off the bra clasp, he pressed her hand against his erection. Her eyes went wide.

"I can't fight it anymore, Halley. I don't want to fight it anymore."

Then he kissed her. It was different from the kiss earlier that morning. That had been urgent, carnal. This was languid and moist, her mouth fully open to receive him, their breath mingling together as he tasted her. It was slow and thorough, a hot discovery of each other.

She whispered against his mouth, "I want you too. For months now. I'm going nuts, Evan."

That was the best thing he'd heard in *years*. "Then let's go nuts together, sweet stuff."

Halley's tongue slipped into his mouth and he sucked on the tip lightly. She pulled back with a groan, her hands falling onto his waist. Those fingers touching, fluttering, gripping his belt loops had Evan's breath hitching.

With one hand on the back of her head, he took her mouth again and again, pressing rough and desperate, their teeth knocking together as he slipped across her slick lips.

Control. He needed to go slow. But that was so damn hard when Halley was pressed up against his bare chest wearing nothing but a doily that called itself a bra.

He broke off the kiss, and swallowed hard. They both panted, staring at each other, Halley's expression bewildered and aroused.

"Evan, if we do this, things are going to change between us."

Her nipple brushed against his bare chest as she spoke. "Things have already changed between us. And if we ignore this, the tension will always be between us. I think we should do this, have this one day together, then we can go back to the way we were before."

Not that he could envision ever going back to being pals and watching Halley date other men, but one step at a time.

"So, you mean, we'll just get this strange lust out of our systems?" She was clearly hesitating.

"Exactly."

"And nothing will ever keep us from being friends?"

"Nothing ever. I swear it." That was the whole truth as he knew it. He didn't plan on losing Halley's friendship. But he was going to if he didn't act on these feelings for her. He couldn't bottle this desire up another day.

Taking one step back, he lifted the camera in front of him, adjusting so that Halley was on the screen viewer.

"Take it off, sweet stuff."

There was hesitation, a split second of thought, before Halley tossed back her head, arching her breasts in an unconscious gesture of defiance. The clasp separated between her fingers, and Evan's heart pounded painfully as there was another split second of indecision.

He watched the screen as she made up her mind. The bra slid across each full breast and down her pale arms to land out of view on the floor.

There was nothing but her in front of him. He pushed the button with his thumb to take a picture, no intention of ever putting this on any website. Not even as a joke to teach the hackers a lesson. Not even when no one would ever know they were Halley's breasts.

This view was for him, and him alone, one he'd been waiting five years to see.

It was a damn good view, rivaling the Grand Canyon in natural beauty. Her shoulders were back, her chest rose and fell on anxious breaths, and her nipples were smooth and round, pressing forward with pride.

Halley's breasts were pale and incandescent, rounded and curving in perfect symmetry, not too large and not too small. Just right for him.

He took another picture. And another. He didn't want to risk missing this shot.

Her hands came up to flick a piece of hair out of her mouth, causing her breasts to rise in a fluid motion. Evan groaned, staring at her now, not the screen, and itched with the agonizing need to touch her.

"Did you take the picture?" she whispered, the sound of her ragged edgy voice making him throb.

"Yes." He moved a little to the left, wanting the side view of her, the upsweep of her breast, the graceful arch of shoulder to side.

"Then what are you doing?" She stood still, but turned her head to follow his progress.

"Taking pictures for me."

"Evan!" Her mouth dropped.

He loved the way her waist fell into her pants, with enough room between the fabric and her skin for him to easily slip in a finger or two. Moving slowly, he walked behind her, capturing her long and smooth back, and her ass sitting snugly in her pants.

With a shrug, he said, "I think I may be looking at my next screen saver."

It made her blush. He didn't care.

"You can't do that," she whispered.

"Why not?" It was the best idea he'd had in months. He stepped on her bra as he moved around her other side. Leaning over, he scooped it up. It was warm, the way Halley's skin would be. He brought it to his nose. It smelled like her, soft and citrus and erotic.

"I had no idea you wore such sexy bras. I almost passed out when I saw this little see-through number."

"It's a private indulgence," she said. "A reward for my success."

Lifting the hair on her shoulder, Evan kissed her flushed skin. "That's what these pictures are. A reward for my success."

"Success for what?" Halley stood very still, her shoulders taut and her chest rising a little faster than normal.

"For fixing your website."

She gave a little scoff. "Sure, you fixed it after they made me naked."

He laughed, though it did annoy the hell out of him that his site had been hacked. But the first thing on his mind right now was her soft warm flesh, uncovered and so close to him.

Her head tilted back. She added, "The pictures aren't for you. They're supposed to be for the website, for the hackers."

Revenge would have to wait. "We'll talk about that later. Right now, I've got to touch you." He set the camera down on his desk and reached for her, putting his hands on her warm waist above her pants.

"Are you sure we should?" Her voice was a little whimper that didn't fool him for one second. She was trembling now, leaning toward him, her nipples hard and rosy. Halley looked as if a breeze blowing between her thighs might make her come.

Evan wanted to make her come. He wanted her to let go. To completely give it all up, to break and shatter beneath his touch, no thoughts of anything but their bodies and the pleasure he was giving her.

"I want you," he whispered in her ear. "Can I have you?"

He pulsed with desire, ached with the need to bury himself in Halley. There had been quite a few women in his life over the years, but it had always been casual, a little company and enough to take the edge off. He had wanted women, but had never needed.

He needed Halley.

He loved her. She knew him backward and forward and there were no games between them ever. There wouldn't be now. He could never be anything but honest with her, which was why he could no longer hide his desire for her.

Halley, eyes glazed with passion, turned to stare at him. She swallowed.

Then said, "Take me, Evan."

Evan just about came on the spot.

Chapter Five

Halley watched Evan's eyes go wide with shock and desire. A little laugh bubbled up and out of her. It felt so good to see that look on his face, to know that he wanted her just the way she wanted him.

Finally, after all these months she was going to have him.

Only he wasn't doing anything, he was just standing there, eyes rolling up and down over her as he looked his fill.

What the heck was he waiting for, an embossed invitation?

"Do something," she said, feeling a tinge self-conscious standing there like a topless waitress.

Evan gave her a lusty smile. "You're always so damn impatient."

There was no point in arguing. He knew her well. Halley put her hands on her hips and frowned at him, wondering if she was going to be forced to grab his crotch to goad him into action.

It felt suspiciously as if he was teasing her, which he should know she wouldn't like.

"I've been waiting a long time to see you. I want to look awhile first."

She applauded the sentiment, but couldn't he touch her first, then look later?

The camera came back up. She narrowed her eyes at him, not the least amused. "Evan, put that down."

He pressed the button, taking another picture. Halley felt her face burn, part embarrassment, part mortification that she liked what he was doing. He looked so pleased, so eager, that she changed her mind about rushing. They hadn't talked about tomorrow, and he had basically said today was it. One day to be with Evan, to let him explore her and to feel this fevered arousal.

It emboldened her. With a little smile, she ran her fingers through her hair and wet her lips.

Evan's breath caught. "Very sultry, sweet stuff. I like it."

He continued to look at her through the camera screen. "Now let's take your pants off."

"Why?" If he could tease, she could return the favor. She tossed him an innocent smile, arching her shoulders back and resting her hands on the back of her waist.

A little rough laugh ripped from him. "Why? Because I want to see your beautiful body, that's why."

He took a step toward her. "I want pictures of you naked, wanting me. Then I need your pants off so I can drive into you so long and hard you can't see straight."

Oh. That about summed it up then. Halley closed her eyes, need crashing over her, fiery desire making her body ache. Her breasts were heavy and tender, her nipples painful under his steady gaze.

She wanted to do this. She wanted to feel nothing but this passion for Evan, to sink into the past and the future blended together in this perfect moment of right now. No worries, no reality, nothing but the way Evan

could strum and pluck her body until she was singing
with satisfaction.

Eyes still screwed shut, she licked her already moist
lips again. Hot breath spilled across her belly and his
hands fell on her waist, brushing her hands aside. Startled,
her eyes flew open and she watched Evan go down on his
knees in front of her, setting the camera on the floor.

"Let me take them off for you," he said, before his
tongue slid across her skin above her waistband. She
shivered at the warm wet tickling sensation and reached
for his shoulders.

His breath came faster. So did hers. When his tongue
dipped into her belly button, hot desire shot through
her, yanking a groan from her lips. His fingers fumbled
at the clasp of her pants while he nipped at her skin,
tasting around the edges of her navel, sliding up to nibble her side.

The top of his head brushed her breast, teasing her
with light feathery strokes of his hair, first on the underside, then across her nipple. He continued to fumble
with her pants, his jerky movements tugging her a little
left and right.

"Damn it," he said, his teeth clenched.

Halley tried to pull back away so she could hear him
better, but he held her by the bunched front fabric of
her pants. "What's the matter?"

"I can't get these freaking pants undone."

"There's a little hook and eye clasp, a metal thingie. See
it?" Leave it to her to wear pants that were the modern-
day version of the chastity belt.

A lesser man would have given up. Evan brushed
away her fingers when she tried to help.

"No, I'll get it." The metal gave way with a pull that
pretty much assured her he had torn the thread and
the eye was now dangling from the hook, useless.

"Oops, sorry."

The pants didn't matter. What mattered was that she was burning with need and he wasn't doing anything about it.

He pressed a kiss onto her hipbone, his finger playing with the zipper of her pants, drawing it down then back up again. "Stupid thing was too small for a man's fingers. Not very user friendly."

It made her laugh, soft and low, as she ran her fingers across the top of his head, smoothing his unruly hair back into place. "They're women's pants, so men's fingers don't factor in. And *user friendly* is such a computer geek thing to say."

The zipper went all the way down, and stayed down. "Are you calling me a computer geek?"

His hot breath against her made her squeeze his shoulders. "If the software fits . . ."

A damp kiss fell onto her, the heat pouring through her sheer panties and right to the center of her desire.

"Evan," she moaned, rocking forward.

"Nice A drive," he murmured.

She would have laughed, but there was no chance. His mouth still on her panties, kissing and nibbling, Evan yanked her pants at the bottom and dragged them down to her thighs.

Halley couldn't bother to push them farther down, or move to step out of them. She was caught beneath Evan's mouth, lost in a desperate wave of longing, as she gasped under his assault and pushed his head hard against her.

Teeth grazed the gossamer fabric of her panties. He gripped the satin side straps with his hands, twisting them around his index fingers, pulling the fabric still caught in his mouth taut. Then before she could even react, he had ripped right through the front with a sharp jerk of his head.

"Ohmigod." She threw back her head and swallowed hard, want pulsing between her thighs where she was swollen and moist with need.

This was Evan. Her best friend.

Tearing her underwear off her.

"Sorry, I ripped these too," he murmured into her thigh.

"S'okay," she managed to pant.

A cool breeze rushed across her as he leaned back, away from her. She stepped out of her pants and shoved them aside. He returned with the camera and a wicked grin.

"Oh, no. Don't you dare." Alarmed at the thought of herself naked on camera, Halley started to edge to the side.

Evan's thumb slipped through her sacrificial panties and circled her clitoris. She ground to a halt.

"Don't take any pictures of this." Her words were unnecessary, since Evan's hand had gone slack again as he concentrated on stroking her, and the only view through the camera was his country beige carpet.

"But it's so nice looking." His lips tickled her inner thighs as his thumb moved around and around until she was dizzy and weak with desire.

Then his thumb slid inside her, and back out, wetting her clitoris with the dampness of her arousal. Halley felt her legs wobble as she groaned.

"I think I'm going to fall down."

"Back up." His thumb went back to its seductive circles, while his tongue started trailing across her inner thigh.

He was insane if he thought she could move. "I can't. My legs don't work."

He glanced up. She didn't trust that gleam in his eye.

A large rough hand landed flat on her belly. Then he pushed her.

Halley stumbled backward and landed flat on her back on his bed. As she thrust her tangled and eagle-spread legs together, she rationalized this was another time she should be grateful for her midsized breasts. A larger woman would have a black eye right now.

"I can't believe you pushed me." Actually, she could. Evan had tossed her in pools, pushed her in mud, and had tied her shoelaces together once. But that had been when they were just friends. Now that they were naked, it seemed like the rules should change.

Obviously not. And she was the only one naked. He was still wearing his shorts.

"You said you couldn't move. I was helping you out." He leaned over her.

Two could play this game. Halley lifted her foot and pressed her toes against his erection to stop him. "What are you doing?"

He shot her a look of disbelief. "I'm going to lie on you and kiss you like crazy."

He tried to shove her foot away, but Halley squeezed her toes, gathering some of his shorts and a little bit of what was underneath.

"Halley, you're squeezing me." He froze, clearly afraid to move and possibly cause damage.

Halley knew she wasn't hurting him. Yet. But it felt good to have him at her mercy for a change. She threw her hand over her mouth in mock innocence. "Oops. Sorry."

Evan placed his hand on her foot and shook his head. "Hey, you'd only be hurting yourself, you know. You put me out of action and you're going to have a long, lonely day ahead of you."

Geez, he was right. She dropped her foot like a hot potato, not wanting any accidents. She wasn't leaving this apartment without getting an orgasm. And not some little after-the-fact, token-gesture orgasm. She wanted one with him inside her, long and slow with her nails dug in his back.

He smiled knowingly and put his hands on either side of her shoulders. Halley pushed on his chest to prevent him from lying on her.

"Hold on. Let me get my panties off."

Evan sat back to give her room. Lifting her ass in the air, she played with the waist of the shredded panties, sliding them down several inches, then back up.

"Maybe I shouldn't take them off. I might get cold," she teased.

He was staring at her with a mix of fascination and pain. "Very funny. It's eighty-five degrees in here."

It was true. The blinds were closed, but the midday summer sun was heating the room up. There was a thin layer of sweat on his chest and shoulders, and she could smell a faint sweaty heat rising off him. It was masculine and sexy and made her damp between the thighs.

Her skin felt flushed too. Hot and tingling, her hair heavy and moist on her neck.

Evan's hands gripped the sides of her panties, pushing her aside. "Besides, these things wouldn't keep an ant warm. There's nothing to them."

It was nice that he had noticed.

His head bent over her breast. His fingers caressed over and beneath the straps of her panties. His lips came close to her nipple, so close that she felt his breath hitch, but he didn't touch her. All teasing was forgotten as her body responded, aching and throbbing for him. Halley arched her breast up to meet his mouth.

Evan edged away. His fingers slid back and forth as he

dragged her panties down halfway, then stopped. She could see him staring down at her, his thumb rubbing across her curls, skirting her clitoris, while his mouth still hovered tantalizingly close to her nipple.

She wanted him to touch her, anywhere. She could hear her own ragged breathing, loud and fast, and she snaked her fingers down to claw at her panties, desperate to shove them off.

Evan took her questing fingers in his own before she could push the panties down, and he held them tightly against her hips, pressing her fingers into her flesh. She squirmed and tried to tug her hands loose.

He pressed against her mound with his erection, with so little pressure and so briefly that she groaned in frustration. She wrapped her legs around his and tried to pull him back down, but Evan shook her off.

"Not yet."

When? When the next ice age came through? Halley was about to complain when he bent his head down and plucked at her nipple. She cried out.

He pulled back.

"More," she panted.

This time Evan bent down and licked all around her nipple with his tongue, wetting her and circling her until she wiggled back and forth, trying to force his tongue onto her. His hands held hers harder, holding her arms down tightly by her sides, so that she couldn't move.

He felt big and hard leaning over her, and she forced her eyes open long enough to see him sweep his gaze across her chest and down her belly. He drew in a deep breath before dropping his mouth to her breast again.

This time he pulled her nipple in hard, and pain mixed with pleasure.

"You taste so good," he said as he licked her. He lavished his tongue all over her nipple, around and around until she thought she might explode just from his wet movements.

Her panties were barely covering her, twisted and rolled and caught between her and him, and it added to the excitement, to the decadence of what they were doing.

As he pulled her nipple deep into his moist mouth, thoroughly wetting it, she moaned.

"Evan." She tried to rip her hands out from under his, but he still held her, more from his weight bearing down on her than from any effort on his part.

He pulled back from her chest, tugging her nipple out with his mouth before releasing it. "You like that?"

No, she always moaned and panted whenever she detested something. "I like it better when you don't stop."

Evan liked that better too, though he had to admit it was a turn-on to tease Halley a little. Of course, in teasing her, he teased himself, and her breast tasted so salty and eager, he just wanted to keep going.

"Then I won't stop, sweetheart. I'll just suck and suck until you can't stand it anymore." Evan trailed his tongue along the underside of her breast. "How's that sound?"

That strangled whimper from Halley could count as a yes.

Evan didn't wait for further verbal confirmation. He took Halley into his mouth, rolling his tongue around the sweet hardness of her nipple. He had been wondering how she would feel beneath him, he had been dreaming about tasting her, and now that he was, he was fighting hard for every ounce of control.

Her hand ripped free of his hold, and reached up to grip his shoulder, squeezing and scratching along his flesh as she made little encouraging gasps. Evan didn't need encouragement. He was reveling in every stroke of his tongue, every inch of her soft warm flesh in his mouth, and everything rational was skittering away from him, lost in agonizing need.

He switched breasts. Halley groaned.

Her tight smooth thighs had clamped around him again, grinding her rounded mound against his all-too-eager cock, and he struggled to force himself to move away. But every time he leaned back an inch, she rose upward, meeting him again.

Giving up the battle, he let her bump against him, and he concentrated on breathing. It was a hell of a challenge.

Halley's grip was getting tighter, her back arching farther, her cries louder and more ragged. Evan lapped his tongue back and forth over her, brushing his thumbs along the underswell of her breast. He could feel her orgasm closing in on her.

"Touch me," she begged.

"Where?" Evan pressed his thumb into her belly button. "Here?"

"No."

"Here?" He brushed her wet nipple.

She groaned. "Yes."

Halley was in delicious agony. Every part of her body ached and throbbed, begging for Evan to stroke, taste, slide in wherever he could, and pleasure her.

"Touch me more," she said shamelessly, finally pulling her other hand free of his heavy hold.

With both hands, she went straight for his hair, tugging and urging him downward, trying to force him to suck harder, touch her between her thighs, anything to release the ache inside her. She was strung too tight, tense and violently needy, vibrating everywhere.

Evan pulled his mouth off her again, obviously not

the least bit intimidated by her desperate aggressive-ness. A slow grin crossed his face.

"Should I touch you here again?" he said, and put his lips on her nipple, lightly closing his mouth over it, hot breath dancing across her.

She squeezed her eyes shut and gasped. When he laughed, she could feel it. His mouth wrapped around and sucked, but the muffled sound of his pleased laugh-ter wafted up to her.

His lips, tongue, and moist inner mouth vibrated around her, onto her tight sensitive nipple. As Halley glanced down in agony at Evan's caramel-colored hair falling into his eyes, she came hard.

With nothing touching her but his thigh resting against her, the orgasm was painful and throbbing, her clitoris swollen and in need of release. Shuddering, Halley let out a cry and went still, riding out the waves of tight pleasure.

Evan pulled back and gaped at her, his lips shiny and wet. "Holy shit. You just came, didn't you?"

Unable to speak, she nodded.

"Damn, that's sexy." He buried his face in her navel and dipped his tongue into her belly button.

Her shoulders relaxed a little and she stroked his hair as her body settled.

"Thanks," she murmured. New desire was already building as his tongue delved into her, but it was less ur-gent, more sensual this time.

Halley suspected she had needed to take the edge off, and could now look forward to enjoying Evan even more thoroughly. "I think I needed that."

He dropped a warm kiss on her abdomen. "What are friends for?"

Not for sexual gratification, she was pretty sure, but

if he didn't mind, she wasn't going to stop him. She laughed. "Usually not for this."

Now he was stroking her inner thigh. "I think we're on to something here."

As he tugged her panties down past her thighs, she murmured, "Or we could be making a huge mistake."

Her panties were around her knees when he stopped pulling and looked up at her. "Hey. I love you, you know that. I'd never hurt you, Halley."

"I know." He wouldn't hurt her on purpose anyway. And as long as she told herself this was all about sex, with a man she could trust above all others, she would be okay. If she went and started imagining this was more than enjoying each other in a spontaneous day in bed, then she would be in trouble.

"Should I keep going?" he asked, his thumb caressing her knee.

His breath landed on her inner thigh.

Did a bee like honey? If she'd already gone this far, she might as well get the full treatment.

"Yes, keep going."

"Thank God." He took her panties in both his hands, and yanked them down hard to her ankles.

He tossed them over his shoulder as she lay there stunned in a pool of wet paralyzing lust.

"You're not going to need those anymore."

"Ever?" she said dumbly.

"Not for a long time," he confirmed, his brown eyes so dark with desire they were nearly black.

"You're not going to need these shorts either."

Sliding next to him onto her side, Halley trailed her fingers along his waistband, pausing at the button of his khaki shorts. She glanced up at Evan. He raised his eyebrows up and down.

With two hands, she popped the button. The grin fell off Evan's face. She bit down on her own grin, then unzipped his shorts.

Evan gave a sharp intake of air.

Halley slipped her hand inside his shorts, under his boxers, stroking his hard flesh and tugging lightly on the springy hair there. Evan was breathing hard, a sound that emboldened her, raising her own desire another aching notch.

Her fingers enclosed around him, holding the warm satin length of his erection in her hand, feeling the pulse beneath the skin.

"Halley."

She saw his eyes were half closed, his chest inflating and collapsing like an accordion. He looked like a page from the calendar she had hung in her locker at school when she was sixteen. A gorgeous bare-chested man with his pants unsnapped.

Only he was real. He was hers right now.

An arousing thought came to her. Her eyes landed on the camera Evan has discarded at the foot of the bed.

Giving a little squeeze to his penis, she let go and pulled her hand back. Evan gave a groan of disappointment.

Bending over, she retrieved the camera and stood up, pointing it at Evan's chest.

He sat up fast, alarm all over his face. "Whoa. What are you doing?"

"I'm going to take a picture of you. Use it as my next screen saver." Halley clicked the button and gave him a cocky grin.

Though he looked amused, Evan's hands twitched as if he was fighting the urge to cover himself with a blanket.

"Put the camera down."

She laughed. "No. Tit for tat, Evan." She took another shot of him frowning.

Then he relaxed back a little. "*Tit* for tat, huh? But tell me you don't want to slap these pictures of me up on the web."

"Oh, are you shy?" Halley tilted her head, fully aroused and enjoying herself. It felt good to be free like this, the only tension in her body sexual. Being with Evan was different from being with any other man. With him, she was still herself. They could tease and play like this, just like they always had, and it was because of their friendship.

With the added bonus of red-hot desire.

"But come on, Evan, why would we use your body? That would be like a dream come true for those guys to have your biceps attached to their heads."

Evan smiled and popped his arm up, flexing his bicep with mock arrogance. "You like my muscles, sweet stuff? I've got a muscle you'll really like."

Boy, did he ever. His penis had come through the hole in his boxers again, and this time Halley wasn't so startled as she was eager. It was time to put that crazy-looking thing to good use.

Her mouth went dry as she studied him on the camera screen, about to suggest they do just that. Then Evan made the muscle in question flex, winking up and down at her. Halley went wide-eyed and nearly dropped the camera.

"Ohmigod!" After a startled second of silence, she started laughing so hard a snort threatened to emerge from her mouth.

"You think that's funny?"

He clearly did too, since he was grinning like the village idiot.

She nodded, unable to speak.

Then Evan's eyes dropped to her chest, and his grin turned lascivious. "Keep laughing all you want," he said.

Heat rushed through her cheeks. She had forgotten she was totally naked. Everywhere naked. Not-a-stitch-on naked.

Laughter probably did all kinds of weird things to her stomach and her chest from his point of view. She pictured buoys bobbing up and down in the surf. Or in her case, something significantly smaller, like a couple of toothpaste tubes.

To emphasize his point, Evan made himself flex again, resting back on his locked arms. She refused to laugh again, even though it was hilarious. Only she was trying so hard not to laugh, that a snuffling sound emerged from her nose and mouth.

She should have forced him to button the little button on his boxers earlier. "You're very talented."

Evan said, "I have all kinds of hidden talents."

Despite the absurdity of his words and his Adam Sandler expression, Halley was intrigued. Aroused. Yearning for him.

If he could make her come just by sucking on her breasts, what else could he do?

Her thighs slid against each other restlessly, the hot dampness between them about to become embarrassing without panties on. "Why don't you show me your many talents?"

The camera found a place on his desk. Halley walked toward Evan, climbing up onto the bed, debating whether she wanted to be on top of him or beneath him.

First.

Chapter Six

Halley naked should be illegal. Damn, Evan could barely breathe, let alone think or move. He'd thought his bikini-stripping dream was pretty hot, but that was nothing compared to the real Halley standing in front of him with nothing on.

She looked so good, it was a wonder his shorts didn't burst into flames.

Evan quickly stood up as Halley sat down, falling back against the sheet. She looked at him puzzled, her pale fingers already reaching up for him. Mouth dry, he put a hand on each of her smooth thighs and yanked hard, pulling her to the edge of the bed.

Her knees fell open as she let out a small cry and tried to sit up. Evan pulled her again, causing her to fall back down, arms over her head. The crook of each knee lined up with the edge of the mattress and Evan dropped to his knees in front of her.

"This isn't funny," she said, trying to pull herself up again, but unable to because he held each leg against the bed.

"I'm not trying to be funny. I'm very serious." He

studied her inner thighs, stroking above her knees with his thumbs to relax her.

He could feel the heat from her, smell the musky dampness of her arousal, and his gut cramped into painful desire. He blew onto her lightly from just a few inches away. She twitched.

"I'm as serious as that Cupid was," he murmured.

She made a sound that could have been a gasp, a smothered laugh, or a moan. It almost sounded to his eager ears as if she were having an orgasm. She wasn't, of course, but the sound made his blood go south.

Evan swallowed hard, leaning in and running the pad of his thumb across her plump clitoris then down into the dewy heat below. His thumb sank inside her, and she pulled him in, clenching on with tight muscles.

Holy hell, she felt good. He closed his eyes for a second, feeling her skin pulse around him, and listening to her breathy little moans of pleasure.

He couldn't get enough of those moans.

"What is that?" she asked, spreading her knees farther, the movement urging him to sink deeper.

"The bottom of my thumb." Evan buried his face in her thigh, breathing in her scent deeply. Then he flicked his tongue over her clitoris, his thumb still deep inside.

Halley let out a wild cry and suddenly her fingers yanked his hair hard, jerking him back. So hard, water popped up into his eyes. It was a good sign. Evan laughed at her response and pulled his thumb out.

"Don't stop!"

"I'm just getting started."

Evan loved to look at her, to see her swollen pink folds in front of him, aching and throbbing for his touch. She moved with quick jerky movements, wiggling down farther, trying to entice him to touch her.

He was happy to oblige.

With his tongue, he tasted her, running up and down each side, swirling over her clitoris before finally sliding down the middle. He gave a long teasing probe deep inside, then pulled back.

"Put it back," Halley panted.

Evan was drowning, his control shredding under her desperate and vocal need. Halley was aggressive, intent on getting what she wanted. It was that part of her that made her successful in her business, and mixed with her loyalty and her kindness, it made her all the more fantastic to him.

She was everything he liked in a woman.

He liked giving her pleasure. And if he could keep himself from exploding in his boxer shorts, he could enjoy it a little longer.

So he continued to tease her with his tongue. Gliding lightly up and down, skirting her clitoris, never going deep enough to satisfy her, but brushing with a feathery touch of his mouth.

Halley's legs thrashed, her hand clawed at his shoulders, and she made alternating sounds of ecstasy and agony.

"I want you inside me. Now." The words came out harsh and nonnegotiable.

Evan paused. Then he looked up at her, met her glazed eyes over the length of her flushed body, and said, "Really? I couldn't tell."

In spite of his holding her legs over the edge of the bed, she managed to sit up. She scooted forward, toward him, a dangerous gleam in her eye.

He was in for it now.

He couldn't wait.

It wasn't long in coming. She shoved on his chest,

her fingers gripping the dusting of hair there, tugging on him until he felt the sharp jerks of stinging pain.

Then she was in his lap. All of her. Every warm, wet, pink, flushed, salty inch of her. A nipple was tantalizingly in front of his mouth. He reached for it.

She jerked back, head arched, voice insistent. "No. No more playing. I want you inside me."

"Yes, ma'am." He wasn't about to argue with the Naked Caterer. Not when it would be so much fun to give her what she wanted.

Her arms locked around his neck, and her breasts brushed across his chest. Evan shifted and settled her down in his lap more comfortably. Her hot little mound was pressing against the base of his cock, making him sweat with need.

He was still wearing his shorts, but was loath to let her go even long enough to shuck his clothes. Yet there was a more urgent concern about what he wasn't wearing.

The tangy taste of her still hovered in his mouth and he wiped at his moist lips. "Someone needs to stand up and get a condom."

For a second, he thought she was going to tell him to hell with the condom. Panicked alarm skittered through him.

He should have known better. Halley wasn't stupid.

She sighed. "Damn. Where are they?"

"Nightstand." His voice was a relieved croak. He was mature, he had control, but hell, how was he supposed to stay strong against the temptation of sliding into Halley skin on skin?

It was like waving steak and dried kibbles in front of a dog and telling him to choose.

No, that wasn't right. Making love to Halley wouldn't be anything like dried kibbles, condom or not.

She disentangled herself and went over to the night-stand while he ditched the rest of his clothes. In a minute she was back, with not one condom, not even two. But four condoms.

His body hummed in anticipation while his brain froze. Who was this woman? His best friend, naked, with a handful of condoms.

Damn, he liked it.

Reaching for her, he felt a strange thickness inside his gut area.

He loved Halley. Of course he'd always known that. But it felt different now, more intimate and satisfying.

She slid into his lap as if she belonged there, as if they had done this dozens of times before. Evan dropped a kiss onto her shoulder, trailing his tongue across her salty skin as she rolled the condom onto him.

He nuzzled into her neck and stared up at her, tenderness mixing with passion.

"What?" she said as her fingers finished their task and she looked up.

"Nothing." He shook his head and smiled.

Did she even know what was happening here? That this had become way more than just sex and had nothing to do with hackers or websites or work?

This was about them, moving from friends to lovers and eventually to more.

She didn't see it now. But by the end of this, when she was sore and satisfied, boneless and carefree, he would explain it to her.

It might take some convincing, but he had every intention of having more than one day with Halley.

* * *

Evan was looking at her strangely, like she'd gone and grown a third nipple. As if he was simultaneously horrified and yet intrigued by the possibilities.

"Why are you looking at me like that?" She didn't expect an answer, and she didn't get one.

Not an honest one, anyway.

He smiled and said, "You're beautiful."

Evan's arms were around her, pulling her forward against him. Her chest molded to his, and she had her legs wrapped around his waist.

It put her right flush against his erection, and the press of him right on her soft spot was deliciously distracting. She didn't pursue the conversation. Evan could look at her any way he damn well pleased as long as he did it while inside her.

"Come here." Evan urged her forward, with a hand on the back of her head. "Taste yourself on me."

He gave her a drawn-out, languid kiss, teasing his tongue past hers. The musky taste in his mouth was from her, she knew. From her desire for him.

Yanking her head back, she moaned, "Evan, please."

"Please, what?" Evan's thumb ran across her bottom lip and she could smell the rich scent of her body there as well. "Take out my garbage? Hack the Three Commandos? Fuck you senseless?"

"The last one." Without thought, she pulled his finger into her mouth and sucked. Her eyes drifted closed and she started to bump against his penis. She was losing her patience here. How could he just sit there naked with her and maintain his control?

Halley felt close to howling.

"Fuck you senseless, okay, I can do that."

Nipping his finger, she let go of it. "Today, not next year."

Then Halley lifted herself and joined them, with a quick downward thrust.

Now the moan came from him.

Followed by a matching cry from her. He was big, filling every inch of her, reaching nearly to her throat, so deep she wasn't sure she could take him. But she would find a way to take him. She leaned against his chest and sucked in air, adjusting to the fit, thrilling over the feel of him inside her.

She had wanted this for so long. Too damn long.

His hands caressed her back with a tenderness that brought unexplained longing to her. Ignoring it, she closed her mouth around his taut small nipple and sucked, luxuriating in the throbbing of his penis inside her, vibrating her with pleasure.

"I love doing this with you," he said, his hand dipping down below her back to her behind, sliding into the crevice between her cheeks.

A shudder went through her.

She held on to his shoulders and sat back a little, spreading her legs wider to encourage him to move. Evan did. Dropping his hands to her waist, he thrust up, pitching her forward with the power of his motion.

Then he pulled back and she sank back down a little. Another thrust, and she was up again, gripping his shoulders and biting her lip.

Then down, and she was crying out from the loss. Back and forth, over and over, he filled her, then took away, his movements a taunting fulfillment, yet not enough to satisfy.

She wanted more, something, what she didn't know.

His short fingernails were digging in to her side, his hands squeezing her flesh. "Sweet stuff."

The silly nickname sounded strange, out of place, but

oddly in tune with what they were doing and the way she was feeling. He said it like an endearment, and she took pleasure in that. In everything.

He slowed his own thrust, and urged her with his hands on her waist to take over, to slide up and down on him. Bending her knees for leverage, Halley lifted herself, sank back. Sweat started trickling between her breasts from exertion and pleasure, and she tossed her hair out of her eyes.

"Why did you stop, Evan? Is something wrong?" She felt very erotic and free, as if she had nothing better to do than sit on Evan's cock and fuck the day away.

It felt so damn good she could see the temptation to do just that every day. But they could talk about that later.

Right now, there was only she and Evan, and this wonderful feeling that pulsed and jerked through every inch of her sensitized body. There was only now.

And now she was going to enjoy every second of being with him.

"Nothing's wrong. Not at all. Just wanted to see you do a little work," he said, breathing hard.

His grip on her was so tight, Halley knew she would have bruises tomorrow. But she didn't care. She wanted his mark on her, proof of his desperate desire.

Halley bent her head over again, this time sneaking a peek, watching herself. Watching her go down on the length of Evan's shaft, taking him into her, covering his skin with hers.

"Oh," she moaned.

"Like that view?"

"Yes."

"It looks good from my way too." He shuddered, his eyes fixed down below her waist. "So good, I'm going to come."

Triumph surged through her, surprising her. She had never taken a man's orgasm personally before. But then she'd never been moving on Evan, and this time everything was personal.

There was one shot at this. One time, now, today, to get this right.

She wanted this, she was entitled to this moment of safe, pure freedom with a man she both trusted and cared about more than anyone else.

A man who pleasured her like no other guy before.

"Good," she told him as she felt the first shudders of his orgasm ripping through him. "I think I'll come with you."

Then Halley couldn't speak as she broke over him, her head arched back and her hands on his shoulders. He was deep inside her, and their shudders and pulsing bodies blended and fed off one another.

Halley made a sound she'd never heard from her mouth before, a bizarre wail that reminded her of tornado warning sirens. Then as the pulsing throbs receded, she dropped against his chest and laughed softly, amused with herself, her thoughts, her body, and Evan.

She felt fabulous. No wonder she had been craving Evan for months. Her body must have known instinctively that he would be incredible.

He dropped a kiss on her sweaty head. "Are you laughing at me?" he teased her with a low growl. "I don't think my performance deserved to be laughed at."

Evan was still firmly inside her, her breasts still flush against his chest. His lips were inches from hers, his hard sweaty forehead locking her head in place.

"Not at all. It's a 'Damn, that felt good' laugh."

The kiss he gave her was deep and possessive. "Good. You want some more?"

There was more? She shivered in anticipation. But she felt compelled to say, "Are you sure? Maybe we should quit while we're ahead."

"Where would the fun be in that?" He scoffed at her, running his hands through her damp hair.

Stricken with a conscience a bit after the fact, Halley still felt the need to say something. "Well, you know, this isn't what friends normally do, and I don't want to push. And what if . . . we don't like it?"

It was time to close her mouth, before something even more absurd rolled out. Halley bit her lip.

Evan pulled his head back, frowning, and slid out of her. She gave a sigh at the loss, both physical and emotional. She wasn't sure which was worse and she was annoyed at herself. The man gave her a couple of orgasms and she had morphed into a sappy love-struck idiot. Who wanted to talk, of all things. And was having disturbing visions of a relationship.

She commanded herself to knock off the needy babbling and focus on the here and now.

Evan had removed the condom and rolled on a new one while she had conducted her mental self-help seminar.

Without preamble, he thrust back into her. "Do you like this? Do you like it when I fuck you?"

"Oh. Yes." She was still wet and aching, and his thrust ripped her thoughts out of the uncertain future and into the present. Where having him inside her just felt fabulous.

Evan bent his knees and wrapped his arms around her. In one impressive lurch, he stood up, their bodies still joined. "Not on the floor this time, though."

They could do it on broken glass for all she cared. "Standing?" she asked, dropping her legs down to the carpet, forcing him deeper inside her.

"Good idea." Evan gave a slow thrust.

Halley had the sudden idea that this would make a great shot with the camera. "Do we . . . have all the pictures we need? You know, for the hacking we're going to be doing? Not that I want pictures of this on the website, but you know . . . the other things. We took." *Shut up,* she commanded herself.

"Any pictures we take will be just for our pleasure, sweet stuff."

His hands on her ass, holding her in place as he softly moved inside her, he gave her a sly smile. "Besides, taking pictures of you for the website was just a plot to get you naked."

She had suspected as much. Halley found she didn't give a damn. "Oh, shoot, and here I really wanted to see my breasts online."

Evan groaned. "Well, we still can if you want."

Straining on her tiptoes, Halley gripped his shoulders and shook her head. My, oh my, this felt good.

"That's okay. I don't care about the stupid hackers anymore."

The strange thing was, she meant it. The website wasn't important. Revenge wasn't important. Just being with Evan. Just this feeling that nothing was more right than being with him, naked, pleasuring each other.

He still moved inside her with slow, steady thrusts, only now his eyes held hers. She blinked once, licked her lips, and still he stared at her, his dark eyes unreadable.

Finally he said, "Damn, am I dreaming?"

Any reservations still buried deep in Halley fled at the wonder in his voice. It was the same words he'd spoken to her just hours earlier, then in a teasing flirtatious voice. Now he looked as stunned and bewildered as she felt.

"Why would you say that?"

"Because I can't believe that I could be lucky enough to have you as a friend and as a lover."

Halley didn't know what to say, and the myriad of emotions crashing through her were confused and jumbled. But she could show him how she felt. She moaned and gripped his back to show approval.

Then without warning he stopped moving.

She dropped to the balls of her feet, her calf muscles straining from standing on her toes for so long. She was no ballerina and ten seconds away from intense muscle cramping.

"Why are you stopping?" She pushed herself against him, giving a little whimper as he sank deeper into her.

He laughed softly. "To tease you."

It was working.

Then he started thrusting again, harder and faster this time, lifting her back up onto her toes and driving the air from her lungs.

"I love you, Halley."

A cry flew out of her mouth as an orgasm built inside her, her passion blending with confusion as their sweat-slick bodies touched each other.

"Evan." She wanted to believe him. There was nothing she had ever wanted quite as much.

But it wasn't that simple. Or maybe it could be.

"Do you love me?" he whispered into her ear, his hot breath tickling her.

There was no way to lie, nowhere to hide, not with him holding her in his arms and his body making her feel as if she could rip apart.

"Yes."

He swallowed the word as she spoke it, covering her mouth in a crushing kiss of possession.

There, she'd done it. Told him the truth, exposed herself to pain and loss if this didn't work out. But those thoughts were shoved resolutely to the back of her mind as she tasted Evan, slipped her tongue into his mouth and wrapped her arms around his smooth warm neck.

If this was a mistake, she was going to enjoy it while she could.

Evan urged, "Let me feel you come."

And so she did.

Chapter Seven

Halley left Evan in bed, making an adorable little snuffling snoring sound, and went over to his dresser. She
pulled out a pair of his boxer shorts and stepped into
them. After dragging one of his T-shirts on over her unruly hair, she went down the hall to the kitchen, walking
softly so she wouldn't wake him.

There had been plenty of times in the past when she
had worn his clothes for various reasons, but this was
different. For one thing, she wasn't wearing any panties,
since hers were beyond repair. But she'd also never made
love to Evan before, and his scent was still on her skin,
mixing with the clean softness of the clothes, making
her feel practically delirious with happiness.

In a matter of minutes, she had found enough ingre-
dients in Evan's refrigerator to have an omelet cooking
on the stove as she hummed to herself. She caught herself and laughed. Geez, she was humming. Something
she never did. While cooking for him.

How pathetic was that?

But it didn't feel pathetic. It felt . . . right.

Like this was where she was supposed to be. But she
was terrified to tell Evan. Sure, he had said he loved her,

but she had always known that, had heard him say it before. What she didn't know was what Evan wanted from her. Just a roll in the hay here and there, or a relationship.

If she asked, he might give her an answer that she didn't want to hear.

Working so hard to build her business, she had never had time to make a lot of friends. She had met Evan her first day at college, and had been friends with him ever since. She couldn't imagine him not being in her life.

Loading the dishwasher with what looked like a week's worth of dirty dishes, Halley knew she and Evan were going to have to talk sooner or later.

Just not today. Today she just wanted to enjoy him.

Glad to see he'd taken out his trash, she flipped the omelet, then squirted soap into the dishwasher and shut the door. She turned the machine on, then spun around to find Evan standing in the door yawning.

Naked.

He sniffed the air. "Mmm. Something smells good."

Halley backed up a foot as he strode into the kitchen, filling the room with his masculine presence. Her butt hit the counter, and the dishwasher buttons pressed into her.

"It's an omelet, no big deal." It felt ridiculous, all of a sudden, that she had cooked for him.

Which made no sense, since she had done that dozens of times before. She had known sleeping together would change their relationship for the worse, make it uncomfortable, and here it was, happening already.

"It is a big deal." He kissed her forehead. "Thanks."

Brushing him aside, she reached over and turned off the heat. "Shit, it's burning."

His finger snaked out and ripped off a piece. He tossed it in his mouth and said, "It tastes perfect."

Damn, why did that please her so much?

And why did she like that he was nuzzling into her neck?

"You look cute in my clothes."

"Well, I had to wear something." Halley tried not to be turned on, but she was failing miserably.

Evan was nibbling on her ear, his hands reaching up under the T-shirt to cup her breasts.

"You're naked under those boxer shorts, aren't you?"

Halley heard a roaring in her ear, then realized it was the dishwasher as the water started shooting through the clean cycle. "Yes."

"Good." Strong hands gripped her waist, tossing her onto the counter.

Halley sat down with a hard thump and stared at Evan in disbelief. "Geez, what are you doing?"

Actually, she had a pretty good idea what he was doing. "I just turned the dishwasher on, you know."

She was sitting right on top of it, and could feel the vibration through the countertop, jiggling her thighs where she was already starting to feel uncomfortably aroused.

"Even better." He moved between her legs, forcing them apart.

He gave her a long, slow kiss that left her breathless.

The slit in the boxer shorts she was wearing was yanked apart. "Are you okay to do this?" he asked. "Or are you getting sore?"

Okay was an understatement. She was dripping in pleasure. "I'm okay."

The T-shirt was tugged up and over her head. Evan bent over her breast and sucked lightly on her nipple, making her squirm in need.

"This tastes even better than the omelet."

The counter was still vibrating, and steam was floating out from around the dishwasher door, rushing between her legs and causing her nipples to tighten. Halley gripped the backsplash and arched her head, crying out as Evan drove a finger into her.

He stretched her with two, then before she could blink, had moved himself into place and thrust into her through the opening in the boxers. It was unexpected and rough, the urgency on Evan's face exciting her.

There was no slow buildup of rhythm, but just fast strokes and his hands on her hips urging her to meet him thrust for thrust. Still gripping the counter, she could do nothing but take and feel. His hard abdominal muscles bumped against her clitoris with each push into her, and she felt it all the way down to her toes.

Halley was burning hot from the steam and her own passion, and when Evan leaned forward and kissed her, his tongue pushing past hers, she broke on a long, slow, shivering orgasm.

As she grabbed the strength to push forward and meet him, stealing the last shudders of pleasure, Evan followed suit, calling her name out into her shoulder.

It was a sound she wanted to hear again and again.

"Damn, how do you do that?" he said a second later, rubbing his lips across her clavicle bone.

"Do what?" Halley dragged in a breath.

"Make me so hot so fast?" He shook his head. "It must be the years of repressed lust."

Halley jerked up. "Years?" What exactly did that mean?

He pulled back, out of her. "Listen, Halley, I think we need to talk."

Oh, geez, here it was. The weird, awkward conversation where they both fumbled for the right words. The talk where it was possible her heart just might break.

"Here, you eat first before the food gets cold." Brushing past him, she hopped off the counter and pulled the boxers out of her rear, where they were wedged. "I'm going to grab a quick shower, then we can talk. Okay?"

Halley got the hell out of there before he had time to respond.

Evan watched Halley run out of the room and sighed. He didn't want to upset Halley, but they did need to talk. She had to know that he couldn't go back to being just friends. He wanted more.

Marriage. That's what he wanted. And just why the hell not? He loved Halley. She loved him. They knew each other with all their faults, and still got along fantastically.

Today had proved they were more than sexually compatible. They were so good together, they could make a freaking instructional video.

Reaching into the silverware drawer, Evan pulled out a fork and started munching on the eggs. He heard the shower turn on.

It didn't take long to finish the eggs and drop the fork into the sink. Evan turned toward the door, then stopped himself. He shouldn't go into the bathroom. He should give her some privacy.

But somehow he found himself standing in the bathroom a minute later, holding his breath so she wouldn't hear him. He just wanted to watch her undetected for a minute.

She was in his shower, the clear glass door displaying every inch of her as she tilted her head back and let the spray hit her face and roll down her chest.

The heat from the shower had turned her skin pink on her back and her little curvy behind. With her arms in the air digging into her hair, her breasts rose and beckoned him.

He wanted to step into the shower.

He wanted to take his hands and rub them all over her damp body.

But for now he was content to watch.

Leaning against the door frame, Evan crossed his arms and settled in for a good long show.

Halley had said she loved him. He had believed her. Halley wasn't the kind of woman to ever say anything but the truth, whether he wanted to hear it or not. This he had wanted to hear.

But he still felt the strange urge to watch over Halley, to hold on to her, as if this might very well be a dream after all.

Halley turned, bending over to grab the shampoo bottle. Evan appreciated the picture she made, leaning over without bending her knees, her round ass slippery and wet, his hand itching to reach between her legs from behind.

Halley saw him and yelped. "Geez, you scared me!"

She clutched the shampoo bottle to her bare chest.

"Sorry. I didn't mean to scare you."

"How long have been standing there?" She looked embarrassed, though the flush could be from the steam of the shower.

"Long enough to have a fantasy or two."

"I'll be done in a minute." She popped the top on the bottle and squirted a huge amount of shampoo into her hand.

"No hurry." He watched her reach up and work the shampoo into her hair, a lather quickly building as she roughly scrubbed.

"Are you just going to stand there and watch?"

"Yes."

She gave a gasp and flicked suds off her fingers. "Well, don't."

"Why not?"

"It makes me uncomfortable."

"We can't have that." Evan started toward her, unable to resist another second.

"Oh, no." She backed up until her behind hit the tiles on the wall.

The demure act was cute, but he had no patience for it. He opened the door. "Come on, I'll just help you wash your hard-to-reach spots."

Though she held her arms out to ward him off, Evan also noticed the little gleam of interest shining behind her embarrassment. As well as her firm nipples, and open mouth.

"I just bet you will."

Steam rose around them, and water was pelting him in the face in a fine mist. Evan stepped into the shower and clicked the door shut behind him. "Have you ever done it in the shower?"

It was a stupid question to ask. Jealously stabbed through him painfully.

"No."

All right then. He smiled. "And here I thought you were such a bad girl."

Halley tilted her head and flattened herself farther against the wall. "I've never been a bad girl. I'm more like an occasionally-veers-into-the-unorthodox kind of girl. Like washing colors with whites. Not bad, just not what you should do either. And I thought you wanted to talk."

Evan wiped some shampoo suds off her temple and stroked a moist finger down her cheek. He moved in until he was hard against her, the water falling between them onto his chest and pooling over her breasts.

He blinked to shake the water off his eyelashes and said, "We'll talk in a minute. First, I'm going to make love to you. Here. In the shower. While you're all warm and wet."

Halley looked ready to give in. She was sighing and gripping his arms as he licked water off her chin.

Then she said, "Wait."

The most hated word in the English language. Evan forced himself to say, "Why?"

"I want to do this first."

Halley put her slippery, sudsy warm hand on his cock and stroked.

Fuck. Evan went from semihard to granite in one brush of her eager fingers. Fingers that slid and stuck as the pelting water washed the soap off her.

He groaned.

She said in a thoughtful voice, "Hmm. My hand's getting stuck. I think I need more shampoo or something."

Evan couldn't answer, but braced his legs farther apart as she filled her hand up again. Then she touched him with a squeeze, before moving up and down, going all along the length of him before climbing back up and rounding over the head of his cock.

He panted like a Saint Bernard in the desert.

"This feels good," she murmured.

If it felt any better, he was going to rip the shower door off its hinges.

In fact, he was ashamed to admit it, but he was just about done for. Another minute and he would be spilling all over her like a garden hose.

"That's enough, Halley."

Her hand paused. "You don't like it?"

Damn, she sounded heartbroken. Her lower lip even trembled a little and her big blue eyes shone brightly. Then he realized she was faking it. She knew damn well he liked it.

He brushed a wet strand of her hair back and shook

his head. "You know that's not what I meant. I just can't wait anymore. I'm going to . . . if you don't stop."

Her expression changed, a smile splaying across her face. "Oh. In that case . . ." Her hand started moving again.

Evan closed his eyes. "Halley," he warned.

"Bad girls keep going."

And she did, her smooth hot fingers working over him until he gave up the fight and let himself come into her hand, feeling out of control, very turned on, and seriously in love with Halley.

Halley unwound herself from Evan, who was once again snoring, and grabbed the sheet to pull over herself.

Evan had been dead to the world for the last hour, but she couldn't sleep. Her mind was racing, her body exhausted, satisfied, and sore, and reality was slowly starting to encroach on her bliss.

She had no idea what time it was. There were probably a thousand things waiting for her to attend to at the office, and Nora probably thought she'd been run over by a garbage truck by now, she'd been gone so long.

Evan didn't have a clock in his bedroom, a fact that didn't surprise her. He wasn't exactly chained to the normal conventions of appointments like most people.

Like her. If she leaned far enough over, she could catch a glimpse of the clock on his computer. Holding on to the edge of the mattress, Halley strained forward, nearly toppling off the bed when she saw it was three fifty-seven.

Her first reaction was to have a cow. Her second reaction was the same.

Holy shit.

How could she have spent the day in bed with Evan when she had a business tottering on the brink of financial disaster?

Biting her lip, she shifted carefully out of the bed and started searching for her pants. She didn't want to wake Evan up, nor did she really want to leave him just yet, but she couldn't slough off her responsibilities. She had a catering job at a ladies social club at five o'clock and there was no way she couldn't be there.

The club was a solid twenty-minute drive and she needed to go home and change still. Crawling around on the floor naked, Halley started to wonder if Evan's smoldering glances had disintegrated her clothes, since they appeared to have vanished. All she had stumbled across was a sandal and her tank top.

Pulling on the tank top without a bra, she wrapped the sheet around her waist and checked to make sure she hadn't woken up Evan. He was still breathing slowly, mouth open, muscular arm up over his head.

Damn, he was cute. Maybe it was a good thing she had to leave, or she might be tempted to throw herself at him and beg him to let her stay forever.

Which, if the sex didn't ruin their friendship, *that* surely would.

This way she could avoid the embarrassing talk that Evan wanted to have, in which she had to presume he was going to remind her this was a one-time deal. Since that sounded about as much fun as eating maggots, she was glad to be spared that. If she ducked out now, then maybe tomorrow they could act as if nothing had happened.

She was very good at avoiding. Hadn't she successfully avoided her attraction to Evan for nearly a year?

Halley caught a glimpse of herself in the mirror over his dresser and jumped back, slapping her hand over her mouth. She didn't look as if nothing had happened. Taking a cautious step forward, she took in the mussed frizzy hair without an ounce of hair product in it, the clean shiny face sans makeup, the pouty plump lips, and the wrinkled tank top clinging to her breasts.

This woman looked exactly like someone who'd spent the day in bed having the best sex of her life. This woman staring back at her looking pleased and territorial. This woman looked relaxed and in love.

Halley liked her. She didn't want that expression to go away.

Except that she was really damn late and still couldn't find her bra or her pants.

Tripping over the sheet wrapped around her lower half, she grabbed Evan's desktop phone to check her voicemail messages. Scanning the floor for her pants, she listened to Nora rambling on in her ear asking her where she was and when she thought she'd be back in the office. Then Nora suggested she check her e-mail before carrying out any plans for revenge on the hackers.

Halley stopped looking under the bed for her pants and swore under her breath, disconnecting her phone. Dragging her sheet behind her, she logged on to her e-mail through Evan's computer and checked the time again. Yep. Still late and totally screwed. After deleting several unimportant e-mail messages, she ran across one with no title.

The message was from her hackers.

Sorry. Wrong caterer. But you look great wearing nothing but a smile. The Three Cs.

After a moment of shock, it struck her as wildly funny. That's it? That's all she got for being subjected to humiliation and financial devastation? A lukewarm apology?

A choking snortlike laugh escaped her mouth before she could stop it and she clicked on the sender to see if there was a return address. Of course there wasn't. Somehow they had sent the message without a sender address, and she was certain if she tried to hit Reply to sender, it would just bounce back into her own e-mail.

Not that she knew what she would say to them. *Next time, try better breasts* probably wasn't a good idea.

"What are you doing?"

Halley whirled around. Evan was sitting up in bed, yawning but looking ready to devour her all over again.

"Go back to sleep," she told him. "I've got to go."

He grinned. "So soon? But we haven't even done it in the living room yet."

That gave her momentary pause before she mentally shook herself. No, she had to leave. A half an hour ago.

"I can't. I have a catering job in less than an hour and I have to change and drive there."

Evan scratched his chest. She was tempted to throw a shirt at him so she wouldn't weaken and stay. And just where in the hell were her pants?

"Okay, I understand. But you're coming back tonight, right? Pack yourself an overnight bag and come over after the job's done. I'll wait up for you."

Halley wanted to say yes. But she had the sneaking suspicion that if she came back, she was going to wind up sorry. Friendless, heartbroken, and sorry. Better to leave now and when she returned, pretend they had never been naked together.

Taking little geisha steps, she held on to her tightly wrapped sheet and swallowed hard. "I think I'll just go home afterward. I'm going to be tired."

Tired of pretending she didn't love him.

"So? I'll let you get some sleep. In the morning."

Evan's voice was coaxing, seductive. Halley fought the urge to look at him. Frantic, she darted her eyes around the room, then gave a cry of triumph when she spotted her Capri pants bunched up by the closet.

"No, not tonight." Or any other night, if she wanted to keep her sanity.

The teasing tone left his voice. "But we need to talk, Halley."

"There's nothing to talk about." She headed toward the closet. "We had a fun day and now it's over. End of story."

That was not the end of the story as far as Evan was concerned. He watched Halley wiggle her way around the room like a giant fruit roll-up, her hair frizzy and lopsided and her breasts doing an enticing little jump with each jerk forward.

Did she really consider what they had shared nothing more than a fun day? Damn, that hurt. But Halley was a busy woman and he knew she didn't date much. Maybe he had been nothing more than a sexual diversion. An oversized stress ball.

She bent over carefully, trying to grab her pants off the floor while still holding on to the sheet. A painful lump formed in his chest.

"Halley."

"What?" Halley was hopping on one foot as she tried to step into her pants, all while keeping the sheet wrapped around her.

Exasperation rose in him. "Jesus, drop the sheet. You're going to fall and knock your teeth out." It wasn't as if he hadn't seen every inch of her body. And tasted it.

"I'm fine." She continued her one-footed dance.

He stood up and stalked over to her. He held her arms so she wouldn't wind up in a heap on the floor.

"No, you're not. Why are you running out on me and acting like you don't want me to see a flash of your ass?"

She blew her hair out of her eyes and stopped struggling with her pants. "Because now we have to go back to being friends and that's not what friends do."

"Friends don't show friends body parts, huh?"

Wiggling her pants up her calves, she said, "Yes."

"What if I want to be more than friends?" He started to caress her arms with his thumbs, and leaned forward to place a kiss on her warm shoulder.

She stiffened. "Knock it off. You can't change the rules now. If we do this again, then what happens eventually when the lust burns out? I don't want to lose you, Evan."

If that's what was bothering her, then maybe there was hope for him after all.

He nibbled on her ear, noticing the way she drew in her breath. "Do you love me?"

She sighed. "We've been over this. Yes. But there's love. And then there's *love.*"

"Well, do you *love* me?"

Hot fingers shoved on his chest. He stayed firmly next to her.

"I've got to go."

"Answer the question, then I'll let you go."

Halley looked over his shoulder and rolled her eyes. "I plead the fifth."

That was promising. He teased his tongue into her ear. She gasped.

Evan wanted it all, and he wanted it now. Halley was the woman for him and he wanted to spend a lifetime loving her. "I love you, you know. Always have, always will. I want you to marry me."

"What?" Halley squawked, wondering if she was hallucinating. "What are you talking about? This was supposed to be about sex, remember?"

Her heart was beating like a hummingbird's wings and she was so hopeful she was sick. He couldn't mean it . . . but if he did, she was going to be really excited. She couldn't kid herself anymore that she just wanted Evan's body. She wanted everything.

His heart.

He whispered in her ear, "This whole day was about love, not sex."

Oh, damn, that was romantic. Her knees gave out, she loosened her grip on the sheet, and her Capri pants puddled to her ankles.

He kissed her jaw, his hands cupping the sides of her face. "Marry me."

Who was she to say no? "Yes. Yes, yes, and yes."

Leaping into his arms, she almost fell down as the sheet trapped her legs. Evan caught her and smiled down at her.

"I'm so glad you said yes. Because I was going to have to hurt you if you said no."

She laughed, feeling a little punch drunk on happiness. She tried to force herself to back up, but her body wasn't having it. Neither was Evan. He still held her tight.

"Now let me go, I've got to leave!"

He kissed her full on the mouth, a deep, possessive kiss that had her sighing with pleasure. Oh, yeah. Waking up to this every day would be a dream come true.

"So let's just clarify. That's a yes, you'll marry me?"

"Yes." Every day with her favorite person. She couldn't ask for anything better.

Evan squeezed her hard enough to collapse a lung. "Now tell me that you *love* me and I'll let you go."

"I do." Halley sniffed a happy sniff and let go of her sheet altogether.

"Keep saying those words, sweet stuff, because you'll be needing them soon." He grinned at her.

A shiver went through her. When she had spotted that angel between her legs, she could never have imagined this would be the result.

"Hey, I forgot to tell you, the Three Commandos sent me an e-mail apologizing."

"You're kidding." Evan moved to the computer.

Wearing nothing but a smile suited him. She said, "No, I'm definitely not kidding."

Evan started clicking on the computer. "Well, we'll have to e-mail them back."

"I don't want to hack their site anymore, Evan. And I don't want to send them a nasty e-mail. Let's just forget about it." Her conscience wouldn't let her torment them in return and she had no desire to start an online feud with the Three Cs. Besides, she didn't want anyone but Evan to see those pictures they had taken with his camera.

He glanced back at her, tossing his light hair out of his eyes. "I wasn't going to send them a nasty e-mail. I was going to thank them. After all, they're semiresponsible for us getting together."

She stepped out of the clinging bits of the sheet and went to stand behind him, wrapping her arms around his waist. Her thighs rubbed against his and she dropped a kiss onto his back. "I have to leave now."

"Promise you'll be back tonight?" Evan abandoned the computer and stood up.

"Yes." As soon as the last slice of raspberry cheesecake was served, she was out of there.

Evan turned around and Halley found herself pulled into his arms. Before she could blink, her tank top was gone, tossed over his shoulder and lying crumpled on the keyboard.

"How long until you have to leave?"

"I needed to leave a half an hour ago."

Halley moaned as his hand moved between her thighs. "I'll be quick."

Halley tried to dredge up the strength to say no. "How quick?" she asked, breathless.

"Just long enough to do a quick Cupid imitation."

All kinds of perverted analogies involving Cupid and arrows ran through Halley's mind.

"As long as it doesn't involve any hacking."

What Evan whispered to her made her laugh, before the sound was swallowed by a very friendly kiss.

He'd told himself he wouldn't kiss her until she showed interest, and so maybe alarm couldn't be classified as such, but she wasn't smacking his hand away either.

"Houston . . ." She licked her lips. "We have a problem."

His fingers stopped sliding across her cheekbone as Josie realized what she had said and giggled.

"I guess you've heard that one, before, huh?"

There was a bright sparkle in her eyes, so adorable that he couldn't bring himself to be annoyed the way he usually was when someone made an Apollo 13 reference. "Once or twice." Or a thousand times. He'd lost count.

Leaning forward, he kissed the corner of her mouth, then the other. A little gasp left her, but she didn't move away. Her lips were soft and moist from wetting them with her tongue, and they fell open as he brushed over her a third time. Right in the center, flush on her mouth with his.

Josie sighed, her mouth receptive to him, relaxed.

She tasted like apple juice, sweet and ripe, willing, and

he fought to keep his eyes open and his hands off her
body as he pulled back.

This wasn't what he had intended to do with her in
here. He had meant to clear the air, make sure she didn't
have a more serious problem than chronic klutziness.
But he couldn't be sorry that he'd kissed her.

Nor did he feel sorry for what he was about to pro-
pose.

"The problem, Josie, is that you're driving me crazy."

"I am?" She shook her head, flustered, eyes unfocused.
"Oh, right, with all the dropping and the tripping. I don't
mean to, you know, it just happens."

"That's not what I meant." He buried his nose in her
hair by her ear and breathed in deeply. Strawberries.
Damn. She was practically a fruit farm.

"I meant you're driving me crazy because I want you."

"Want me?" Her breath hitched, and he felt goose-
bumps rising on her jaw and neck, but she still didn't
pull away. "Want me for what?"

That she could even say that, so innocently, made
him hard.

"I want you for this." He plunged his hand into her
short hair, drew her flush up against him, and gave her
a real kiss. A lip-sliding, mouth-open, tongue-tasting kiss
that had them both panting and wide-eyed.

"Oh," she said, looking up at him before darting her
eyes over to the closed door to the hallway.

He could hear the standard hustle-and-bustle, voices
carrying down the hall as business went on as usual in
the hospital. This was risky, inappropriate, and he was
still new on staff. He should care that someone could
walk in at any second, but he didn't.

"Are you serious?" she asked.

Seriously out of his mind with lust. "Very. I'm attracted

to you, Josie, and we need to discuss what we're going to do about it."

Josie gave an awkward laugh. "I thought you couldn't stand me."

Had she just missed the kiss he'd given her? "Hardly. Now tell me that you're attracted to me, too." So he could lean her against that door to prevent a possible interruption and kiss her again.

Josie worried her bottom lip with her teeth than gave another heartfelt sigh. "Okay, here's the thing. I am something of a klutz, but I've never been this bad before and it's all your fault."

Her fingers gripped his shirt and pushed him lightly to emphasize her point. "I feel like you're always watching, waiting for me to screw up, and I've had this sort of ridiculous crush on you."

Her cheeks were pink, eyes wide, and Houston kept quiet, liking the sound of this, wanting to hear where this could go. Desire punched him in the gut at her admission that she was attracted to him.

"Silly, really, because you're . . ." She waved her hand around in front of him. "And I'm . . ." Gesturing to herself, she blew a loud breath out of the corner of her mouth.

He had no idea what that was supposed to mean, and he was about to ask her, when she glanced toward the door again.

"But anyway, I don't think this is the place to discuss this."

Josie stepped back out of his reach. He took her hand, pulling her to a stop, not about to let her escape now that he'd gotten a teasing taste of her. She had admitted she was attracted to him as well, and that was just the green light he'd been looking for.

He knew he should let her go. He should forget he had started this and walk out of here with his sanity intact. Except that he would go crazy if he couldn't have Josie. The ache was too strong, too burning, deep inside where it plagued him and distracted him every minute in her presence.

He had to have her.

Put a Little Romance in Your Life With
Melanie George

Devil May Care
0-8217-7008-X $5.99US/$7.99CAN

Handsome Devil
0-8217-7009-8 $5.99US/$7.99CAN

Devil's Due
0-8217-7010-1 $5.99US/$7.99CAN

The Mating Game
0-8217-7120-5 $5.99US/$7.99CAN

Available Wherever Books Are Sold!

Visit our website at **www.kensingtonbooks.com.**

Contemporary Romance By
Kasey Michaels

__**Can't Take My Eyes Off of You**
  0-8217-6522-1   **$6.50US/$8.50CAN**

__**Too Good to Be True**
  0-8217-6774-7   **$6.50US/$8.50CAN**

__**Love to Love You Baby**
  0-8217-6844-1   **$6.99US/$8.99CAN**

__**Be My Baby Tonight**
  0-8217-7117-5   **$6.99US/$9.99CAN**

__**This Must Be Love**
  0-8217-7118-3   **$6.99US/$9.99CAN**

__**This Can't Be Love**
  0-8217-7119-1   **$6.99US/$9.99CAN**

Available Wherever Books Are Sold!

Visit our website at **www.kensingtonbooks.com**.